RISK THE HEART
BY:
JASMINE ALEXANDER

Noire Passion is an imprint of Parker Publishing LLC.

Copyright © 2008 by Jasmine Alexander
Published by Parker Publishing LLC
12523 Limonite Avenue, Suite #440-438
Mira Loma, California 91752
www.parker-publishing.com

ISBN: 978-1-60043-060-2
First Edition

Manufactured in the United States of America
Printed by Bang Printing, Brainard MN
Distributed by BookMasters, Inc. 1-800-537-6727
Cover Design by Jaxadoradesigns.com

Parker Publishing, llc
www.Parker-Publishing.com

DEDICATION

Thank you, God. With you, all things truly are possible.

To my mom and dad, thanks for teaching me to believe in myself, encouraging me to chase my dreams, and loving me even when I'm not perfect. To Kim, I thank you for being my first fan and looking past all the typos! To Lloyd, my heart. I may not have known you for the first chapter, but thank you for all your love and support as we move into the next.

ACKNOWLEDGEMENTS

To Andrea, thank you for allowing me to "hook on to you" and learn everything I can! Any beginning writer would be fortunate to have you as a mentor. To the world's best critique partners, Denise, Lawan, and Cheryl. Thanks for the advice, guidance, support, laughter, and friendship. To my bestie, Janseen, thank you for always picking up the phone and knowing exactly what I need to hear. To my God Sister, Valerie, for allowing me to keep my head stuck in a laptop when I visit. Last, but surely not least, a huge thank you to all the friends and family that agonized over a title with me. The good news…it was worth it!

RISK THE HEART
BY:
JASMINE ALEXANDER

CHAPTER ONE

He found her.

Well, if Marcus Cortland had to be honest, he wasn't looking for her. However, when he heard her laughter he knew he'd found something he hadn't even known he was waiting for. The melodic sound reached him over the din of conversations floating around the ballroom of the Richmont Country Club. Tingles ran down his spine. The sensation passed through him and he turned away from the conversation he was engaged in to do a quick scan of the room and the other guests close to him.

She stood about six feet away.

She wore a simple black dress that hung to the floor and fitted her small, curvaceous frame to perfection. Her almond-colored skin was flawless. Her brown hair draped in curls over her shoulders and down her back. Her full lips begged to be kissed. She had the face of a seductive angel, heart shaped with soft features. But her eyes captivated him. They were deep brown pools.

He wanted to meet her. To know her. It had been a long time since he'd felt drawn to a woman. She was involved in conversation with two other ladies, who he recognized as wives of two of his business associates. What would they think if he walked over and introduced himself to the Angel? Then, he wondered how to even go about it. Usually, women sought him out. If only she would look up at him, smile, offer some sort of encouragement. One of the other women made a comment and her enchanting laughter filled the air once again and left him wondering; was it possible to feel somebody's laugh?

"Well that's impossible! Wouldn't you agree Marcus?"

At Anthony Delton's voice Marcus turned back to the people surrounding him. Five expectant faces stared back at him.

He had no idea what that was, better yet whether it was possible or not. "Yes, I agree... impossible," he offered, trusting in Anthony's general intelligence not to lead him astray, and the debate picked back up.

Letting out a relieved sigh, Marcus excused himself. He had a seductress to meet. He may be unsure of what the first step was going to be, but he'd never backed down when he wanted something. Yet, when he started in her direction, he realized she'd disappeared. Marcus set out to locate her.

Ten minutes later, he was ready to conclude that finding a cure for cancer would've been an easier task. She was nowhere to be seen. Marcus scanned over the hundreds of heads in the room, not too difficult since he was taller than most of the guests. The charity event was a success and people were packed into every nook and cranny. Dancing was taking place in the center of the room to the accompaniment of an orchestra. He moved through the crowd, eyeing every black dress, keeping his ear tuned for her laugh. Finally, he spotted her slipping out the doors leading on to the terrace. Perfect.

Maneuvering through the crowd without being blocked or stopped took skill. As a veteran of such events, he accomplished it with ease. He stepped out on a well-lit terrace that emptied onto a sprawling lawn and golf course. Other people wandered onto the terrace in small groups and were conversing on the lawns and moving along the walkways. He caught a glimpse of a black dress before it disappeared behind a bush. She was walking toward the gardens. His family had been members of the club since he was young, he knew the grounds well.

Walking along the gravel path, Marcus located her. She leaned against a classic gazebo, the moonlight shining down on her as though it was illuminating her way home. Her head tilted, leaving only her profile visible to him. She held what looked to be a cell phone. She was gorgeous. She was...

Muttering? He stepped closer.

"Stupid shoes." She reached down and snatched the offending shoes off her feet and dropped them on the ground. "Stupid purse." Her handbag joined the shoes. "Stupid, stupid, stupid phone." Turning her back to him, she walked further into the gazebo.

"I wouldn't be so quick to drop that if I were you," Marcus drawled out.

She spun around, her curls falling like waves on her shoulder. Her eyes widened. "Drop what?"

"That phone." He motioned with his head at her cell, stepping into the entrance of the gazebo. "They don't bounce."

Her mouth formed a silent "oh" as she stared at him with a blank expression. Then she blinked. "I didn't know anyone else was out here."

"There wasn't." He smiled, stepping closer, extended his hand. "Marcus Cortland and you are?"

"Seeking a moment of privacy." Ignoring his hand, she bent down and scooped up her purse and shoes. "If you'll excuse me." She moved to step around him but he blocked her way.

He didn't know what had overcome him. This had to be the first time in a long time that his name had no effect. Didn't she know who he was? "If it's a phone you're in need of please allow me to offer mine. It has excellent reception."

She tipped her head to the side.. Her eyes were clear and direct. "Sir, it's nice of you to offer, but I assure you I'm not in the habit of taking offers from strange men."

His lips twitched. "I don't know that I've ever been called strange."

"Well, if the shoe fits." She held out one of her shoes as if to demonstrate, then slipped both on to her feet. She tried to maneuver around him, and found her path blocked.

"I wouldn't call us strangers."

"I didn't. I called you strange," she interrupted

"But if you would tell me your name." He ignored her interruption. "Then we would no longer be strangers. We are, after all, guests at the same party."

She paused. "I have to go."

"So you've said."

Her eyes narrowed. "And you have yet to move."

"I'm still waiting on a name."

Her shoulders squared, right before his eyes and if possible she got taller. Which wasn't saying much considering the top of her head only came to his chest.

"I don't know if these intimidation tactics are how you pick up women, but I'm not impressed." She planted her hands on her hips. "Furthermore, if you don't get out of my way, I'll be forced to scream. So loud that everyone attending the party will come running. Then I can promptly inform them of how you are holding a defenseless woman against her will. So, unless you already possess a reputation for holding women hostage, which at this point I'm half convinced of, I suggest you move."

There was a long pause. Then he stepped to the side.

She walked past, and without a backward glance disappeared through the gardens heading back toward the ballroom.

Well, he thought smiling as he leaned against the railing, train wrecks had occurred with more finesse. This wasn't going to be easy.

Sabryna Givens hurried back along the path as though the devil was at her heels. Which could be the case, considering her harasser was as handsome as sin. She tried not to dwell on his tall, muscular frame or his fathomless dark eyes set in a face that had left her breathless. After all, she wasn't here to play. She was here on business.

Here to keep the Middleton Youth Center in business. As the assistant director, her purpose for being at this party was to inspire some of the rich guests to contribute to the center.

She stopped at the edge of the terrace doors, resisting the urge to massage her aching temples. The headache she had when she woke up this morning was increasing in strength. Sabryna glanced out over the party, a glittering sea of colorful dresses and sparkling jewels. She'd met a handful of nice people tonight. The rest she could classify as snobs. If she was forced to endure one more conversation about who knows who or who has what she would scream. The knowledge that she didn't belong here was solidified the minute she'd stepped foot into the room and a beautiful young woman, whose diamond necklace probably cost more than her monthly salary, gave her the cold shoulder. The future of the much needed community center gave her the courage she needed to brave the condescending glances of the women and inappropriate stares of the men.

Spotting her boss, Grant Morganfield on the other side of the room, she moved to his side. He was easy to spot, tall, dark, and large. He reminded her of an aging football player. His face like stone, rarely showed any expression. Sabryna knew his gruff exterior hid a huge heart. After all, he was the founder and director of the Middleton Youth Center. He was talking to an older couple, she waited until they moved on then approached him.

"Grant, I'm ready to go." She didn't waste time with small talk knowing that he appreciated directness and would see past her weak smiles.

He sighed. "Sabryna, we haven't been here long –"

"We've been here for three hours."

"And there are still other people here we need to talk to," he continued as though she hadn't interrupted. "Do I need to remind you why we came here tonight?"

"You mean why you dragged me here tonight." She glanced around. Grant didn't share her dislike for attending such events, but one of his big contributors and friend, Jeff Sampson, sat on the board at the Club and often gave him invitations to these parties to recruit more supporters for the Center. However, tonight was the first time he'd asked her to attend. "Besides, I want to go by the center and check on the lock in slumber party."

Grant smiled and nodded at another couple walking past them. "I thought you called."

The words brought her mind back to the encounter in the gardens and dark eyes flashed through her memories. "I couldn't get any reception." She heard the distraction in her voice and hoped Grant didn't notice.

Concerned eyes met hers. "Are you okay?" he asked.

She nodded, purposefully staring at spot past his shoulder. "I do have a little headache. If you want, I can catch a taxi home. I know you need to stay."

Grant took her gently by the arm and led them to a corner housing a large plotted plant. "Do you need a drink? Some air?"

Sabryna shook her head. "I need to go home. You don't need me here, Grant. You're always so good at these types of things."

Grant seemed to search for his words. "You have a way with people. They like you."

"Thank you. But I think they would like me a lot more after I've had an Aspirin."

"All right, we can leave." Her grateful gaze swung back to him and before she could voice her appreciation, he qualified, "after you meet one more person."

Sabryna almost groaned. "Grant, I'm tired of meeting people who think life's biggest tragedy is having to fly coach."

"Well unfortunately, we need these people or have you forgotten?"

Her grumbles were his only response.

"Sabryna." His tone was unbending.

Realizing she would reach her goal easier if she gave in, she rolled her eyes to the heavens and muttered, "Who is it?"

There was a short pause. "I forgot his name. You know how bad I am with remembering names. Jeff introduced us earlier. He owns a successful IT firm. He started it right out of college and since then has turned it into a multimillion dollar business."

"Did you speak to him about the center?"

"I mentioned it, but I thought he might be more willing to hear it coming from you."

"Why me?" Her puzzlement showed in her voice.

"Well....Oh there he is."

"Where?" Sabryna looked at the multitude of guests in front of them.

"By the terrace doors. The tall one wearing the dark suit." Grant gave her a slight nudge so she would look in that direction. "Now what was his name? Something that important you think I would remember..."

Grant's words slid into the background. Her eyes locked on the tall man standing by the door. In the weak light of the gardens, she hadn't been able to appreciate just how handsome he was. His face was hard with well sculpted features, and dark hair cut close to his head blending almost even with his skin. He scanned the ballroom, moving with lion-like grace, as though he was on the hunt. Her heart skipped three beats. She had a name for him. Sin!

"Marcus Cortland." Grant's pleasure at remembering the name rang in his voice. "Come on, I'll introduce you."

Before she could protest, Grant was dragging her across the room. He'd certainly take one look at her and give her the set down she earned earlier. What had she called him? Odd? Weird? Strange- she called him strange! She opened her mouth to speak but her breath froze in her throat as the object of her anxiety turned and leveled the full force of that devastating gaze on her. He noticed her direction and the most amazing smile spread across his face. Next thing she knew they were standing before him. Gathering her courage, she raised her gaze to his and lifted one challenging eyebrow. She would be prepared for whatever came next.

"Mr. Morganfield, I hope you've been enjoying your night," Sin spoke with smooth charm to her boss.

"Please call me Grant. I wanted to introduce you to someone. I believe I mentioned her earlier." Grant placed a gentle hand on her elbow giving her a slight push forward.

"Ah, yes, your revered Assistant Director." His eyebrow lifted to match hers. She read the message. Challenge accepted.

Grant shot her a speculative look before he made the introductions. "Yes. Sabryna Givens. Marcus Cortland."

"It's a pleasure to meet you." Sabryna offered her hand.

She wondered if he would fling her greeting back in her face, inform her boss of her earlier rude behavior, and storm off.

His smile widened as his large warm hand closed over her smaller one. His thumb brushed the inside of her palm, her heart skipped five more beats. At this rate, she would have a stroke by the end of the night. "It's a pleasure to meet you, also. Your boss has been singing your praises. Tell me, do you walk on water?"

Her amused glance slid sideways to Grant. "Only when it rains."

Marcus bit back a laugh.

"I need to speak with Jeff before I leave, if you two will excuse me." With a smile for Marcus and a warning glance for Sabryna, Grant took his leave.

Sabryna felt as though she had just been left alone with a lion. A sinfully attractive lion! She stared. Her mouth went dry.

"In case you missed your cue, this is the part where you convince me to fork over thousands of dollars for your center," Marcus suggested, his dark eyes caressing hers.

Her temper stirred inside of her, but she quickly squelched it. He had, after all, done her a favor. "No, this is the place where I thank you for not making a scene in front of my boss."

"That's all right, you made an obvious mistake. You're forgiven."

Sabryna's lips straightened. "Well then, that would be the first time that I was forgiven without first offering an apology."

"I thought I would save you the breath."

"I don't need to be saved a breath that I was never planning to spend."

His eyes widened. "You weren't planning to apologize?"

"Absolutely not." She turned to look at the other guests.

"You were rude," he accused.

Sabryna looked back at him. "I was cornered by a stranger in a dark garden," she pointed out. "For all I know you could have been a dangerous criminal."

"Do I look like a criminal?" His gave her a look of mock innocence.

Her laughter filled the air. "That has to be the most idiotic question I've ever heard."

Marcus's lips lifted in a wide grin. He extended his hand to her. "Dance with me."

⋙━◈━⋘

Pure and utter madness made her accept his hand and allow him to lead her onto the dance floor. Heat spread through her at his touch. She resisted the urge to snatch her hand back and run for safety.

When he pulled her into his embrace, she forgot all about breathing. His strong arms circled her waist and she forced herself not to clench her fingers on his hard muscles. Ordering herself to pull it together, she fought to ignore her reaction. She focused on the dance, but found herself taking note of how well they moved together. She listened to the music, but found that to be an inadequate distraction. So, she turned her attention to the one thing that mattered. Her sole purpose in being there.

"I imagine Grant gave you an entire dissertation on the center." Her voice sounded strained. She tried to find her usual lightheartedness.

Above her head, she heard a soft chuckle. "He was very thorough."

"Well he loves that place," she defended. "He's passionate about it."

"So tell me Miss Givens." He leaned down, his breath brushing past her ear as he asked, "What are you passionate about?"

For a moment she couldn't speak. She took a deep calming breath. "Our...our center provides something positive for the youth of a neighborhood that many would prefer to write off." She warmed to her topic and outlined some of the finer points of the center. After listing certain challenges they faced, she then shared with him examples of how the center had helped the children in the neighborhood. "I know it all sounds exhausting, but when you see a young person make a positive choice for the first time you realize the battles are worth the victory."

Marcus was transfixed. After a while he'd stopped listening to her words and more to the sound of her voice. Her tone was smooth, like warm honey. In it he could hear the pride and love she felt for this center. It took him a moment to realize she was done talking. "That...sounds nice." He wasn't referring to the center.

"Do you have any questions?" The song ended and she stepped out of his arms.

He looked down at her as an unfamiliar swell of emotions caught him off guard. For a moment he was paralyzed with fear. He shook it off. She couldn't be dangerous to him. He wouldn't allow it. Sure he enjoyed their verbal play, their dance, and listening to her. She was sexy with a great sense of humor. An intriguing combination. But the simple truth was, he wanted her. Now. He zoned in on that single thought. "Just one."

Her wide-eyed expectant look was so innocent, he took a second to rethink his next words, but decided she couldn't be that naïve. Only a comatose patient wouldn't have felt the sparks flying between them. "Have dinner with me."

She stared. Then blinked. Then stared some more. "Dinner?" she repeated in disbelief.

"Yes, dinner. The last meal of the day." He ran one hand down the side of her bare arms, smiling as he felt her shiver. "I'll pick you up tomorrow at eight."

Her expression blanked. "I thank you for the...invitation. But I already have plans."

"Cancel them."

"Excuse me?" A fire lit inside her eyes. "Mr. Cortland…"

"Call me Marcus."

"Mr. Cortland…" she restated stubbornly.

"Listen, even you cannot deny there's an attraction between us. Come to dinner with me and we can explore our mutual interest further."

"The only interest I have in you is as a potential patron of the Middleton Youth Center." Her tones were clipped, angry.

"Fine, we can talk about the center over dinner." Stepping closer, he lowered his voice. "Or in bed."

Her eyes narrowed. He heard her sharp intake of breath.

He knew he was being forward, but if she was waiting for empty promises and flattery, she would have to keep waiting. He'd sworn off making promises to women a long time ago. "I wish you would just give in to the feeling."

"And I wish that you could see all of the wonderful things going on at the Middleton Youth Center. Maybe then you would realize there is more in life to be…" She aimed a condescending look up at him. "mutually interested about. Goodnight, Mr. Cortland." She turned on her heel and left.

Marcus watched as she disappeared into the crowd. He squelched the impulse to chase after her. There was only so much rejection a man could handle in one night. And he wasn't a man often faced with it. However, the few minutes he'd spent in her company left him craving more. His heart was racing with the thrill of excitement and the skin on his arms still felt warm from her touch. Grabbing a glass of champagne off the tray of a nearby waiter, Marcus swallowed it in one gulp. She was going to be a challenge.

CHAPTER TWO

Pleasantly absorbed in a daydream where he was undressing a certain woman in the moonlight, Marcus almost missed the voice of his secretary through the intercom. "Mr. Cortland, your mother is on the phone."

He glanced at the work piled on his mahogany desk, untouched. "Tell her I'll call her back later."

"Yes Sir."

He ignored the question he heard in the voice. It wasn't in his character to brush off his mother. He came from a close-knit family, but today he was distracted, by Sabryna.

After she'd walked away from him for the second time that night, she'd disappeared from the party. Finding nothing else worth holding his attention, he returned home. Alone. Gone straight to bed. Alone.

That must account for his irritable mood.

"I hope this lack of desire to talk to your mother doesn't extend to every member of your family," a familiar voice announced from the door of his office. "If so then you and I are going to have a very quiet lunch."

Marcus leaned back in his chair and grinned at his younger brother David lounging in his doorway. "How did you get past Marie?"

David shrugged. "What can I say? I impressed her with my smile."

"You impressed her with your gun," Marcus shot back, rolling his eyes.

"Occupational hazard." David walked in and lowered his lean frame into one of the cream leather chairs facing his brother's desk. "People seem to respond to it."

A grunt from Marcus was his only response as straightened papers on his desk. David glanced around the large immaculate office. "I see you've nothing better to do but redecorate your office." He smacked his hand on the plush arm of the chair to emphasize his point.

"Would you like a drink?" Marcus asked, nodding his head toward the side bar.

"No. Do you want to tell me why you're avoiding mom?"

Marcus looked his brother straight in the eye hoping he would let it go. "Actually, Detective Cortland, there's no story behind that. I was busy, you know how mom can talk, and so I'll call her back later." David was smart and perceptive, which made him a good detective but an annoying brother. Two years apart, they'd been close growing up, always getting in and out of trouble together. Marcus hid few secrets from David.

David stared at him until Marcus felt as if his brother was reading his soul. No matter that Marcus was the oldest, whenever David employed that penetrating gaze he felt like the roles reversed. "You looked distracted when I came in. Not busy."

Marcus faked a grin. "Do I need an attorney present?"

David chuckled. "All right. I'll back off. For now." David stood. "Besides, I hate interrogating anyone on an empty stomach. Let's go to lunch."

They headed to Mama's Soul Food Kitchen, a personal favorite for both brothers and were seated at a small table in the corner.

Once the food arrived, David attacked his plate with a zest that surprised Marcus. "Have you eaten lately?" he asked David sarcastically.

"Nope." David spoke in between bites of crispy fried chicken. "I veen bery phisy. Vig pase."

Marcus rolled his eyes. "You're going to choke one day."

David swallowed and smiled. "So are you going to tell me what had you so distracted when I came in?"

"Are we back on that?" Marcus took a swig of cola.

"Yes."

"It was nothing."

David's copper colored eyes held a teasing light. "Was it a woman? A pretty brown-eyed vixen you met at that party the other night."

Marcus choked on a piece of cornbread.

David's smile widened. "Ahh. I see I've hit the nail on the head. Some fine young lady has you by the balls."

"Please, David." That wasn't a fate Marcus planned on succumbing to. "There are many things in this life worth being distracted by. A woman isn't one of them."

David shook his head in disbelief. "Brother, you need a new set of priorities."

"My priorities are just fine." Marcus scowled at his brother's laughter.

"Women are a dime a dozen. There's no need to be caught up by one, when ten others will do just fine."

"Well, you wouldn't be taking them for granted if you weren't Mr. Big CEO." David laughed. "I guess I might be a little jaded if women were always throwing their unwanted attention at me, too."

"I haven't noticed you lacking in female company."

"Well, big brother, you know me." David's smile had melted just as many hearts as it had broken. "I love a good distraction."

"Well, I have one for you." Marcus reached into his pocket, pulled out a small white card and flicked it on the table near his brother's plate.

David glanced at the card and then back at Marcus. "You got another one? When?"

"Two days ago. I figured it could wait until we met today."

David picked up the card and examined it. It was a plain white card with no marks, words, or pictures on the front or back. He flipped open the card and the inside read: I HAVE NOT FORGOTTEN. I WILL NEVER FORGET. He let out a slow sigh. "Well, I'll take it to the lab, but I figure just like the other ones, we won't get anything from it. But, it's worth a try."

These words were familiar to Marcus. The strange cards had started coming about seven years ago. Always showing up in different spots clearly placed for him. The first one had been on the windshield of his car. This one he found in his gym bag. There was never any clue as to who had sent them or why. All came with cryptic messages written inside.

When he found the first one, it had put him into a mild panic. The card read: ONE DAY I WILL MAKE YOU PAY. At that time, his brother wasn't on the force, so he informed the local cops. They told him to keep his eyes open and remain on his guard. So he did. And nothing happened. Every couple of months another card came, the message always threatening. At one point, he'd hired a private detective. That proved to be a dead end. Now, seven years later, he had a sizable collection of cards. They seemed like a normal part of his life. They came, they threatened, he put his guard up for a few days, and nothing happened.

With these thoughts in mind, Marcus reached for another piece of cornbread. "Well, tell me if anything pops up." He switched to the discussion of sports. As David ranted about the loss his team had suffered, Marcus once again let his mind drift back to seducing Sabryna in the moonlight.

She never saw it coming. One minute Sabryna was rounding the corner of the building and the next a hard object slammed into her head knocking her to the ground, leaving her sprawled on her back examining the back of her eyelids. A sharp agonizing pain formed in her forehead. She was aware of some commotion around her but the loud buzzing in her ears was drowning out everything but the pain. She groaned.

"Is she dead?" The question came from a voice that sounded as though he was hovering near her.

"I think so," answered another young voice. This one she recognized. It was Gabe Lucas, one of the kids who frequented the center.

"She's not dead, stupid." That was the voice of Latisha Wilder, one of the young girls. "Didn't you hear her moan. But both of you are going to get it when she wakes up."

Sabryna sensed someone kneel down next to her. Blinking her eyes open, she caught sight of Latisha. "Miss Sabryna, is you okay? Do you want me to get help?"

Sabryna's vision blurred for a few seconds and then snapped into focus as she looked at the three young faces leaning over her.

Gabe pushed his hand past Latisha's shoulder and stuck up two small fingers. "Can you tell me how many fingers I'm holding up, Miss Sabryna?"

"You don't even know how many fingers you holding up, Gabe." Latisha helped Sabryna sit up.

"Johnny? Gabe?" Sabryna glared at both boys. "You have a five minute head start."

They only needed five seconds. Latisha's laughter rang out as the boys dashed around the corner sure to stay out of her way for the rest of the day. Sabryna picked up the volleyball that had assaulted her five minutes ago and wondered if she could squeeze it hard enough to burst it into smithereens. A million times she'd instructed the boys not to throw the ball against the outside wall. She handed it to Latisha. "Make sure that this ball does not see the light of day for several weeks."

Latisha took the ball from her and dashed off in the opposite direction. Sabryna rubbed her head. After five years as an Assistant Director at the Middleton Youth Center, she was more than used to a bump or two. Standing up on her feet, she made her way into the large brick building, through the common rooms filled with activity and into her office. Sitting down behind her metal desk, she massaged her throbbing head. One of her office walls housed a huge window that permitted her to observe the main room of the center. It was an advantage that allowed her to intercept most problems before they began. Suppressing the urge to pop some aspirin, she began shifting through papers on her desk, looking for the grant proposal she had been working on that morning. Perhaps if she could hurry up and get more grant money, her boss would stop asking her to attend those ridiculous functions.

As if her thoughts had summoned him, Grant Morganfield walked into her office and took a seat. "You look like death hung over. Twice."

"Thank you, Grant. I can't tell you how much I look forward to your daily boost of self-esteem," she walked over to her file cabinet and pulled so hard she rattled the mirror on the wall next to it. Catching sight of her reflection, she grimaced.

She wasn't feeling pretty today. Not that she often felt like a beauty queen. She knew she came to work most days looking drabber than fashionable. But when she was at work, she needed to be functional. Today, she was dressed in a pair of dark blue Levis and a white blouse. Her hair, as usual, was pulled back into a tight bun, and she was sure, looked disarrayed after being knocked with the ball. She rubbed her forehead hoping it would release some of the pain.

From his chair, Grant cleared his throat. "I wanted to come in and say…"

His voice broke off as Lena Martinez, a youth counselor, popped her head into the door and remarked in a voice laden with a thick Spanish accent. "Hey, I've been waiting for you to get here so I could hear about the gala."

"We were just about to talk about that," Grant told her.

"Good." She came further into the room and propped her petite figure on the corner of Sabryna's desk. "So tell me, how was it?"

"It was productive," Grant answered.

"It was irksome," Sabryna stated at the same time. She located the file and went back to her desk.

"Sabryna, how can you say that?" Lena asked in disbelief. "You went to a ritzy ball and got to be like Cinderella!"

Sabryna laughed. Lena was a hopeless romantic who believed every moment in life was blessed with a chance for something fabulous to happen. She was one of the most open and expressive people Sabryna knew and she loved her for that. In fact, Lena had become her closest friend. "Lena, it was the farthest thing from a fairytale."

"I don't know." Lena shook her head. "A beautifully decorated ballroom, scrumptious cuisine prepared by the best chefs, and handsome, rich men waiting to waltz with the woman of their dreams." Lena propelled herself from the desk and did a quick swirl that had Grant rolling his eyes to the heavens. "I could think of worse things."

Lena's words sent an image of a handsome Marcus Cortland pulling her close for a midnight waltz. A shiver raced down her spine. Sabryna shifted, uncomfortable. "Lena, you would be very disappointed by the real thing. Nothing but a room full of pretentious snobs gathered together to discuss how much better they are than everyone else."

"Sabryna," Grant admonished. "It wasn't all bad. I'm sure you met some nice people."

And one pushy, intoxicating, handsome jerk, she thought. "In all fairness, I did meet some nice people." Then she qualified. "But, they were few and far between."

"And did one of those benevolent souls include Marcus Cortland?" Grant asked.

Sabryna kept her eyes focused on the file on her desk. "No, it did not."

"You met Marcus Cortland?" Lena exclaimed rounding on her at the desk. "I can't believe you met him! What was he like? Was he handsome and sexy as all hell? Was he sophisticated? What am I talking about, of course he was all those things. I want to hear everything." She finished her ramble and dropped into the seat next to Grant, an expectant look on her face.

Sabryna stared at her in open mouth fascination. "How do you know who he is?"

"Are you kidding me?" Lena cried out. "He's in the society columns all the time. Or the business section of the paper. He's rich, handsome, and single. Did you know he was born into money but started his own business from scratch?"

"What are you, his biggest fan?" Sabryna couldn't hide her surprise. Was she the only one who hadn't known this guy existed? "Anyway, it was a brief meeting, barely nothing."

"Nothing?" Grant didn't sound convinced. "The two of you talked for quite a while and you danced together."

He also invited me to share his bed, she thought. Lena's already dropped mouth would fall on the floor. "Yes, we danced. However, he didn't appear interested in the center."

"Well, what did he say?" Grant and Lena asked at the same time.

Sabryna hesitated. "He asked me to dinner and I said no."

"What were you thinking?" Lena shot out of her chair. "You were asked on a date by a fine, rich, successful business man and you said no." Lena threw her hands up in the air. "I just don't know what to say."

In a much calmer tone, Grant remarked, "You should've said yes."

"Why?" Sabryna asked. Grant rarely made comments on her personal life.

"If you went to dinner with him then you might be able to change his mind about donating to the center," he told her, proving once again where his priorities would always lie.

"You want me to prostitute myself for the center?"

A look of disgust crossed Grant's face. "Absolutely not! I'm suggesting that a friendly dinner might encourage him to be more generous in our direction."

Lena rose from her chair. "Ya'll are going to have to fill me in later, somebody has to do some work around here or these kids will tear this place apart." She shot Sabryna a quick girl-we-have-got-to-talk-about-this-some-more look and took off.

Sabryna looked back at her boss, wished he would follow suit. "Grant, you can drag me to these events and I'll do my best to raise money for this center, but don't ask me to do something I'm not comfortable with." She was definitely not comfortable with having dinner with Marcus Cortland, it was too dangerous.

Grant let out a sigh. "Okay, you're right." He lumbered up from his chair and headed for the door. "Anyway, maybe you'll get another chance to talk on Saturday. I'm sure he'll be at the Charity Golf Tournament." With those words, he left. Sabryna's heart raced at the thought of encountering him once again.

❦

"Sabryna?"

Startled to hear her name called by a familiar male voice, Sabryna stiffened before she turned around to see who it was. She'd been preparing herself all week for a run in with Marcus. She turned and scanned the crowds of people moving around on the lawn, partnering up and preparing for a day of golfing and networking at the Richmont Country Club Annual Charity Golf Tournament. Her eyes alighted on a tall man weaving his way through the crowd toward her.

She recognized him. "Steven?" Allowed a smile of relief to spread across her face. Steven Barclay and she had attended college at the University of Virginia together. She was a freshman when he was a senior. Steven was a handsome male, standing at over six feet tall with coffee colored skin and soulful brown eyes. He had a great sense of humor and seemed to enjoy life. Of course enjoying life was simple for a good-looking guy born to a rich family. At one point, they'd attempted to date, but that had fizzled, dissolving into a comfortable friendship. Sabryna never expressed it, but she always sensed his heart was with someone else.

"Sabryna, I didn't expect to see you here. How have you been?" Steven asked as he approached her. He pulled her into a brotherly hug.

"I've been good. And you, are you still breaking hearts?"

His smile was relaxed. "Every chance I get."

Sabryna laughed and gave him a quick update on what had been going on in her life. As she spoke, she realized that everything centered around work. Nothing in her list seemed to be about her personal life.

Steven must have noticed it too, he glanced at her ring finger. "No husband?"

She smiled tightly. "No not yet. Work keeps me too busy." It was her standard response. "In fact, that's why I'm here today. The center is going to receive a percentage of today's profits so my boss and I are here as representatives." Wanting to change topics she asked, "How is the banking business going?"

They continued to swap stories for a few more minutes and then he made her promise that they would have lunch soon. He left to join the group he would be golfing with that day, reminding Sabryna that she needed to sign herself up for a group. She had been headed to the information table to do just that when Steven had called her name. Returning to her earlier task, she set out to locate the information table. Distracted, she ran into a hard male body. Looking up, she came face to face with Marcus.

His lips curved upward in a smile. "Were you looking for me?"

She managed not to humph. "Actually, I was looking for the information table so that I could sign up for a partner, Mr. Cortland." She took a step back.

He took a step closer. "Marcus. And I could help you with that."

Her heart skipped a beat. "Thank you, but no. I can find it on my own."

"Why do you say no to everything I ask you?"

"Because you have yet to ask me anything I want to say yes to." Sabryna loved her cheeky answer. She could do this. She could engage in verbal warfare with him and not feel her knees go weak when he looked as though she were the biggest gift on Christmas morning. Did he have to look so fine? He was golfing for goodness sake. Weren't people supposed to look ridiculous when they golfed? Yet his white pants and vest with a red polo shirt underneath brought out the golden specks in his eyes. She started to move past him.

"I noticed you talking to Barclay," he told her. "How do you know him?"

Freezing in her get-away tracks, she stared at him. "Why does it matter?"

His eyes lifted from her to scanning the crowd over her head as he spoke. "No reason, I would just be more careful of the company I keep."

How dare he, she thought. He was the one who invited her to share his bed after knowing her for ten minutes, and here he was casting aspersions on someone else. On someone else that she considered to be a friend. "I thank you for your advice." She looked him up and down. "And I think I'll heed it. Now if you'll excuse me." She moved to step past him and froze anew when he reached out and locked his hand on her arm. The contact was enough to send the blood pumping through her veins. Bewildered and a little off balance, she looked from where he touched her to where his eyes studied her.

"Why is it that you're always angry with me?"

Sabryna almost laughed in disbelief. "Let me think." Sarcasm laced her tone. "I haven't spent more than an hour in your company, yet, in that time I've been cornered in a dark garden, propositioned for a night of meaningless sex, interrogated about my choice of friends, and forced to tolerate aspersions on my character in reference to my choices. Tell me, don't you think I've had enough provocation?"

His smile stretched from ear to ear, causing the flecks in his eyes to shimmer. "Did anyone ever tell you that you have a very impressive vocabulary?"

Shocked at his words, she caught herself smiling. "Mr. Cortland…"

"Marcus," he insisted.

"Marcus," she conceded. "I really need to…"

"Let me guess, go?" he asked. "I have a better suggestion. How about if you and I…"

"Marcus?" A female voice all but purred, bringing their conversation to a screeching halt. "I've been looking for you."

They both turned to look and Sabryna found herself facing what had to be the most beautiful woman she'd ever seen. Her skin was a rich mocha brown and her dark eyes were exotic. She had a face that caused men to fight wars just to impress her. Sabryna used her free hand to push a strand of hair out of her face that had escaped from her bun and tried not to feel too frumpy. As the woman walked toward them, her body swayed as if moving to a rhythm.

A young man, most likely in his thirties, accompanied her. He was tall, slim, and carried himself in a debonair fashion, as he strolled in the lady's wake.

"Marcus," she drawled as she drew up in front of them. "I was wondering where you were. And now that I've found you, I'm guaranteed to have an interesting afternoon. Are you partnered yet?"

"Hello Adrina, Anthony." He greeted both individuals then turned toward Sabryna. She held her breath and waited for him to excuse himself. "Sabryna, please meet Adrina Howell and Anthony Denton. Adrina, Anthony, Sabryna Givens, my partner."

Adrina turned sharp eyes to Sabryna, and Sabryna felt herself become the object of condescension, as the other woman looked her up and down as though she was lacking. She could sense the shock of the other woman. But, she thought, they could not be more surprised than she was. When had she agreed to be his partner? What made him want to partner with her when this beauty was begging to spend the day worshipping at his feet?

Anthony smiled. "Great, now Adrina can partner with me and save me the bother of finding someone else. The four of us can make a group." His announcement caused Adrina's perfectly arched eyebrows to furrow. Marcus released Sabryna's arm and moved to gather up his clubs.

Startled that he was acting as though everything was settled, she followed behind him. "Umm, I don't think this is a good idea."

"Of course it is," he told her.

Sabryna leaned toward him. "You don't understand. I'm really bad at golf."

"Then why are you here?" asked Adrina, her voice laced with repugnance.

Sabryna cut her eyes toward the other woman. "It's a charity event and I…"

"Oh, I get it now." Adrina's face suggested she'd just solved a confusing puzzle. "You're here for charity. That is sweet, but the players here take their game seriously. Isn't that right, Marcus?" She smiled at Marcus as though they were co-conspirators. "Perhaps you would feel better starting off at the driving range. I can point you in the right direction."

Already annoyed, Sabryna was seething by the end of the speech.

This chick obviously made a sport out of sharpening her claws on other people. But Sabryna was not a passive scratching post and she would not let this woman intimidate her.

Once Marcus saw how horrible she was at golfing he might throw money at the center just to get her to stop playing. She turned to Marcus, whose face was expressionless and placed her free hand on his arm. His eyes lowered to where her hand rested on him. "I'm ready when you are."

CHAPTER THREE

So she also enjoyed a challenge, thought Marcus with a smile, as he watched Sabryna standing off to the side examining the different clubs in her bag. Her profile was to him and once again he was struck by how attractive she was. Her slim figure was draped in a pair of green and blue plaid pants and she wore a matching blue polo shirt. Her hair was pulled back in a severe bun and a few tendrils had escaped, falling enticingly over her right eye. His fingers itched to pull the rest of her hair free and watch as her curls danced down her back.

He enjoyed watching her spar with Adrina. Yet he wasn't surprised. After all, she had no trouble standing up to him. Adrina had decided a few months prior that he would be the perfect husband. He was sure it was his money that did the trick, and had no interest in her, marriage, or anything else that resembled commitment. At times, he would humor a woman like Adrina. She was smart, beautiful, aggressive and could prove to be an enjoyable lover. But she would want more and he refused to let anyone expect more than he was willing to offer. In such circumstances, it was best to stay away from clingy women like Adrina.

"Isn't that the girl I saw you dancing with at the benefit the other night?" Anthony asked as he approached Marcus. They were standing at the first hole and he had just finished putting. It was Adrina's turn now. "Is there something going on between the two of you?"

Marcus didn't turn to his best friend when he answered him. "Yes. And soon." Anthony let out a low chuckle. "Does she know that?"

"She will." Marcus glanced up just in time to catch a bemused look from Sabryna. He immediately walked over to where she stood. "What's wrong?"

Sabryna held up two clubs. "I have no idea what I'm doing," she whispered. "And I refuse to let that idiot woman know."

She was asking for his help. Her vulnerability was endearing, even more so because she had dropped her guard. A small step, but a step in the right direction all the same. "Use this one." He handed her the nine iron. "When we get to the next hole watch which one I grab and do the same. If ever you get too close to the hole…" he paused as she raised a disbelieving eyebrow, "Use this one, it's a putter."

She gripped the nine iron and faced the course, sheer determination fell like a veil around her. She turned half way around and then looked over her shoulder at him. Her eyes told it all, but her beautiful lips still formed the words. "Thank you."

Marcus folded his arms across his body, strangely satisfied with himself. This was going to be an interesting day.

They lost horribly. After they returned, and parted from Adrina and Anthony, they began to make their way toward the tent that was set up for the evening's festivities of dinner and dancing.

Sabryna glanced at Marcus strolling by her side and attempted not to smile. She hoped he would take their loss in stride. "If there was an award for the biggest losers today we would win hands down."

"We?" he remarked with dry amusement. "I don't believe I contributed to that particular victory. I at least hit the ball near the hole it was supposed to go into."

Sabryna laughed. "I tried. Is it my fault they placed all those trees in the way?"

His laughter joined hers. "Well, if you were aiming in the right direction the trees may not have been such a problem."

"Maybe I should stick to the driving range."

"You, sweetheart, should just stay clear of anything golf related," he joked and her laughter began anew. She just couldn't help it. Despite her desire to show up Adrina she had been a miserable failure on the course. She knew it would happen, she had only played the game two other times with similar results. However, no matter how far behind she had set them Marcus never once lost his temper. He helped her choose the right club, encouraged her when it was her turn to swing, and smiled every time she sent the ball flying in the wrong direction. He was so supportive that even Adrina's facetious comments or obvious attempts to ingratiate herself with Marcus hadn't set her off. Much to her surprise, Marcus had remained attentive and agreeable, and after awhile she started to enjoy herself.

One of the attendants came up to her and handed her a note. "This is from a Mr. Morganfield," he told her before taking off. She opened the note and scanned it.

"Is there a problem?" Marcus asked.

She glanced up. "Grant's wife wasn't feeling well. He thought it best if he went home. I wasn't planning to, but he wants me to stay for the dinner."

"Excellent," Marcus declared. "Now we can have dinner together."

"I…I don't know," Sabryna responded. She wasn't surprised he asked but she was surprised that she wanted to say yes. "I'm not sure if it's a good idea."

"What can happen in a tent full of people?" He gestured toward the tents. "Besides, you owe me."

"I owe you?"

"If it wasn't for me you would still be in the woods at the ninth hole trying to hit your ball out of the dirt."

Sabryna burst into laughter. "Do you think they figured out you hit the ball for me. Your friend Anthony did give me a strange look when we emerged."

He waved the comment aside. "Anthony may have guessed but he's smart enough not to say anything."

Sabryna smiled. She had enjoyed his company today and she wasn't ready for it to end. He was right, what could happen in a tent surrounded by people? " I'll have dinner with you."

"Thank you." He took her hand in his.

The heat from his palm traveled up her arm and warmed her. Reminding herself it was just dinner and there were hundreds of people around, she squelched the impulse to run and once again followed temptation.

<hr/>

Dinner was a scrumptious affair. Each course was a culinary delight. Sabryna thought, as she savored her third glass of Chardonnay, no matter what she thought of this world there were definite perks.

However, despite her lack of desire to admit it, she had to confess dining with Marcus was also a pleasurable experience. His conversation was amusing and intelligent. He could converse on all kinds of subjects and he kept her entertained with anecdotes about the people around him. She was surprised to learn that when it came to the society where he was such a prominent member, he possessed a certain amount of cynicism.

Despite this cynicism, those around Marcus admired and respected him. The tables were set up so that there were ten people at each. Unlike other events she attended with a similar crowd, with Marcus leading the discussions, the topics of conversation were interesting and engaging. When he spoke, the other occupants at the table hung on his every word and seemed to put a lot of stock in his opinions. As she listened, Sabryna could understand why. Marcus knew his stuff. He was blunt without being callous. He was matter of fact and confident in his statements. Maybe she had been too quick to judge.

Even as she thought it, she dismissed the idea that she had been hasty in her judgment. For all his enigmatic charm, he was still the man that offered her sex after knowing her for a few short minutes. That too had been the real him, another side of the man that she was meeting today. It would be a mistake to forget it. She hadn't gotten this far in life without knowing when to protect herself. Her heart skipped a beat each time he looked at her, or that he was the most handsome man she'd ever met. It didn't matter that when he draped his arm over the back of her chair during dinner and leaned in close to whisper something to her, his nearness elicited a strange tingling feeling in her bones.

Yet for one night, she could relax, and enjoy her third…no now it was fourth, glass of wine and forget she was a fortress.

Marcus leaned in closer to her. "I could use a quiet moment. Would you like to take a walk?"

Sabryna looked out into the clear night. Other guests were dancing, laughing, and seizing the moment. She resolved to do the same. She had never had so much fun at one of these events. She looked into his eyes and melted. He rose and extended his hand to her. Just one night, she thought, and nodded in answer.

Marcus told himself not to question his luck. He hadn't expected her to say yes, but he wasn't going to quibble. As they followed an isolated but well-lit path that took them away from the tent area, the music became a faint melody in the night and Marcus's shoulders were relieved of their tension.

As they lapsed into a comfortable silence, he allowed his mind to explore his reasons for wanting to stroll. His plan was to seduce her, after all, and he couldn't do it with an audience. Tonight, he'd simply wanted to enjoy her company. And he had. That was until he noticed the inquisitive gazes of other men. They were wondering if he would get bored with her and leave her to them. He almost growled on the thought. For her part, she appeared not to notice. But he did, and refused to watch them ogle her. He experienced the same level of annoyance when he sighted her earlier that day talking to that fool Steve Barclay. It was safest not to think too much on why he felt this way. All he knew was that he couldn't think past the need to get her to himself.

How long before he could have her crying out in passion in his bed? He bit back the words and asked instead, "Did you enjoy yourself?"

Her smile broadened and she glanced at him. This action must have been too much, because she tripped up. He put a hand out to steady her. She giggled. "It would seem I've really enjoyed the wine."

He laughed. "Maybe, I should take you home."

She turned to face him, halting him in his tracks, she poked him in his chest. "Mr. Cortland, I'm not going to sleep with you."

"Are we back to Mr. Cortland?" He reached out and grabbed her elbows, yanking her into his chest. "And here I thought your opinion of me was improving."

"It did…it has."

"Well, then you'll understand when I tell you I just want to see you safely home." He wanted more than that. The effect of her body so close to his was enough to solidify that fact in his mind. But he was determined that when they hooked up, she would be willing and consenting, not loaded up with wine. "You don't drink often do you?"

She shook her head. "I guess I may have overdone it."

He chuckled. "That's a pretty safe guess. Will you let me take you home?"

She raised a skeptical eyebrow, but still she conceded. "I'd appreciate it."

Sabryna's apartment was located about twenty-five minutes from the golf course. They took Marcus's car and left hers at the club. She gave him directions to her apartment. She lived on the first floor near the front of the complex and situated on a slight hill. As a result, five steps led up to her front door. She stepped up to the fourth one and then stopped. She turned and looked at Marcus who had followed her out of the car.

Marcus came to the first step and stared up at her building. The area was well lit. It had an attractive façade, a white wash with royal green trim. He wondered if she would invite him in. Prepared himself to say no if she did.

"Thank you for seeing me home."

He heard the words but his attention was focused on her mouth, imaging what it would be like to kiss those luscious lips.

"I really enjoyed dinner, and the game, and even though we lost, I had a great time."

She was rambling, he noticed, and rummaging through her purse, he guessed for her keys. He stepped onto the second step.

"And I want you to know I don't usually drink so much, I mean I'm not a raging alcoholic or anything, but I just…"

He stepped up to the third step, towering slightly over her. Her intoxicating brown eyes lowered to his lips as her words died off. He bent toward her, wanted to taste her. He leaned to touch his lips to hers, felt something give away beneath him, and went tumbling to the ground.

Flat on his back, Marcus had a wonderful view of the clear night sky.

"Oh my God, are you okay?" Worry and shock laced her voice as her face hovered into his vision. She dropped to the ground beside him, looking at him as though he needed fixing and she didn't know where to start. "Are you okay? Did you break anything?"

He groaned. "Just my dignity." She slapped her hands over her mouth, but it didn't catch the giggle that escaped. He couldn't help but notice how her eyes sparkled when she was amused. "I can't believe you are laughing at me at a time like this."

She clutched her arms to her side and laughed harder. He smiled, despite himself. "I'm sorry," she told him in between fits of laughter. "That step has been loose for a while. I should have warned you, but I never would've suspected that would happen."

"Is that what happened? The step crumbled under me?" And here he had just thought God was getting revenge because he was daring to touch one of his Angels. He sat up and took inventory of his injuries. His back and his elbows were a little sore, but other than that, he didn't think there was any real damage. He looked back into her smiling eyes. "You are so beautiful."

Marcus didn't know where the words came from. He hadn't so much thought them as he had just felt them. She sobered before his eyes, as she tucked a wayward strand of hair behind her ear and glanced down as though embarrassed.

"Thank you for…Oh my goodness your arm."

He looked at his arm at the same time she grasped it and pulled it into the light. He was sure she had been about to thank him for his compliment. He found her habit of being super polite when she was uncomfortable or angry endearing. Now his arm distracted her. He examined the damage. His sleeve had ripped and his arm was scraped and bleeding.

"Come on, come inside so I can bandage that up for you." Her hands on his shoulder urged him to stand and come with her.

"That's okay," he told her. He didn't trust himself not to take things to far if left alone with her. "I think it'll be okay until I get home."

"No, that wound should get cleaned up right now." She helped him stand.

Reluctantly, he followed her up the steps. He could rein in his raging hormones, let her slap a quick band aid on his over sized paper cut, and remain honorable in light of her somewhat inebriated state. If for nothing else, this episode should advance her seduction along.

In contrast to her earlier nervousness, she efficiently located her keys, unlocked her door, and ushered him inside. "Have a seat on the couch," she ordered, gesturing in the general direction of the living room. She flipped on a light, dropped her purse on a table by the door, and headed off "to gather supplies" she announced over her shoulder before disappearing.

He wondered what constituted "supplies." She wasn't cleaning a gun shot wound. Shaking his head at the thought, he took stock of her apartment. It was a small space. In fact, the apartment he lived in while attending college had been larger. Granted he couldn't see her bedroom, but what he could see was a tiny living room with a fireplace and a tidy kitchen area. A counter separated the two rooms. To the right of the kitchen was a breakfast nook hosting a round table. However, despite the lack of space the apartment was well decorated. He strolled in to the living room and looked around. The center of the room housed a cushy light blue couch with matching love seat. Books were stacked up on the mahogany coffee table. There was a small television in the corner, with more books stacked up beside it.

Noticing the picture frames lined up on the fireplace, he walked over to get a closer view. Most of the pictures appeared to be taken at the center. One of Sabryna smiling, surrounded by a group of giggling girls. Another of three boys holding up paintbrushes wearing broad smiles. And another of Sabryna and Grant, standing with a young lady in a high school graduation gown. There was only one picture that didn't look work related. It was a family portrait of an attractive young black couple and their daughter. He would've recognized those mahogany colored eyes anywhere. It was Sabryna at about five, with what must be her parents.

"Sorry it took so long." Sabryna walked back into the room with her 'supplies.' She sat on the couch and laid the items out on the coffee table.

He joined her. "Okay, Dr. Givens." Marcus presented his scraped arm. "I'm all yours."

"Well, in that case. I'm going to need you to get undressed."

Marucs just stared at her as though an alien head grew from her body. Sabryna grinned, it was nice to be able to shock him for a change. "Just your shirt," she clarified, having mercy on him. "I can't clean and bandage your wound through your sleeve."

He looked down at his shirt as if he was seeing it for the first time. Then he reached down and took off his vest. As his hands went to the buttons on his shirt, Sabryna braced herself for what came next. Her earlier cockiness slid off her with the same ease as his shirt fell from his body when she found herself looking at a broad, muscular chest. Her mouth went dry.

She picked up the rag, dipped it in the bowl of warm water that she'd brought, and started to wring it out. "I'd like to apologize for any inconvenience or discomfort that's been caused by my faulty step, I'm …"

"Sabryna?" he interrupted with a gentle smile. "I'm okay, just clean the cut."

She began to clean his wound.

"Your parents are a handsome couple."

Startled, she glanced up from her task. With his head, he gestured toward the fireplace and told her, "I saw their picture."

"Oh."

"Do they live around here?" His breath fanned on to the back of her neck and a shiver raced down her spine.

"My father lives in Georgia, and my mother is…dead."

"I'm sorry." Finished with cleansing his scratches, she looked up and for a moment their eyes locked. There was something in the recesses of his eyes and in the quiet solemnity of his words that reassured. It was as though he understood, and not just in that way that people were naturally sorry for any death. It touched something inside of her.

"Thank you." Sabryna cleared her throat. "But, it was a long time ago. I was very young."

"What happened?"

"She was killed in a car accident. My parent's were driving home one night when they were hit by another driver. My father survived with nothing more than a broken arm. My mother wasn't so lucky. She died three days later."

"How old were you?"

"Ten." She reached over and grabbed the bottle of alcohol.

"It must have been hard on you."

She shrugged. "It was tough on my father. He never quite recovered." Her thoughts stretched backed into the past and she felt the familiar sadness reach out. Shaking herself out of its hold, she held up the bottle of alcohol with a smile. "This might sting a little."

She wet the washcloth and applied it to his wound. He sucked in his breath. "I thought that was just going to sting a little."

She let out a low chuckle. "Aren't you supposed to be Mr. Big Shot CEO? You should be ashamed of yourself. I'm sure a little alcohol doesn't hurt as much as, a hostile takedown."

His smile lit up his eyes. "I wouldn't know, I've never been 'taken down'," he teased.

She rolled her eyes. "I guess I'm not up on my business lingo."

"I noticed," he quipped.

"I'm going to put some cream on your arm that should take the sting away from the alcohol." She rubbed the substance on his scratches with gentleness and tried not to think how smooth his skin felt. She watched in amazement as his muscles flexed and remembered once again that he was Sin incarnate. After she had applied the ointment, she placed a bandage over the area and gazed on her work with pride. "Okay, I'm finished and you're patched up." She looked up to find his chestnut eyes boring into hers. He lowered his eyes to her lips, subconscious, she licked them. "I, uh…" she started but froze as his hand came up and he traced his thumb over her lower lip. Caught in the moment, her breathing slowed as his thumb moved from her lips to her chin and he tilted up her head so their eyes met. Locked. She knew he was going to kiss her…wanted him to do so, had a split second to be surprised by that realization, before he leaned close and settled his lips on hers.

CHAPTER FOUR

At first, the kiss was tender. His lips slowly touched hers, the barest of caresses. He applied a bit more pressure, until she opened for him and let him in. His tongue explored hers, moving around in a sensual duel.

"God, you taste so good," Marcus whispered. "Like honey."

Sabryna was losing herself in their kiss. Her world had narrowed to the point where their lips met. She couldn't think beyond his touch and she didn't want to. She acted on pure instinct and yet it seemed as though she traveled a familiar route. It was the rightness of the moment that made her feel so wrong.

She had to stop, needed to pull back before she went over the edge. Her intent was to push him away, but when she put her hands to his chest and came into contact with bare skin all intents, all thoughts fled from her mind. Underneath her hands his muscles jumped, her heart echoed the sentiment. His lips continued to make love to her mouth and she could feel herself falling deeper.

No! She grabbed the leash of her self-control. Operating on pure self-preservation, she pushed him back, away from her, breaking the kiss. For a moment they just sat. Both of their breathing was choppy.

She searched for words. Found none, wondered where her ability to communicate had disappeared to.

He spoke first. "Are you...are you okay?"

She nodded, not sure she could give or should give the honest answer. "I, uh, I have to get up early. I think you should go."

His eyes searched hers.

She wondered for a second if he was going to argue, released a sigh of relief when he stood. She walked him over to the door and opened it. The cool night air restored her senses. "Thank you for the ride home."

Marcus flashed a smile and held up his bandaged arm. "Thank you for being my nurse." He stepped out onto the porch, but turned back to her. "Have dinner with me?"

She shook her head. "I'm sorry, I just don't think it would be a good idea. We enjoyed each other's company tonight, can we please just leave it at that?"

He opened his mouth as if to say more. But he didn't. He just turned and walked away.

Shutting the door, Sabryna fell back against it. Sliding to the floor, she wondered just what crazy impulse was it that had made her feel as though she would have been willing to go to bed with him? Not only that, but what was it about her that he seemed to find so interesting.

"He wouldn't find me interesting if he knew I was a virgin," she mused out loud. It was the truth. Guys like that wanted women who knew the game. She wasn't one of those females, had never been. In high school and college, she'd been focused on her studies. Guys had called her serious, nice, and smart - never sexy, beautiful, nor fascinating. Yet, Marcus treated her as though she were all those things. She was use to guys seeing her as a good friend and nothing more. She never got close enough to anyone to have a real relationship. As a result, her virginity had stayed intact.

She wondered if when Marcus looked at her he saw a sex kitten. She giggled at the thought. Yet, he seemed to be pursuing her. She sensed tonight that he wanted her. Knew in her bones if she'd offered they would've spent the night in her bed. Would that have been so bad? After all, who wants to be the twenty-seven year old virgin?

A night of pleasure with a man she found intoxicating was a desirable prospect.

But what would happen in the morning. He would leave, go about his life, and never give her a second thought. Men like that wanted one thing. Marcus had made it clear where his thoughts lay. She was not interested in being anyone's one night stand.

Sabryna stood and headed off to bed, trying to ignore the fact she had declined his invitation when what she wanted was a night like tonight.

Oh well, she thought. She had her moment of fantasy, now it was time to rejoin reality.

"Earth to Sabryna." Steven waved his hand in front of her face.

Sabryna blinked, bringing herself out of a daydream. "Huh? Oh, sorry." She took a sip from her glass of water. "My mind must've wandered." Her mind had wandered all right, back to a kiss that she was still feeling five days later.

It was Wednesday afternoon and she and Steven were having

lunch together at The Cascades, an upscale restaurant located inside of the Grand Regency Hotel. Sabryna had heard a lot of praise for the restaurant, but had never had the opportunity to dine there. When Steven called her on Monday and invited her to lunch at The Cascades, she'd jumped at the chance to catch up with an old friend. Taking a lunch break outside of the center was unusual, and seeing as how the kids were in school, it made that easier. On top of that, Steven was a perfect candidate to sponsor her basketball tournament that she was planning a couple of months from now to raise money. She needed organizations and community members to put together teams and sign up for the event.

However, no matter her list of acceptable reasons, the fact of the matter was that by noon Monday she knew she was in desperate need of a distraction. Something that would take her mind off that spellbinding moment when Marcus Cortland first touched his lips to hers. On Monday, she had buried herself in her work. But that didn't have its usual numbing affect. She was sure this would help, and provide a few moments of enjoyment. Based on her earlier distraction, she could say it hadn't worked.

Five days later and she could still taste him.

"That's okay," Steven assured her with a patient smile. "My mind has been known to do the same thing. But anyway, I was just thinking out loud who I could round up to form a team for your tournament."

Sabryna smiled. She knew Steven would get in the spirit. She hadn't forgotten how easy going he was in college. "I'll fax the registration forms over to you. I really appreciate this."

"Well, since I've put your mind at ease maybe you can do the same for me." Steven took a bite of his pecan-crusted catfish.

Sabryna let her confusion show in her voice. "I'm not sure how, but I'll do what I can."

They paused as the waitress came to refill her ice tea. Sabryna used the opportunity to take a bite of her chicken fettuccini and dwell on the fact that for a low maintenance girl like herself she had sure been in a lot of high society situations as of late. The restaurant, a posh four star establishment, boasted more silverware on the table for one place setting than Sabryna had in her entire apartment.

"What's was going on between you and Marcus Cortland?" Steven's usual relaxed smile was replaced by a more serious expression.

Shocked, she froze, mentally as well as physically.

"I know that we haven't talked in a while. And I know that I have no right to ask. But you're my friend and I wouldn't want to see you get hurt."

She took a drink of her tea. What was going on between her and Marcus? Maybe it was best just to stick to the truth. "Nothing." She hadn't lied. The kiss, if not the memory of it, was safe in the past.

His look dripped skepticism. "Are you sure?"

She fidgeted with the napkin in her lap. "Yes." It sounded weak even to her ears so she added with more firmness, "he asked me out, I said no. That's all."

Steven took a deep breath as if he were contemplating her answer. "You two seemed ...close at the dinner after the tournament."

"We were partners." Now she was starting to feel interrogated. "Steven what is it that you want to know?"

He cleared his throat, readjusting himself in his chair. "I've known Marcus all of my life. We grew up together. I wouldn't call us friends, but we did run in the same crowds as boys. Marcus was always..." he visibly searched for the right words. "Cold."

Cold was the last adjective she would use to describe him. Arrogant, bossy, proud, and sophisticated. Cold, never. Her blood was still warm from where he'd heated her up. "Is that you're polite way of saying he's a bastard?".

Steven chuckled. "That's the Sabryna I remember. Always quick to call a duck a duck."

"Those weren't my words," she reminded him.

He conceded with a nod. "I know it sounds harsh of me, but you have to understand, I know what kind of person he is. The Cortland name is old and prestigious. Marcus is use to having everything handed to him. He takes what he wants and offers no apologies and no excuses."

She couldn't argue with his last point, Sabryna thought grimly. Hadn't Marcus ordered her to cancel her plans, he didn't know they were fictional, and fall into bed with him the first night she'd met him? Yet still there were holes in this character analysis. "Steven, no offense, but didn't you grow up just as privileged?"

"The name Barclay pulls weight, but not the way the name Cortland does." He took a long swallow of water. "When Marcus decides there is something he wants nothing stand in his way. He'll tell you everything you want to hear and seduce you with your own dreams. But once he gets bored, that's it. He moves on to the next challenge."

She told herself she didn't care, but a sinking feeling developed in the pit of her stomach. She had to shake it off. If Steven's information was correct then she had done the right thing. "Didn't he eschew his family's money and start a company from scratch?"

"That he did do," Steven offered in a grudging tone. "No one's sure why, but he sold his families company at a questionable profit and started his own. But that wasn't until he took over as head of the family at nineteen after his father died."

That news startled Sabryna. Marcus' dad had died? He hadn't said, hadn't even mentioned as he listened to her go on and on about her own mother's death. No wonder there was such understanding in his eyes, he too had experienced the loss of a parent, but he had chosen not to share that information with her. Instead, he held back. "Thanks for the warning. However, Marcus was only a potential donor for the center. That's all."

Steven smiled. "I won't lie. I'm happy to hear that. I don't want to see you get hurt."

"I understand," she assured him and not wanting to discuss it further, changed the subject.

However, twenty minutes later the subject walked into the door.

Steven was in mid-sentence when something caught his eye behind her. He froze and a brief look of antipathy crossed his face. His sentence trailed of into obscurity. Curious, Sabryna turned around to see what was responsible for this reaction and her eyes locked with Sin.

Marcus was being seated several tables over from them. He was in the company of Anthony Denton, the guy they'd golfed with on Saturday. Marcus held her gaze for a long minute. Then his eyes went past her to Steven. When his attention returned to her something flashed in the brown depths of his eyes. Other than that, his face was unreadable. Anthony Denton followed his friends gaze and seeing her gave a short wave, then sent a cool nod toward Steven before taking his seat. Breaking eye contact with her, Marcus did the same. Feeling strange and not quite knowing why, Sabryna turned around. "I guess we talked him up," she quipped, hoping to lighten the tension that now crackled in the air.

Steven offered a tight smile. "I guess so."

They could not return back to their light hearted chatting of before. Their lunch ended, and after exchanging goodbyes, they parted ways in the lobby. Steven left, explaining he needed to get to a meeting, but Sabryna made a pit stop by the ladies' room. When she finished, she walked through the elegant lobby, distracted as she searched through her purse for the keys to her car.

Suddenly, she was grabbed from behind. A strong hand locked about her upper arm in a secure vise and she was spun around. She found herself staring into the eyes of Sin. And if the flashing fire in his eyes was any indication, he wasn't happy.

"Enjoy your lunch?" Marcus bit out.

Outraged at his rough manner, Sabryna attempted to jerk her arm from his grasp to no avail. "Let me go!"

"I'm trying to understand why you refuse to have dinner with me, and yet here I find you flaunting yourself in front of Barclay."

She was so astounded all she could do was stare. He was angry. The realization was such a shock that she stopped struggling to free her arm from his grip. "I don't believe it's any of your business what I do, or who I do it with."

The last part of that statement increased his scowl. "Don't be foolish. What type of game do you think you're playing?"

"Me? If you think I'm the one playing a game then you're delusional."

"I warned you to be careful about the company you keep." His tone was scathing "Unless you're hoping to become just another notch on his belt."

"It's so amazing the high opinions the two of you seem to have of each other," she retorted with dry sarcasm.

That took him back a little. "What did that pompous jerk say about me?"

"He didn't tell me anything I couldn't figure out myself," she shot back. "And right now, you seem to be the one acting like a jerk. Steven was nothing but respectful to me."

He pulled her up against his rock hard chest, the contact made her tense in anticipation as he lowered his lips to her ears. "And did he make you burn the way that I did," he whispered seductively into them.

She didn't need the reminder. Not while being this close to him. "Let me go."

At her forceful demand, he conceded. She stepped back. Why had she even bothered to doubt Steven's words about Marcus? Here was living proof that Marcus could be...cold? She'd no intention of being a notch on anyone's belt. Pulling her purse close to give her some protection, she gave him a bold stare. "The other night was a mistake. A stupid, stupid, mistake that will never happen again." And with those words, she left.

It was the sound of gunshots that woke him up. Disoriented and still half asleep it took Marcus several moments before he realized the noise had been a part of his dream. The only sound in his dark bedroom was his choppy breathing. He gazed up into the skylight that loomed over his bed. The sole source of light was coming from the moon shining dully into the room.

He rolled over and to view the clock. It read 3:37 a.m. That nightmare had woke him before. Many times before. It haunted his dreams the same way it haunted his memories.

Knowing sleep wouldn't come soon, he pushed back the covers and headed for the kitchen. Once there, he opened the fridge, letting the light spill onto the ceramic tiled floor. He didn't mind the darkness, it was quiet and serene. Sitting at the counter of the kitchen island, he sipped a glass of water. He lived alone in the penthouse at the top of Elliot Towers.

However, being alone on nights like this, when his memory was in overdrive, was always taxing. There was no one around to distract him from his thoughts or his dreams.

Once again, his memory recreated the sound of gunshots. Why was he thinking about this tonight? It had been so long since it had crossed his mind. Well, that was almost the truth. It was always there, a part of who he was, the reason he was who he was. Never let any one get to close. It was dangerous. Not to him, but to them. The past had proven that.

He shook himself out of his reverie. He needed something stronger than water. He walked over to the bar in his spacious living room and poured himself a brandy. With his glass of brandy secure in his grip, he padded over to the large bay window his feet sinking into the luxurious carpet. His condo had an excellent view of the city and he gazed unseeing into the quiet of the night.

He turned his thoughts away from the darkness of his past toward the light that shone from the eyes of one beautiful Angel as she laughed and walked with him in the moonlight. Or the light that dulled in sadness as she had talked about the death of her mother, minimizing her pain in lieu of her fathers. Or the way that light had turned to lightning as she spit fire at him that afternoon. He didn't know if his fascination stemmed from her or from the way he reacted every time she floated into his orbit.

What had he been reduced to? Either he was acting like a jealous barbarian wanting to whisk her away to a secluded tower, or like a pathetic schoolboy allowing her to doctor a few scratches just so that he could be close to her.

Had she been any other woman he would have had her in bed several times by now. He was now sure that once would not be enough. Not after that kiss.

But Sabryna was different. She had a sense of pride and purpose that prevented her from jumping mindlessly into bed with him. Although, he was sure she'd been tempted, she held back. Was it a show of great morality and innocence or was she playing the game at another level? He wasn't sure. As beautiful as she was, she must have had plenty of lovers. What did they possess that convinced her to lower her guard? The thought of her lying naked in another mans arms made his stomach churn.

What did he know about her?

Well, she was beautiful, maybe the most beautiful woman he'd ever met. She carried herself with grace and elegance. She was funny. Outside of his family, he had never enjoyed so much being in one person's company. She had a quick wit and a dry sense of humor. She had the ability to laugh at herself, she wasn't afraid to stand up to him, and she didn't tolerate foolishness. She was opinionated, kind, when he wasn't provoking her, and she was willing to rise to a challenge.

And she tasted like honey.

He grew hard just at the thought of their kiss. It had taken every ounce of control not to push her back on the couch and make love to her.

Uncomfortable, he shifted. Time for him to take her seduction to the next level. But, how did he regain the ground he'd lost earlier when he acted like a jealous idiot.

Of course, he did feel justified. His warning hadn't been for purely selfish reasons. He'd known Steven Barclay all his life. They'd grown up together, gone to school together, chased girls together. And in that category Steven and Marcus has used a similar practice, tell a girl what she wanted to hear, get what you want, and move on to the next. From all he had observed in recent years Steven's script hadn't changed, but Marcus's had. An unfortunate incident had taught him that it was unwise to play with anyone's heart. If a woman got involved with him, she did so with her eyes wide open and no illusions.

Even now, he couldn't place the emotions that had gripped him when he walked into The Cascades and seen his Angel calmly having lunch with a playboy. The thought that they might already be lovers had sent him spiraling down a dark path.

Marcus could admit it had been a bad move on his part to act the aggressor in the lobby. It had surprised him and alienated her. But what was he to think, she hadn't explained her relationship with Barclay to him. Still hadn't, but he would have his explanation.

It was time to gather the troops and lay siege at his Angel's stronghold.

CHAPTER FIVE

"We're headed for trouble," Lena announced as she walked into Sabryna's office the next afternoon.

Glancing up from her desk where she was pouring over the budget, Sabryna responded, "I agree." She continued holding up the papers as though she just didn't know what to do, "I keep working and reworking the numbers, but the money is just not adding up. I can understand why Grant has been so pushy to get sponsors. We need a lot more funds or we're going to have to start cutting programs."

Lena waved aside her remarks and walked over to stand in front of the windows that overlooked the common room. "I'm not talking about the budget. I'm talking about that kid over there." She pointed at the glass.

Wondering who had her friend's feathers ruffled, Sabryna joined Lena at the window. "Which kid?"

She pointed again. "The one sitting next to Lamont Cross." Sabryna looked to where Lena indicated. She recognized Lamont, a junior in high school. He was a regular at the center. Her eyes moved to the boy sitting next to him. He was tall, she guessed about six foot two. She also pinned his age to be about 16 or 17. He was wearing a pair of baggy blue jeans and an oversize black hoodie. He and Lamont were at one of the Playstation centers. Lamont and another boy were playing a game, and he sat watching.

"His name's Damon. I haven't gotten the last name yet," Lena told her. "He's new to the neighborhood and he came in with Lamont today."

"And why is he trouble?"

"Well, all the girls are going crazy." Lena threw up her hands in exasperation. "You'd think Kanye West had just walked in the door."

Sabryna laughed. "I'm not surprised. He's not a bad looking kid."

"Yes, well, unfortunately Alexis Houston has also noticed that he's not a 'bad looking kid,'" Lena explained. "She's been gawking at him since he walked in. However, it seems her 'boyfriend' Carlos is not too happy about this. And you know how Carlos can get."

They both turned their attention to where Carlos and a group of his friends stood near the pool tables. Indeed, Carlos didn't appear happy. "Lena, your ability to keep up with the kid's gossip circuit is amazing."

Lena just shook her head. "You have to know these things to keep up with them."

"Even so, you know how everyone gets when a new kid comes around." Sabryna walked back to her desk. "Sizing each other up and ready to protect their territory. But Carlos, Lamont and all the rest know the rules, and soon they'll learn to coexist."

"I don't know." Lena turned around and leaned her back against the glass. "Damon's only been here a month and he's already been suspended from school five times. Latisha told me he has a very bad attitude."

Sabryna raised a skeptical eyebrow. "Latisha doesn't even go to the same school that he does, so how would she know?"

"She lives a couple doors down from him," Lena told her. "You know how nosy she is."

"That's true," Sabryna agreed. "Well, it doesn't matter. Most of our kids were trouble makers, some of them still are. But he's here, which means we have the chance to make a difference in his life." Sabryna returned her attention to the papers laid out on her desk. "As for now, I am up to my neck getting ready for this tournament. There's so many loose ends."

"Anything I can do to help?" Lena offered.

Sabryna smiled as her friend settled into the chair in front of her desk. "You could take over my anger group this afternoon." It was one of the groups they offered to help the kids learn certain life skills. Most of the members were younger and signed up by their parents.

"Oh, no," Lena declined. "I'm leaving early tonight. My husband is taking me out to dinner." Lena had gotten married two years ago to a wonderful man.

"Oh yeah, where are you two going?" asked Sabryna, happy for her friend.

"Well, I wanted to go to The Cascades," Lena told her. "But George is cheap. So, we're going somewhere else."

"The Cascades is nice," Sabryna informed her. "I had lunch there the other day."

"With Marcus Cortland?" Lena asked surprised.

"I had lunch with a friend of mine from college who I ran into at the golf tournament."

"Look at you," Lena whistled. "All these rich men wanting to wine and dine you. I'm impressed."

Sabryna leaned back in her chair and rolled her eyes. "Don't get too impressed. Steven is just a friend," she said firmly. "Marcus Cortland doesn't merit a mention."

"So, I take that to mean you're not going out on a date with him?"

Sabryna could hear the disappointment in Lena's voice. She shuffled her papers. "Lena, I don't have time to date. This center keeps me so busy."

"That's an excuse and you know it," Lena admonished her. "If you wanted to date you could find the time. Don't you want to get married and have children?"

The papers were shuffled and restacked again. "Sure, some day." She glanced toward the window. "But for now, this center is my priority."

Lena leaned forward. "Sabryna, it's great that you're so dedicated. Lord knows you have enough commitment for all of us here, but the fact of the matter is that at the end of the day these kids go home to their families. One day, they will grow up and have families of their own. Where does that leave you?"

Sabryna couldn't quite meet her friend's eyes. Lena was good at getting to the point.

"I'm sorry to put it to you like that, but I just want you to be happy. I want you to find a nice man and fall in love. You'll never do that if you're always pushing them away. You don't want to be a virgin forever do you?"

"Lena!" Sabryna shot her a look of embarrassment. "I should never have told you that."

Lena laughed. "It's amazing what a couple of glasses of wine will reveal."

Sabryna flushed. If only Lena knew what a few glasses of wine had lead her to the other night. She made a mental note to stay away from all alcoholic beverages.

Lena grinned. "Besides, I want my babies Godmother to be happy."

Confused, Sabryna said, "But you don't have children."

Lena patted her stomach. "I will in about seven months."

Sabryna shot out of her chair. "You're pregnant?" She embraced her friend. "That's wonderful. When did you and George find out?"

Lena settled back in her chair. "About two weeks ago. We wanted to wait to tell anyone."

Sabryna listened as Lena told her about how she first learned she was pregnant. Her friend glowed. For the first time Sabryna was cognizant of pangs of envy. What would it be like to have her own family? She could vaguely recall the time before her mother had died. The memories were random and foggy. The truth was she had no idea what it meant to be part of a family. Her father had been so devastated after her mothers' death that he'd hit the bottle. Providing his only child with a safe and secure home had been the last thought on his mind. And now that he was sober, he chose to be hundreds of miles away in Georgia. Their relationship was rocky, their conversations few and far between.

Until this moment, she'd never let herself imagine what it would be like to be part of a network of people who supported and loved each other. If she couldn't have it in her own life, then the least she could do was provide it for the children here.

Lena's voice trailed off as two girls entered the room and asked if they could speak with Sabryna. Lena excused herself and Sabryna turned her attention to what she did best. Her job. Sabryna let the whirlwind of her job relieve her mind from the sad turn it had taken her earlier.

She was back in her office that afternoon, finalizing some plans for the basketball tournament when Lena came rushing in. She slammed the door behind her, rounded Sabryna's desk and pulled her from it.

"Lena, what's going on?" Sabryna asked at her friend's strange behavior.

Lena didn't answer. She gave Sabryna a head to toe inspection, assessing her light colored khakis and white button up blouse. "I guess its okay, but let's undo those top buttons." Her hands went toward the buttons on Sabryna's shirt.

"What are you doing?" Sabryna slapped Lena's hands away. "Is this the crazy trimester?"

Lena went on, ignoring her comment. "Take your hair down. No, to obvious. Leave it up, but brush it back. And here I brought my make up case because I knew you wouldn't have any here." She dug through the bag. "You're in luck, I brought my Luscious Red lipstick with me."

Sabryna stared at Lena as though she were speaking Russian with an Italian accent. "Lena? I don't care if you brought the cosmetics counter at Macy's with you. I'm not doing anything until you tell me what's going on."

"Marcus Cortland just walked in."

"What!" Sabryna's frantic gaze swept her cluttered office.

"He came in just a minute ago," Lena informed her. "Grant is talking to him now, but I know he's headed here. He has flowers."

Sabryna stared at her friend. He was here! In the center. With flowers. Soon he'd be in her office. With flowers. She couldn't think, didn't stop to think, as she grabbed the makeup bag out of Lena's hand, and promptly dropped down to the floor behind her desk.

Lena knelt down beside her. "There's a mirror in there."

"Would you go and look out?" Sabryna dug for the mirror. She was sure her hair was in its usual disarray.

Lena hustled to the window and peered out. "He's still talking to Grant. Mios dios, he's good looking," she reported. "I thought you didn't care about Marcus Cortland," she teased.

Sabryna groaned. What could she say? She didn't want to look like a mess in front of Marcus, she had her pride. "What are they doing now?"

"They're headed this way." Lena turned from the window just as Sabryna stood up from behind her desk.

Sabryna smoothed her clothes. Sat down, stood back up and smoothed them again.

Lena waved for her to sit. "Don't be so obvious."

Sabryna did as ordered and wondered how she could be subtle and keep her heart from beating out of her chest all at the same time. Her door opened and she seized her customary cool. If she could deal with angry teenagers, she could deal with one infuriating man.

Grant stepped through first; his eyes passed over Lena and landed on Sabryna. He raised an eyebrow when he saw her luscious red painted lips. "Sabryna, you have a visitor."

Sabryna squelched a groan.

Marcus came through the door next taking up all the space in the room. She heard Lena emanate a soft sigh and in her mind she echoed the sentiment. He looked striking in a dark gray suit that fitted his large frame to perfection. He had a bouquet of tulips in his hand. She rose as he entered. "Hello, Mr. Cortland. Please allow me to introduce you to Lena Martinez one of our counselors here at the center." She extended her hand and prided herself on her calm.

"It's nice to meet you, Ms. Martinez." Marcus shot an easy smile toward Lena. His eyes, unreadable rested on Sabryna. "Good afternoon, Miss Givens. I hope you'll excuse my dropping by, but I had some free time this afternoon, so I thought to take you up on your invitation."

"My invitation?" Sabryna searched her memory.

"Yes, on the night of the charity ball," he informed her and then turned to Grant. "Miss Givens shared with me some of the wonderful things you all are accomplishing here and invited me to come see for myself."

Sabryna's memory snapped together in perfect clarity. Those weren't her exact words and it hadn't been an invitation.

Grant was looking from her to Marcus like a pleased papa. "Well, we're glad you were able to come visit."

Marcus spoke to Grant but his eyes burned into Sabryna. "I wasn't sure if Miss Givens would be too busy to meet with me. Especially, since my behavior may seem to come off rude." As he continued, he extended the bouquet of tulips toward her. "I hope you'll forgive me."

He was apologizing! This arrogant, overbearing, powerful man was apologizing to her. In quiet awe, she accepted the flowers. Her fingers stroked the long silky stems and ivory bulbs. She could feel Grant's and Lena's eyes on her. They would think he was apologizing for showing up unannounced, but she knew the truth. He was asking for forgiveness for his behavior at The Cascades. She raised her eyes to his and gave him her answer. "It's no problem. We're always happy to have a visitor to the center." She raised the flowers to her nose and inhaled the sweet fragrance. "Thank you."

Grant cleared his throat. "Well, if you'll excuse me I have to check on something. I'm sure Sabryna can show you around." He and Lena both left the room.

Alone with Marcus in her office wasn't the direction she'd expected her afternoon to go in, but here she was. She would have felt safer if a pterodactyl was flying around her office. "The tulips are lovely."

"The lady at the floral shop told me they meant forgiveness." His lips quirked up. "I thought it was fitting."

Folding her arms, she lounged against the corner of her desk. "We've had some rocky meetings, haven't we?"

His eyes lowered to her lips. "I wouldn't call all of them rocky," he said in a seductive drawl, then abruptly turned away. "However, my behavior the other day was uncalled for. So I wanted to apologize." He glanced around her small office. "And I admit, I was also curious about where you work."

She gestured into the air. "This is it. Would you like to see the rest of it?"

There was something likeable about the Middleton Youth Center, Marcus decided as his "tour guide" showed him around. It was a large two-story building, populated by a multitude of children and teenagers. There was a large common room with a television, several game stations, pool tables, and other rooms meant for meeting groups and studying.

He was impressed. He strolled beside Sabryna and listened to her soft husky voice as she explained the different facets of the center.

She certainly knew her stuff.

He was grateful she'd accepted his apology. He'd imagined himself being thrown out and chased by angry kids wielding sticks.

Time and time again, she was stopped by children wanting to talk to her. Each time, she gave a gentle redirection for them to wait before interrupting and then she introduced them to him. The kids would stare at him in open-mouthed fascination, but it was Sabryna they seemed to adore. He could understand why. It was obvious that she cared about them. They were just stepping on to the second floor, when the sounds of commotion reached them from around the corner. Two angry male voices drifted into the air along with a huge thud. Before he blinked, Sabryna took off running in that direction. Worried, he followed.

Rounding the corner, he took in the scene all at once. Two boys were fighting in the middle of a lounge area. Three other boys looked on to their credit, they were urging the other two to stop, but none seemed intent to break it up.

Sabryna ran straight to the boys and attempted to get between the two. Seeing her, one of the boys stopped, the other more like a charging bull, kept going. He sure wasn't about to watch her get pummeled by an enraged teen. He intervened quickly, grabbing the charging bull, holding him around the shoulders.

The boy struggled to break free. "Man, you betta let me go."

A furious Sabryna rounded on the calmer of the two. "I want to know what is going on right now, Carlos," she demanded.

"He was looking at my girl." Carlos jabbed his finger at him.

"Tell your girl to stop lookin' at me," sniped the other kid.

"Man, you better…" Carlos started forward.

Sabryna put her hand out to stop him. "Carlos, you know the rules here. There's no fighting."

"He started it…" Carlos started to argue but his words trailed off as Grant stepped on the scene.

"It doesn't matter who started it. We don't fight." Sabryna looked at one then the other. "If there's a problem, we mediate it. We fix it."

Carlos dropped his head. She placed a hand on his shoulder. "Don't worry, we'll work it out. Why don't the two of you go with Grant and discuss it?"

Carlos nodded, but the other kid spat in anger, "Man, I ain't got to do nothing. I don't want to discuss nothing with that punk." He shook himself free of Marcus and went ripping down the stairs.

"Come on Carlos, let's go to my office." Grant led Carlos away.

The rest of the kids sensing the drama had been diverted, and more than likely feeling guilty that they had not intervened, slinked away.

Marcus turned toward Sabryna, who started in silence in the direction that Damon had disappeared. "That was intense."

She let out a shaky breath. "I'm sorry you had to witness that."

He shrugged. "I survived." he quipped. "Do you make a habit of jumping into the middle of fights?"

She shrugged. "I do what I have to do."

"Maybe," he treaded with care. "It would be best if you could let Grant intervene instead."

"Grant can't always be there. If I'd waited they could've hurt each other."

"You could've gotten hurt." Part of him wanted to shake her until she admitted that truth.

Sabryna regarded him. "I don't want you to think that this kind of thing happens here all the time. What you witnessed is not what the Middleton Youth Center is all about."

"I can see the wonderful things you all are doing here." He reached out and took her hand in his, wanting to soothe her nerves with his touch. "I want to be a part of your mission. I want to donate."

Her eyes grew round with suspicious. She opened her mouth and before she could misunderstand him, he added, "No strings attached. I'm truly impressed. I want to help."

"Thank you."

Marcus waved her thanks aside. "It's important that we put back into the community. I want to donate, and I want to sign up for the tournament that you're planning."

Her smile grew wide and he felt like a hero. They went back to her office, where she retrieved the registration forms for the tournament, and he scribbled off a check. Her eyes went round at the figure on the check, but he ignored it.

He knew his stock had gone up. It was time to take a risk.

"Before I leave, I have one more question for you," he told her.

She looked at him.

"I want to take you to dinner."

Her copper eyes hooded. "Marcus, I..."

"Before you say no, hear me out," he interrupted. "I didn't do all this to set you up and I'm not expecting anything. I gave to the center because I wanted to. I asked you to dinner, because I would like to spend time with you. I want to know more about you." He heard the words, and the subtle ache in his bones told him he meant them.

She hesitated, and then smiled lightly. "Okay. I'll have dinner with you."

"Great." Marcus released a breath. "I'll pick you up at 8:00 on Saturday." He walked to the door and as he was about to exit he looked back. "Oh, and Sabryna," he called and then winked. "Wear something sexy."

CHAPTER SIX

Sabryna stood in front of her wardrobe and wondered for the fiftieth time what exactly constituted as sexy in Marcus Cortland's opinion. It may as well have been a foreign concept to her. Sure, she knew how to dress to the occasion, but to dress to appeal, to make Marcus's eyes pop out of his head? She was at a complete lost.

Lena called during one of these moments of deliberation with specific advice to offer. "Whatever you do, don't wear that bun on your head."

Somewhat offended, Sabryna said, "There's nothing wrong with my bun."

She could picture Lena rolling her eyes. "No, there's nothing wrong with your bun." Then she continued, "If you're planning to attend church."

Sabryna laughed, but when she got off the phone with Lena she went straight to the bathroom to curl her hair. She caught sight of her reflection in the mirror and for a moment wondered, what the hell was she doing.

It had to be impulse. A pure, unfettered, impulse that led her to accept his invitation to dinner. A quality that was not a trademark of her. She wasn't the kind of girl who lived on impulses, nor did she often give into temptation. But when he smiled at her, when his eyes devoured her, when he even simply walked in the room, she found herself being drawn to him. This, she thought, was the definition of crazy. The one person her mind told her to avoid her heart was begging her to get close too.

Best not to think too much into it, she decided, not when she still had to find something sexy. Returning to her closet, she decided on a cute red slip dress that she bought on a rare shopping trip to New York with Lena almost a year ago. The dress possessed a square cut neckline held up by spaghetti straps and it hugged her curves in all the right places. It fell to just above her knees, and was accented around the edges with a black lace threaded pattern. She knew the matching shawl would help keep her cool and she had the perfect shoes to go with the dress. She admired her reflection in the mirror, understanding the saying; if you feel sexy, you'll be sexy. In excitement and anticipation, she laughed out loud. The sound blended with that of the doorbell.

Marcus stood on the doorstep. The scene of the now infamous kissing crime. Or at least that was how he remembered it. The door swung open and a vision in red liquid silk filled his world. For a second he just stared. He'd wanted her to wear something sexy not give him a heart attack. That dress fit her like a glove and accented every perfect curve of her graceful form. Had she plucked it straight out of his imagination?

Sabryna smiled noting his reaction. "I take it you approve." She draped a matching shawl around her shoulders.

"You follow directions perfectly." He extended his arm and she accepted.

Sabryna felt like a princess as she allowed him to lead her down the steps, then caught sight of their ride and felt like a queen. A sleek black limo waited at the curb. A chauffeur in a starched black suit waited to serve them.

As they approached, the chauffeur opened the door and she slid in, feeling Marcus's weight as he settled beside her. She could've been awestruck at the limo. She had never ridden in one and she found it impressive, from the soft leather seats, to the shiny interior. There was even a small bar inside.

However, she was more impressed with her date. The arrogant, urbane man who was sitting next to her. As usual, he was dressed impeccably. She didn't know labels too well, but she could tell from the sharp cut of his black suit that it was expensive. He was at ease in these elegant surroundings. It was hard to be awed by anything but him when he was around.

"Where are we going?"

He stared at her for a long time, then reached out and tucked a wayward curl behind her ear. "I want you to be surprised."

She sat back and decided to just enjoy the moment.

From the corner of his eye, Marcus observed her. She seemed to be relaxing, but he was aware of a fine tension in her. He would aim at making some of her tension disappear before the night was through.

He sat back. His strategy was progressing right along. He did a quick review in his mind.

His first step had been to regain some of the ground he'd lost at The Cascades. That had been simple, an apology, which, thank goodness she accepted. The second had been even easier than the first. He knew he would need to show an interest in the things that concerned her. Nothing seemed as important to her as that community center. So he'd gone, and discovered his pretend interest had become real when seen through her eyes. He had been truly impressed by all that they were accomplishing there and it was nice to donate money and know how it would be used. That particular trip had been beneficial on so many levels. The third part of his plan was the step he was taking at this very moment.

Dazzle her.

The fact of the matter was that despite her large vocabulary, strong convictions, and incredible stubbornness, she was still a woman. A woman who had not been exposed to the type of lifestyle he was privileged to. He wouldn't lead her on, he wouldn't make promises, but he would allow her to experience all that she desired. As time progressed, she would lower her inhibitions.

The limo came to a stop and Sabryna peered out the window. "I recognize this area." The chauffeur opened her door. "The Cascades?" she said as they stepped from the limo.

"I thought it would be nice to have a repeat of our earlier visit," he told her.

She laughed. "You mean our encounter."

Smiling at her comment, he led her in. He was conscious of a strange anticipation gripping him. Her surprise wasn't complete just yet.

His eyes were trained on hers as they walked into the restaurant. At first she didn't notice. Then she blinked, followed by a quick scan of the restaurant. When she finally looked at him he was waiting, pleased with her look of confusion.

"It's 8:30 on a Saturday night." He nodded in agreement. "Where are all the people?"

He laughed, guiding her further in. "They decided to stay home and let us enjoy this place. Alone."

At his words the maitre'd appeared. "Good evening Mr. Cortland, Miss Givens. We're pleased to have you dining with us tonight. Please follow me."

Sabryna waited until they were seated in the empty dining room, next to a glass window with wonderful views of the downtown Richmont district, before stating the obvious, "you arranged all this."

"I wanted the night to be special."

She looked as if she wanted to ask why, but she didn't. She cleared her throat, and then calmly placed the napkin on her lap. Best she not ask why, he wasn't sure he wanted to explain the need to have her all to himself.

"This place is very elegant," she complimented, sounding unaffected by the extremes that he'd gone through.

He laughed. "You don't seem very impressed." He told her. "I take it you're used to men shutting down restaurants for you?"

Sabryna smiled. "Of course, all over town, they shut things down for me, restaurants, malls. In fact, just yesterday they shut down the power company so I could pay my electric bill in privacy."

His amusement mingled with hers. From there they enjoyed a delicious meal coupled with wonderful company. The sole fly in his otherwise flawless ointment had been their waitress. They had only one, and she either had been poorly trained or very clumsy. She mixed up their plates, got their drink order wrong, and on a whole seemed to be somewhere else. Marcus's growing irritation with the waitress was eclipsed by Sabryna's patience. By the time the chef came out to speak with them, his mood had once again turned agreeable. —

The sound of the phone interrupted an ensuing political debate. He excused himself to take it, then had to excuse himself away from the table. "We've been working on a serious project in Japan, and that's where the call is coming from. I need to take it," he explained and she reassured him it was okay.

His phone call took longer than he would've liked and he was anxious to get back to Sabryna. The scene he walked in on was not what he was expecting. Sabryna had pulled her chair closer to his, but the waitress was sitting in it. And she was crying. Had Sabryna laid into her because of her poor service? Doubtful, he thought. Even when faced with Adrina's rudeness on the golf course she hadn't been nasty. Besides, he noticed as he stepped closer, she was holding the waitress's hand.

"Don't worry Lucy," she was saying in a calming voice. He hadn't even remembered the waitress's name. "It's common for girls her age to rebel. You're doing the right thing. She needs firm boundaries and limits, and she'll appreciate you for them later."

Lucy nodded, sobbed, and nodded again. "I'm so sorry to burden you with this, but thank you for listening to me."

Sabryna continued her soothing strokes on Lucy's back. "Anytime. You have my card if you need to call me about your daughter or anything else."

Lucy glanced up, spotting him, she stood. "Sir, I'm sorry." She wiped hastily at her eyes. "Is there something I can get you?"

"No, thank you," he said with real warmth and she headed back to the kitchen. He focused on Sabryna. "I know you don't know her, so how did you know that stuff about her daughter?"

Sabryna shrugged. "I asked her what was wrong. She told me."

"How'd you know something was wrong?"

"I watched her. She seemed distracted," she explained. "Are you done with your call?"

He reached down, lifted her hand, and raised her to her feet. When she was only inches from him he said, "You're amazing."

He took her up 25 floors to the roof. The cool night wind ruffled the curls in her hair as they gazed out over the city skyline. "The view is amazing," she breathed in wonder. "How did you know about this spot?"

Marcus's lips quirked into an odd smile. "I have a thing for rooftops."

"You're definitely going to have to explain that comment."

He hesitated, coming to join her near the ledge. "When I was growing up I knew two things for certain. I would one day take over as head of the company and that my father was grooming me for this task. He was determined that I would know everything he knew, I guess you could say I was his protégé."

Was that a slight sneer she heard in his voice?

"This was okay with me as it meant he took me everywhere and I... worshipped him." For a second he was quiet as he peered out into the night. "One day, I guess I was about seven, we were in New York City. He took me on a helicopter ride. This was a big deal to me, because I was going through my airplane fascination phase." His lips rose up at the edges as he remarked with wistfulness, "Most boys have them at some point. Anyway, we landed on the top of Trump Tower, and I remember running over to the edge and looking out at that incredible city. My father walked up behind me and whispered in my ear 'you were born to own the world.'" Marcus sighed. "I don't know why it stuck with me, it just did. Whenever things get a little crazy I find a building, come up to the top, and I start to feel more in control again."

"It reminds you that you're strong," she suggested when he grew silent.

His eyes searched hers, this time he turned away first. "Yeah, I guess it does."

"Your father sounds like an amazing man."

He regarded her until she wasn't sure he was going to speak. After a while, he did. "He had his moments. What about your father?"

She pushed away from the ledge. "Sorry, no rooftop visits to share."

"I'm sure you have your own stories." He observed her progress. "After all, it was just you and your father. My guess is you were Daddy's little girl."

It was her turn to hesitate. Then she said something that she thought she could never bring herself to admit, "I don't think my father was even aware that I existed."

"Now you're going to have to explain that comment," he remarked turning her words back on her.

She walked over and sat on the ledge, facing away from the scenic backdrop. "I guess it's unfair of me to say that he was unaware of my existence. He knew but he just didn't care. When my mother died, she took most of my father with her. He was helpless without her. All that was left of him was the guilt that she had lost her life and he had survived. He couldn't deal with it, so he buried himself in his work and in the bottle."

"He became an alcoholic?" Marcus asked.

Sabryna nodded, pulling her arms around herself. "He drank all the time. When he wasn't working, he was drinking himself into a stupor. For his part, he held down a job, always made sure we had a roof over our heads and food on the table. But that was it. I didn't have any siblings, and all of our extended family was in Georgia. No one knew or understood the seriousness of the situation."

"What ended up happening?"

"As time went on, I just got angrier and angrier. I had decided that if my father wasn't going to care about me, then I wasn't going to care about myself. I started skipping school, failing classes, and running with the wrong type of kids. Lucky for me, I had a school counselor who could see this was a problem and she connected me with a youth center that changed my life."

"Middleton Youth Center," Marcus guessed.

She shook her head. "Not quite. I lived in another part of the city. That center was closed a couple years after I graduated high school. That center saved my life. Having adults who cared about me helped me to believe in myself again."

"So in turn, you graduate from college, and return to give back to the neighborhood," he finished.

She flashed a brilliant smile. "That's right."

"What about your father? Where is he now?"

"He went to rehab when I was in college, then moved back to Georgia. Claimed the memories here were too painful and he felt it was best to start a clean slate."

"Are you close?"

Her smile grew sad. "As close as two strangers can be."

To her surprise, Marcus reached out and pulled her close. It felt so good to be held up against his large frame Sabryna didn't even think to protest. He enfolded her in his arms. A sense of safety and protection wrapped around her, and then she realized what he was doing. He was comforting her. And, Sabryna realized with no small amount of amazement, she needed it.

His lips brushed a butterfly kiss across her forehead. She wanted those lips somewhere else, and she shamelessly tilted up her chin to offer him her mouth. He took all that she gave, seizing her in a ferocious kiss that belied the gentleness of his hold. Their tongues dueled until their hearts were beating to the same speedy tune. She wound her arms around his neck and stretched her body against his, craving contact. He responded by pulling her closer to him, as though to absorb her into himself. She supplied the need, he filled it.

When the kiss was over, she rested her head on his shoulder until she could catch her breath. He ran his hands up and down her back in soothing strokes. The ride home was also as calming. He walked her to the door. They shared a lingering kiss that left a warm smile on her face.

It wasn't until she went to bed that she realized, he hadn't asked to see her again.

CHAPTER SEVEN

Marcus climbed the steps to his family's home, reminding himself to school his features. The thought was almost as difficult as the act. After all, he hadn't been this pleased with himself in a long time. That morning he woke up feeling the rush of a fresh challenge, sensing his impending victory. Relishing the thought when he would have Sabryna right where he wanted her.

A man couldn't do anything but smile when faced with such provocation.

The door opened as he crested the last step. He walked into the large entrance hall. "Good morning, Hinton," he greeted his mother's butler who was pulling the door shut behind him. "Is my mother home?"

"Yes, sir," Hinton confirmed. "She's in the kitchen."

Marcus stopped short. As always, the butler's face remained expressionless. There were thirty-seven rooms in the house, and of all the places he expected to find his mother, the kitchen was not one of them. He shrugged, she was full of surprises.

He found her seated at the counter island in the middle of the large airy room with a stack of books in front of her. Two diligent maids were going about their task as if his mother's presence there was an ordinary site.

"Did you get lost on the way to the dining room?"

His mother's head popped up and a broad smile spread across her face. At fifty-five, Elaine Cortland was still striking with her slim figure and chestnut brown skin. Her hair was cut short, with curls just touching her ears, and a few distinguished streaks of gray. She looked as though she were headed to lunch at the country club dressed, stylish as usual, in a cream-colored Prada pant suit. She held up one the books. "I'm learning to cook."

He swore he heard one of the maids groan.

He laughed, dropped a kiss on her forehead and took a seat on a stool across from her. "Any reason why?" He took an apple out of near by bowl and bit into it.

His mother didn't cook. She didn't clean. She didn't work. She'd been born a rich Senators daughter, and then she had married into even more money. She'd always had a privileged life.

She put her hands under her chin. "I wanted to try something new."

"Did you get bored already with knitting?" His mother had decided a couple of years ago that she wanted to, in her words, 'learn to do something.' What had followed was a series of hobbies, she tried them out which often resulted in something horrendous and then she moved on to the next one. "And here I was hoping to get another sock."

"I already knitted you a sock."

"Yes, but socks tend to come in pairs."

"Oh, yeah. Well, you'll just have to buy your own sock. I've decided to become a cook."

"And here I was about to ask you to make me a glove."

"You shouldn't tease your mother, it's not nice." She gave him a firm look.

"I only tease you because I love you." He gave her an affectionate kiss.

"I love you too." She closed her cookbook. "Now, when will I get some grandchildren?"

He groaned. "Whenever one of your children give you one."

"You're one of my children, even if you sometimes forget that," she persisted. "Besides, you're the oldest, it's your responsibility to give me grandchildren first."

"I don't believe that was in the contract."

"You must not have read the fine print."

He took another bite of his apple and wisely kept silent. His mother may get older, but she never got slower.

"Now, you're thirty years old," she informed him. "It's time you settle down. I met a very nice girl this week. Sylvia Bryant's niece. You know the Bryant's, wonderful people. She just graduated from college and she's going to be working at her uncle's company. I think you should meet...why are you shaking your head at me?"

"What did I tell you about trying to set me up?" he questioned.

"Don't do it." She folded her arms across her chest. "You're being stubborn."

"And you Mother, are being you," he laughed. "If you feel the need to meddle in someone's life you still have one kid at home."

"Hey, I heard that." His sister, Madelyn, came sauntering in the kitchen with her hands already on her hips. "And I'm not a kid."

He cast a critical eye at his sixteen-year-old sister. "What are you then?"

"I'm a young woman," she announced with a dramatic flair.

"Over my dead body." It was his turn to grumble.

"That can be arranged, big brother." She took a seat next to his. She leaned into him. "Just come back for dinner tonight. Mom's cooking."

"I heard that," his mother announced in crisp tones.

"You were meant to." Madelyn grinned.

"This is why David and Alex are my favorites," their mother sighed, referring to her other two boys, both younger than Marcus and older than Madelyn.

"Her favorites change based on who is not in the room at the time," Madelyn joked.

Marcus laughed and let the easy banter of his mother and his sister elevate his already good mood. He always enjoyed coming home, even though of late his mother had been on some insane kick to get him married off. He just didn't have the heart to tell her that was an impossible goal. He'd no intention of marrying anyone. Ever.

If his mother wanted grandchildren, she'd have to hound his brothers, David or Alex.

It wasn't that he didn't like the idea of a family. He loved his family. They were close, always had been. And, being the head was something he took very serious. It was his duty to protect them and ensure their happiness. At times, it forced him to make some tough choices, and even now, there were things he still didn't dare share with them. But, he knew they would always be there for him and that meant more to him than anything else in the world.

His thoughts shifted to the conversation he had the night before with Sabryna in the moonlight. He recalled Sabryna's recollections about her childhood.

How alone she must have been, losing a mother at such a young age, and having to contend with a father who couldn't see past his own grief. Marcus couldn't imagine. He had always been surrounded by a strong family unit, people who loved him and were involved in his life. Even his father, who possessed many flaws, had been loving and attentive.

He remembered the feeling that had nudged at him last night. It wasn't sympathy, it was deeper than that. He'd wanted to absorb her pain.

Shaking himself out of his reverie, he turned his attention back to his mother and sister. He had enough pain of his own. No need to take on extra.

Sabryna knocked on the door to number 512-B and hoped the sound was loud enough to rise above the volume of the television she could hear coming from inside of the apartment. She knocked again.

"Who is it?" a loud, defensive feminine voice yelled.

Sabryna hated to speak through doors, so she waited with feigned patience.

The door opened a quarter ways, and a pudgy woman peered out. "I said, who is it?" she repeated with pure ice in her tone. She must have been braiding her hair as it was half completed with tight microbraids on the left and loose hair on the right.

"Good Afternoon, My name is Sabryna Givens," she answered, taking in what she could see of the lady. "I work at the Middleton Community center. Are you Damon's mother?"

Her eyes didn't even blink. "What'd he do?"

"Nothing. I just needed to talk to him."

She stepped out of the doorway, leaving it ajar and shouted, "Damon, come and get this door." And then she disappeared.

So much for parental involvement, Sabryna thought with disgust, then stepped back as Damon walked out of the door and pulled it shut. They stood facing each other on the landing of his apartment building. The sounds of children playing, neighbors fussing, and friends talking, rolled up from the ground.

"I came to see how you're doing," Sabryna told him. "We never got the chance to talk."

"Lady, I don't know you." He crossed his arms over his chest.

She nodded. "Well, you didn't stick around long enough." When he remained quiet, she continued. "Listen, you don't know me and I don't know you, but I need some help and you seem like the right person for the job."

He showed no emotion, but she would've sworn his ears perked up. "What job?"

"I need an assistant," she told him. "It doesn't pay much, but, I need someone to help me plan a basketball tournament. Do you know anything about basketball?"

A single shoulder lifted and fell. "I hoop."

"Well, good." She acted as if it had been settled. Sabryna hadn't intended to hire an assistant, had never done so before, but she needed a hook, something to get him back to the center.

"I ain't coming to work for you." He squashed her triumph.

"Do I get an explanation," She asked.

He shrugged. "Ya'll be hatin'."

It was her turn to stare. "That's your explanation."

He didn't speak.

"Let me tell you something," She stepped closer to him so that they were eye to eye. "I won't apologize and I won't excuse what happened. No one fights at my center. You screw up you deal with the consequences. You want to come back to the center, do it the right way."

"And working for you is the right way," he shot at her.

"It's a start."

"Man, I don't need your center." He dismissed her with a wave of his hand.

She paused for a second. "You might be right. But we, I, need you. Think about it. The door is always opened." And with those last words, she walked away.

She may not know how to get a man to ask for a second date, but she knew how to hook a teen.

He called that night.

Sabryna was curled up with a book on her couch when the phone rang. Figuring it would be Grant or Lena, she picked it up. "Hello?"

"Hello, Angel," a familiar sexy voice replied on the other line.

Her book dropped to her lap. "How...how did you get this number?"

"I have connections," Marcus said simply. "Plus you're listed."

"Ahh!" What more could she say? I was thinking about you. I missed you. I was hoping you would call.

"Are you busy?" he asked.

She thought, only if busy included reading a Francis Ray novel for the umpteenth time while wearing a pair of faded jeans and eating a Snickers. "No."

"Good. Have dinner with me. How about a great seafood dinner?"

She played back his words in her mind, no part of them sounded like a question. "Okay, when?" When had she started to find his bossiness charming?

"Right now."

"Right now?" And then because suspicion got the best of her. "Where are you?"

"Sitting outside your apartment."

She shot off the couch and peered out the window. He was leaning against his limo, looking every inch of mischievous. He waved. She broke into laughter. "Give me ten minutes."

Twenty minutes later, they pulled up to the Wachovia bank building in Downtown Richmont.

"I thought you were in the mood for seafood." She glanced out the window. She couldn't think of one seafood place in this area.

"We have to get there first," he said and got out of the car.

Once the chauffeur opened her door, she asked, "Where exactly are we going?"

He pointed straight up.

Ten minutes after that they took off in a helicopter.

"Where are we?" Sabryna asked in wonder as they were let out on an open field.

"Virginia Beach."

She looked around spotting a hanger off in the distance, a limo, and lots of grass. No restaurants, people, sand, or water. "I don't see a beach."

"Oh, you will," he assured her.

And he was a right, a short limo ride later they sat in the Lynnhaven Fish House, savoring an expensive bottle of wine, and enjoying a majestic view of the restaurant's private beach.

"I can't believe I'm having seafood on the beach." She popped a steamed shrimp into her mouth.

"I can't believe it only took you ten minutes to look that good," he replied back.

Pleased at his compliment, she looked down at what she was wearing, a strapless black dress that flared at her waist and ended just below her knees. The dress was complimented with a pair of sling back black sandals. Apparently, she possessed more "sexy" outfits than she first realized.

After dinner, they walked out on to the dark beach. Taking off her shoes, the sand shifted between her toes as they strolled along the beach. The sound of the waves crashing against the shore provided the perfect soundtrack for their companionable silence.

If someone had told her three weeks ago, she would be so easy, so relaxed in his company she would have looked at them cross-eyed. "We certainly have come along way since when we first met."

The corner of his lips turned upward. "You mean from when you first jumped down my throat?"

She laughed. "You cornered me in a dark garden."

"You were perfectly safe."

"How was I supposed to know that?" Did she even know that now?

"Still." His eyes danced with amusement. "You could've been nicer."

She swung around to face him. "Do you have a sister?"

Caught off guard, he answered, "Yes, one, her name is Madelyn."

"How old is she?"

"She's sixteen."

"So, what would you want Madelyn to do?" She paused for dramatic value, a little trick she picked up from working with kids so long. "If she suddenly found herself alone in a garden with a strange man?"

He appeared to give the question serious consideration. His arm snaked and looped around her waist. Before she could think, he yanked her into his chest. "I would want her to be courteous and polite."

"Mmm hmm."

"Especially, if he was trying to be helpful...like say, offering her the use of his cell phone when her own died out."

"Mmm hmm."

"And, if he touched her here." With his free hand, he ran a gentle caress down the side of her face and neck.

Her skin tingled everywhere he touched.

"I would want her to shiver lightly, like you did just now."

"Mmmmmm hmmmmm."

"And, if he kissed her right here…" Once again, he caressed her neck; she angled it for better access. "I would want her to sigh sweetly." Sabryna's breath came out in a soft moan. Marcus kissed the spot. "Like you did just now." He continued his slow ministrations.

"Mmmmmmm hmmmmmm," she purred. His low hypnotic voice was as much an aphrodisiac as his actions.

"And, if he kissed her right here…" Marcus ran his thumb over her lower lips. "I would want her to melt in to his arms." He touched his lips to hers, allowing his tongue to lick them. "Like you're going to do right now."

And true to his word, he took her mouth in a searing kiss, and she melted. She could do little else. He tasted so good, so masculine. The sweet taste of the wine still lingered on his tongue. His lips were firm under hers. His other hand twined with the curls at the nape of her neck. Desire flared between them, an unquenchable tide threatening to take her under. Her hands moved up to his chest, solid and strong beneath her fingers.

His growled emanated from low in his throat.

Marcus had wanted her to melt, had insisted upon it, but this, the way she flowed into his arms, he hadn't expected. Her openness and honesty were incredible. She was so compelling in her desire, her want, and her need. His arousal met the point of pain.

He had known from the very first touch that passion could explode between them. So why hadn't he thought he could get burned by the flame?

When the kiss ended, she rested her forehead against his chest, his arms rock solid around her, fingers sifting through the fine hair on the back of her scalp. The heat from their kiss sizzled and crackled in the air about them.

After a moment, she stepped back. "So is that really how you'd want a stranger to treat your sister?"

He took hold of her hand. "Oh, no. I'd have to kill him."

Laughing, they continued their stroll down the beach.

"Can I ask you a question?" His voice blended with the roaring of the waves.

She smiled her answer.

"Had I approached you differently that night…if I had come up to you in the ballroom and asked you to dance, would our first meeting have been different?"

"I wouldn't have been as defensive," she teased.

He laughed. "Yes, but would you have danced with me?"

She considered. "I might have."

"In other words, no," he supplied.

"I didn't say that." She giggled. "You're very attractive and charming…when you want to be."

Despite being absurdly pleased that she thought him attractive, he continued, "Even so, something tells me you would still have turned me down." When she remained quiet he said, "You don't date a lot."

"No, I don't." Then she clarified, "I guess it's more by my choice, I've never dated much."

He hesitated. "What about Barclay?" Marcus knew it was a dangerous question to ask. But he wanted, needed an answer.

"Steven and I are friends." She squeezed his hand that rested warm in her own palm. "You never…dated him?" Or fell into bed together in a steamy night of passion?

Sabryna shook her head. "In college, my freshman year we...we flirted. It was harmless, and we soon discovered that we just didn't click. I wasn't that into him, and I guess he just didn't feel like that toward me either."

"I always knew he was an idiot."

She grinned, touched. "It all worked out for the better. I think Steven may have been in love with some other girl. He never said, but sometimes you can pick up on these things."

"Barclay is..." he started.

She stopped him by placing a finger on his lips. "No, don't say it. I won't listen to you trash him. Steven's my friend that's all I need to know."

He nodded. He had to applaud her loyalty, displaced as it was, it was still admirable. Besides, he found out what he needed to know and could now breathe a sigh of relief.

Marcus smiled. "I'm glad you're here with me."

"Me too." They continued their companionable stroll down the beach.

◆━◆◆━◆

Marcus settled her in the limo back in Richmont when her cell phone rang.

Sabryna took the phone out of her purse, glancing at the number before answering. "Hey, Grant." After a few seconds she popped up in her seat, alarm evident on her face. "What! Someone broke into the center."

CHAPTER EIGHT

The worry that gripped Sabryna was intense. "Was anyone hurt?"

"No, thank God. But we have a crowd gathering," Grant told her.

"I'll be right there." She gripped her cell phone.

"What happened?" Marcus asked as soon as she flipped her phone closed.

"There was a break in and a shooting at the center. I need to get there."

Without hesitation, Marcus gave his driver directions with instructions to hurry. The limo sped off down the street.

They arrived at the center a short fifteen minutes later. Sabryna didn't wait for the chauffeur to open the door, jumping out as soon as it stopped. Marcus was at her heels. Already, a large crowd had gathered. No wonder, she thought, when she noted the multitudes of police cars and flashing lights on the scene. Ignoring the crowd, she headed for the door, fishing her badge out of her purse. As predicted, they were stopped at the barricade, she flashed her badge and was let in. Marcus stuck close to her side.

They found Grant talking with two cops in the common room. The rooms had been ransacked. Grant looked up when they approached, his eyes took in her black dress in a blink and then slid past her to Marcus. They snapped back to her. "Good, you're here."

"What's going on?" she asked. Introductions were made to the Officers Patrick and Ngobe.

"Someone broke in. They set off the silent alarm and when the cops got here they started shooting at them," Grant explained.

"Oh, my God. Did anyone get hurt?" Sabryna searched the room as if she expected to see someone dead or injured.

"No, lucky for us, whoever it was has bad aim," Officer Ngobe remarked with sarcasm. "However, there was more than one. We're thinking about five to seven."

"Gang related?" Marcus spoke for the first time.

The officer thought about his question. "Quite possibly."

Sabryna took a deep breath. "What did they take?" She didn't want to hear the answer.

"Two play stations, a television, a couple hundred dollars from a safe, six computers, and one laptop were the main items," Officer Patrick read from his list.

Anger bubbled inside of Sabryna. "We can't afford that." How dare they steal from a center that was so devoted to helping the community? The very thought was appalling.

Grant put a hand on her shoulder. "Don't worry, we'll bounce back. We always do."

She nodded, although she knew don't worry was easier said than done.

Grant continued, "Could you take care of that crowd outside. They aren't going to go away until they get some answers."

At that moment, she needed a task. She went outside and answered questions, reassured, and urged everyone to return home, which was no easy job. The community was attached to their center and they needed to know that tomorrow it would still be a safe place for their children. Perhaps, the only safe place for their children.

The sight of the limo was garnering as much attention as the plethora of police cars gathered out front. As Sabryna answered questions, she also found herself dodging and deflecting personal questions. She noticed as she talked to people that their eyes kept darting to Marcus. A handsome guy in a rich suit and limo were not common occurrences in this neighborhood. For that matter, her in a 'sexy' dress was also not a common occurrence.

Marcus watched as she soothed and dispersed the crowd with patient efficiency. She certainly had a way with people. She knew just what to say and when. He'd first noticed that with the kids. It seemed she had a natural talent for taking care of people. Who, he wondered, took care of her?

As if she'd been reading his private thoughts, she turned and looked at him. They'd been on the scene for about an hour and half now, but the difference in her appearance was painfully obvious. Her eyes which had glimmered with brightness on the beach were now layered with tiredness, worry, and half-concealed anger. She crossed her right hand to her left shoulder and massaged it, he guessed to release tension. The demands of the crowd were taking their toll on her. She kept glancing back at the center where Grant was inside answering questions for the police, and Marcus thought if she could be in two places at one time she would've split herself in half in a second. He bit back the urge to snatch her away from the crowd, tell them to wait until tomorrow to get their answers, inform Grant Morgan he would have to handle the situation on his own, and take his Angel home and put her in to bed. To sleep! His sexual need to have her was eclipsed by the intense desire to see her relieved of her stress. He wanted her beautiful eyes to shine again.

What the hell was he being reduced to?

That question sent his mood spiraling into some dark place. The result was a very quiet ride back to her house, when two hours later she was ready to leave. She didn't attempt to make conversation, to drained for the effort. His quiet was due to the thoughts churning in his head.

At her door, she offered repeated thanks. He silenced her with a kiss. Wanting only to calm her, he didn't prolong it. And then he left.

"I didn't do it." The young male voice brought Sabryna's head up from her task. She was in one of the rooms at the center, having just finished a group, and now she was cleaning up the materials she'd used.

She stopped and straightened. Damon stood in the doorway. The look on his face was defensive, his clothes, as usual sagging. "Exactly what is it that I'm supposed to understand you didn't do?"

He stepped further into the room. "What they saying I did. I didn't do it."

She kept her stare blank. She wasn't going to make it easy for him.

"I didn't break into your center and I didn't shoot nobody." He looked her steady in the eyes while saying it. For Sabryna, that carried weight.

"Well, that's nice to know." She turned back to retrieving her material. "However, I don't recall asking you if you did it."

"I know you're thinking it," he accused.

She dropped her materials back down and walked over to stand in front of him. She was eye to eye with him. "The only thing I'm thinking is if you're going to accept my job offer."

His surprise showed in his eyes.

She continued. "I trust that the police are going to do their job and find who was responsible for last night's robbery. It's not my place to make accusations or go searching for a criminal. My responsibility is to you and your peers. It's business as usual here. So tell me, are you going to be a part of that business?"

For a long moment, he just stared, then he nodded.

"Good." She started to walk away. "You can start today. Your first assignment is to get this room cleaned up. Come and see me when you're finished."

She headed for the exit, not waiting to see if he would begin working. At the door, she turned back and looked. "And Damon?"

He turned to her.

"It's not my center, it's our center. Now get to work." She left the room.

A commotion in the common room caught her attention. Hearing a bevy of excited voices, Sabryna headed in that direction.

The scene she came upon was strange. Lena and Grant were standing amidst a bunch of boxes as two delivery guys were carrying in more items. The kids stood around trying to read the boxes to get an idea of what was in them. Those not reading were to busy oohing and aahhing as Grant opened up case after case of brand new computers.

"¡Dios mios!," Lena exclaimed. She opened a box and pulled out a ton of video games. "This box is full of almost every video game you can think of."

The excitement soon attracted the notice of all the kids and everyone tried to pile into the common area at once. Sabryna advanced into the crowded space. "What is all of this?"

Grant looked up, his eyes also wide with amazement. "It seems we have a benefactor."

One of the delivery guys held a clip board to Grant. Grant signed and then read off the list of items that had been delivered. Fifteen new computers, five new laptops, hundreds of video games, and three Playstation III's. Yet, the item that garnered the greatest excitement from the kids was the large flat screen television.

"It's as big as a house!" Gabe Lucas shouted jumping up and down.

"If it was as big as a house then it wouldn't be able to fit in here." Latisha Wilder pointed out.

Gabe rolled his eyes at her. "It's still big."

Grant broke up their little spat and cleared all of the kids out of the common room in a matter of minutes. No one disobeyed, not wanting to miss out on their chance to play with the new items later.

"It's all the things that we lost last night and then some," Lena breathed in amazement. "Do you think the police sent it?"

"If the police reimbursed everyone who got something stolen in this way the city would be broke." The police hadn't sent it so where had the items come from? There was a fortune of electronics in the room.

Lena shrugged. "Well, maybe they think we're special."

"Somebody definitely thinks we are special," Grant replied.

Lena and Sabryna both looked at him in expectation. He held the order form up, his unwavering gaze met Sabryna. "The bill went to

Cortland Consulting."

"What!" Sabryna rushed over and grabbed the order out of his hand. Her eyes raced over the page, confirming what Grant had already said. "He did…I can't…I can't believe he did this." She'd been very aware of his presence last night, a constant by her side, at times hovering to the back. He hadn't interfered, indeed, hadn't said a word at all. She hadn't known what his reaction was to last night's events. Or, she thought looking at the multitude of replacement items scattered around, maybe she did.

Lena caught her eye, a silly knowing grin stretching from one side of her face to another. Grant just stood there in silence, regarding her.

She could almost hear their imaginations churning.

"I have no idea why he sent these things," she was quick to explain.

Grant raised an eyebrow.

"If he did send them then I'm sure that it's because of what he saw last night," she argued.

"Exactly what did he see last night?" Lena questioned with a sly smile.

Sabryna glared. "He was with me when I got the call. He saw the scene for himself."

"He was with you?" Lena eyes grew bigger than when she had seen the television. "Were you two out on another date?"

"Another date?" Now it was Grant's turn to be surprised.

"Yes, yes we were out on a date." Sabryna did her best to downplay the situation. "And yes, it was a second date. However, let us not lose sight of what is important here. I for one think it's wonderful of him to send these things. It's obvious when he saw how the robbery had affected the community, he felt compelled to do something about it. I only wish that more citizens and community members would take ownership of this center. Marcus is to be commended for stepping up to the plate today."

She hoped her speech covered up the beating of her heart. Had he done this for her, because of her? Did she even want the words of her speech to be true, or did she, herself, want to be his inspiration?

Grant was very quiet, yet there was a small spark of humor in his expression. "I agree. He should be commended." Then he added with deliberate slowness, "perhaps you would be willing to…deliver our thanks."

Sabryna straightened. "I believe that would be appropriate. I'll take care of it tomorrow." And she left, leaving Grant and Lena to sort the boxes and their own thoughts.

She ignored the silent laughter that trailed behind her.

CHAPTER NINE

She arrived at his office the next day at 11:30 to render her, their, thanks. She'd dressed with careful precision that morning. Her usual comfortable wear forsaken for more professional dress. As she watched the numbers on the elevator grid flash and change in tune to the soft jazz pumping through the speakers she smoothed down her deep purple cotton pants. Then she did a quick check of her matching short purple jacket concealing a black camisole top. The wardrobe goal for the morning had not been to look sexy but professional. If she ended up looking sexy, it would be by default.

The elevator opened and she stepped off onto a quiet floor. Cortland Consulting took up the top seven floors of this building. The area was very well decorated with rich colors and had a posh feel about it. Two men in expensive suits walked past her to step on the elevator. They were deep in discussion but they did look up and smile as she walked by. She could feel their eyes as she continued through the glass double doors ahead of her.

When she entered through those doors, she caught her first wave of intimidation. The office spread out before her screamed wealth, success, and power. There were two large mahogany desks in front of her. One a little further back than the other, both had a woman seated there hard at work. She paused in front of the first desk.

The lady at that desk, a middle aged African-American woman with stern looking glasses and a head of gray and black mixture looked up. The name plate on her desk identified her as Mary Stein. She smiled. "Good morning, how can I help you?"

Her polite tone eased Sabryna and she smiled in return. "My name is Sabryna Givens. I was wondering if Mr. Cortland was available."

"Do you have an appointment?" She questioned.

"No, I'm a..." Sabryna wasn't quite sure what to call herself. "Friend."

The smile on her face froze. "I'll see if Mr. Cortland is available."

She picked up the phone and Sabryna wondered at the change in attitude. After a quick conversation, she glanced at Sabryna and stated, "Mr. Cortland is in a meeting now."

"Oh, well, thank…" Sabryna started taking that as her cue to leave.

"He should be finished soon. He asked that you wait in his office," Mary continued. She stood and Sabryna followed her down the hallway and into a big office with a large bay window. Amazed, she walked over to the window and gazed out at the incredible view before her. The sun gleamed off the top of buildings and the clouds appeared close enough to touch. Sabryna guessed you could see halfway across the city of Richmont. Marcus certainly did have a thing for being at the top of the world.

"Can I get you something to drink? Coffee? Tea?" Mary asked.

Sabryna turned around in wonder. "A camera!"

Mary cracked a smile. "He'll be right with you."

Not sure if she should settle herself into one of the cream leather chairs, stand in the center of the room, or continue to gape out the window, she settled for exploring his surroundings. She wanted to get a feel for the man who was starting to make her feel so much.

His office was neat, organized, and spacious. She thought of her own cramped office filled to every nook and cranny with boxes, papers, and books. Marcus must've felt like he was standing in a closet. She wandered over to the desk and took note of the one picture on top of its polished surface. It had to be a family portrait, considering how everyone in the picture resembled each other. An elegant older woman, most likely his mother, was surrounded on all sides by three gorgeous guys of similar height and build, one of which being Marcus, and a young woman. The young girl had to be his sister Madelyn.

Muffled voices caught her attention. She noticed the double wood panel doors on the other side of the room. She walked closer to investigate and found that they were ajar. The office connected to another room. She peeked through the crack but could only make out what looked like a part of a long table. Perhaps this was a conference room. As she was standing next to the door, she could better make out the voices.

"I want to apologize for my performance the past few weeks." It was the voice of a man. He sounded guilty and apologetic.

"I'm very disappointed in the reports I'm receiving, Thomas, but I'm not going to fire you." She would know that voice in her sleep. It was Marcus, and chances were he was engaged in a serious discussion with one of his employees that she shouldn't listen to.

She wandered back over to the window as her mind reviewed the reasons she falling for him fast. She felt like one of the teens crushing on the cutest guy in school. He was attractive, God knows, he was attractive. She thought she could stare at him all day. But there was so much more to him than that. He made her laugh with his wonderful sense of humor. The day of the golf tournament he'd chosen her for his partner over the beautiful Adrina, helped her pick the right clubs, been discreet about her lack of knowledge, and playfully teased her when they'd lost. He was arrogant without being boastful. He was full of pride without being conceited, so unlike other men of his kind.

Not to mention the fact that he kissed her in a way she'd never been kissed before, and she doubted ever would be again. He truly did make her burn for him.

There were many layers to this enigmatic man. She had sensed them when he had shared with her memories from his childhood. He was carrying around some inner pain. When he'd talked about his father there had been something familiar in his eyes. The sincere way he seemed to understand how she felt over the loss of her mother and the estrangement of her father told her that not only could he be sympathetic, but he understood what she had been through on some level that no one else before him had. Or maybe, that was because she had chosen to share those parts with him as she had with no one else. However, with him it had been easy, the words had flowed out of her.

Then there was the other night. When she received the phone call about the incident at the center, she didn't ask him to take her there, nor did she ask him to stick around and wait for her. But he did. As if it was the most natural thing in the world for him to offer her support. And whether he knew it or not his presence knowing he was close had created a feeling of security that she hadn't expected. She knew in her bones that if at any moment she had turned to him and asked for his help he would've offered it, without hesitating. Yet he hung back, patient as he waited, not interfering. How could she not fall for a guy like that?

She would never have expected that he would be so generous. He must have seen how it affected everyone and decided to replace the items that had been stolen. Yet, the idea tumbled around her mind, that maybe, just maybe he had done so to please her. It was such a desirable thought, and it would be very telling of his feelings for her, which now that she thought on it, she desperately wanted to know what they were. But, how could she get him to reveal his intentions without revealing too much of her own first?

"Hello, Angel." Marcus's deep voice interrupted her thoughts. She turned around to see him standing in the now opened double doors, wearing yet another one of his well cut suits, this one a dark blue. "To what do I owe this surprise?"

He strolled further in to the room, his office taking on new dimensions with him inside. She smiled. "I wouldn't think that would be too difficult to guess."

He shrugged. "I've never been very good at guessing."

She laughed. "I wanted to thank you for the items you had sent to us yesterday at the center. The children are thrilled."

"I'm glad I could help." Then he added, "I hoped that it would ease your mind...and Grant's."

Sabryna wondered at his words. "Now we won't have to worry about where to find the funds to replace the items, and the routine at the center won't be interrupted."

Marcus seemed pleased at her words, but before she could read too much of his expression he moved past her.

She swiveled to face him. "I was wondering...I was hoping that you would allow me to thank you by taking you out to lunch. Are you available?"

He was opening his mouth to speak when another voice cut across the scene. A clear, crisp female one. "I'm afraid he already has plans." They both looked to the door. Adrina stood there, one hand resting on her hips, appearing for all the world like she had just stepped off the cover of an Ebony magazine. "He has plans with me."

Sabryna glanced from the supermodel to Marcus, she waited for him to call the woman a liar, when he didn't she felt as though she'd just been punched in the gut.

"I'm sorry to interrupt your...meeting." Adrina sauntered into the room. She examined Sabryna up and down. "Neither Mary nor Pauline were at their desk, so I just came on in as usual." She walked right up to Marcus and placed a bold kiss on his cheek. Then she refocused on Sabryna. "Don't I know you?"

"Yes, we've met." Sabryna confirmed.

"Oh, that's right. At the golf tournament. What a long day that was, but it was for charity," she scoffed. "Marcus is always telling me how important it is to support a cause. Has he adopted yours?"

It was clear that Adrina was fishing for the reasons that Sabryna was there. Sabryna's stare remained steady on Marcus, allowing him to read the anger in her eyes. "Yes, he has, and we thank him. Unfortunately, the...center is not looking for any new sponsors at the moment. We thank you for your interest. Goodbye."

She didn't wait for a response, she departed the office as quick as dignity would allow. "Hold the elevator," she called as she noticed the doors were about to close, plus it gave her an excuse to run.

"Sabryna wait!" Marcus called out behind her, but she didn't bother to respond. She stepped onto the elevator and the doors shut behind her.

On the elevator, she kept her eyes trained on the numbers flashing down and ignored the curious stares of the other two occupants. Which was an easy task to accomplish when one was busy drowning in her own humiliation. How could she have been so stupid? Why should a man like that have any interest in her when he was surrounded by beautiful women like Adrina Howell? What a fool she'd been. Hadn't he made his interest in her clear on the first day they met? He wanted her in his bed, but in his life, in his world, that was reserved for woman like the skank upstairs. Later, she'd chide herself for that comment. After all, Adrina was not the one who had led her on.

Thankful when the elevator opened up on the first floor, she got off, praying she could make it outside before the first tear fell.

"Sabryna wait." Marcus's voice commanded. How had he gotten down there so fast? She wondered, but she ignored him and kept going. Seeing the sunshine from outside the front doors of the building, she decided that safety was in that direction.

Reaching the doors she burst through, Marcus fast on her heels grabbed her a few short feet from the door. He swung her around to face him. "Let me explain."

"Let me go," she demanded in a low seething voice snatching her arm back. "I don't need any explanations or anything else from you. Why don't you just go back inside and enjoy your lunch with that…that …woman."

His lips quirked. "Are you jealous?"

"Are you mad?" Jealousy churned in her gut. She spun around. "Don't ever call me again and don't 'drop' by either." Wanting just to get away she looked about, frantic to remember where she'd parked her car. Then she recalled that she come in from the door through the garage that was attached to the building. She was now on the street in the wrong direction. Knowing the last thing she would ever want to do was to go back in that building, she marched toward the street entrance to the garage.

"Sabryna, you're overreacting," Marcus told her, following somewhat more slow at her heels. "Would you just stop so we can talk about this?"

Sabryna paused near the entrance and glared back over her shoulder at him. "I've nothing to say to you…ever," she told him icily. "Goodbye, Mr. Cortland." And with those parting words she stepped out into the street to cross to the entrance, catching the sound of a man's shout seconds before she was jarred with a slamming pain.

Her entire world went black.

CHAPTER TEN

For Marcus, the scene unfolded in suspended horror. Everything else, the sound of metal hitting the sidewalk, the distant scream of a woman, someones voice yelling for someone else to call the ambulance, was muted as the thundering in his heart escalated so loud he could hear nothing beyond its ferocious beating. For one single instant all time stood still, then it fractured. Spurred by nothing but instinct, Marcus raced to Sabryna's side. He didn't notice the other people hastening to the scene, or the biker scrambling up from the cement, he couldn't see anything but the sight of his Angel lying on the ground, not moving.

Dropping to his knees by her side, he put a hand to her chest. She was unconscious, yet, she was still breathing. He released the breath he'd been holding. His eyes examined her body, inspecting for blood, wounds, any sign that she had a fatal injury. He couldn't see any, but how would he know if anything was broken or if there was internal bleeding? For God sake, she'd collided with a man on a bike!

She groaned, but didn't open her eyes.

"Sabryna?" He hoped his fear didn't sound in his voice. "Sabryna?" he repeated with more force. "Open your eyes for me Angel."

"Is she okay?" a tentative voice asked. He looked up into the worried expression of the biker. "I didn't mean to hit her. I swear. I didn't see her there. I swear."

Marcus focused on Sabryna. He didn't, couldn't, care about anything else at the moment. That guy could explode in his own guilt and foolishness for all Marcus cared. He wasn't ready to be even moderately forgiving.

"An ambulance is on the way," another woman's voice announced in the background.

Marcus could only nod, scared to take his eyes off Sabryna, lest she stop breathing in the process. "Please open your eyes, Angel, please," he entreated once more.

She groaned again and this time her eyelids fluttered open. She looked up into his eyes. Blinked. Then blinked again. Her eyes slid sideways to the people hovering near, then back to him.

"Did I get hit by a car?" She sounded somewhat resigned and amused.

Hysterical with relief, he almost laughed. No way would she be making dry comments in such a clear voice if she were dying. "Not quite. It was a bike."

She groaned and tried to sit up. "At least tell me it was a big bike."

Marcus placed gentle hands on her shoulders to hold her down. "Don't move. The ambulance is on the way."

She paused. "Ambulance? I'm okay, I think. Nothing's broken." She shifted and a look of pain crossed her face. "At least, I don't think so."

His face appeared set in stone. "Humor me. Please."

The biker hovered into view. "Miss, I'm so sorry. I didn't mean to hit you, I didn't see you."

"Why don't you back up and give her some space," Marcus demanded. "You can explain later." He was ready to shred the man in two if didn't comply.

Sabryna distracted him simply by placing her hand on his shoulder. When she struggled up to a sitting position, he immediately moved to help her. "It's okay. I'm okay." She addressed the driver. "I wasn't watching. It's my fault."

"Sabyrna…" Marcus warned.

"Marcus, it was my fault." She glared at him and her eyes told him she was recalling their earlier interaction. "Besides, I was too angry to pay attention."

Now, he was the one ready to explode with guilt.

The ambulance arrived in short order, interrupting any further conversations or placement of blame. The EMT's checked over Sabryna and declared she had no broken bones. Still they suggested she go to the hospital to get checked out. She refused, saying that even though she felt a little bumped and bruised now she would feel much better in a couple of hours. Marcus didn't agree, saying that she couldn't see into the future nor her own body to know for certain everything was okay.

The argument had been brief, with the concerned driver and EMT's seconding the motion that Marcus had presented. As a result, a short time later Sabryna sat on a hospital bed in a private room at Richmont Memorial Hospital.

Marcus sat in the chair facing her. He'd been silent on the ride to the hospital, but he'd remained stationed by her side throughout. The EMT's assumed he had some right to be there. She didn't have the energy to argue. Besides, there was something comforting in his presence, especially, after the incident. He'd summoned his own doctor who, over the phone, arranged for X-ray's. While she was wheeled to radiology, Marcus called the center and let Grant know what happened.

"I assured him you were okay and would call him later," Marcus explained. "I didn't want you to worry about work."

She nodded her appreciation. Her body was starting to feel the affects of her accident. She looked across the room to where Marcus sat stoic in his chair. It was nice to have someone step up and handle things for her. She was so used to being the one who took control. In light of her current circumstance, to have a capable stronger hand was reassuring.

She caught the direction of her thoughts and gave herself a mental reprimand. Here she was, ready to praise him, when he was no saint. She almost forgot why she hadn't been paying attention in the first place. He wasn't Mr. Dependable. He was Mr. Take Whatever He Wants.

She'd be a fool to forget again.

"Dr. Simmons will be here soon. He had to come from across town." His voice cut through her thoughts.

It was time she reminded him that she needed nothing from him. "Thank you for your concern, but there was no need for you to call your physician," she informed him with cool politeness. "I'm sure one of the doctors' here would suffice just as well. I'd hate to keep you from any pressing…business you might have."

His smile was warm. "Did you know that you get incredibly polite when you're angry?"

"Well, one of us has to have some manners," she grumbled. "Besides, I'm not uncomfortable, I'm tired and I want to be left alone."

He abruptly stood up. For a moment she thought he was going to comply, but then he prowled over to her, never once taking his eyes from hers. When he was close, he bent down and placed an arm on either side of her. His voice was low and intent. "Get it through your thick skull that I'm not going anywhere."

With those words, he moved back to his chair, she was too outraged to say anything.

From his seat he remarked, "Don't worry, you'll like Dr. Simmons."

"I have my own doctor, you know."

"And I'm sure he's very good," Marcus responded, his tone nonchalant. "If its insurance you're worried about, don't. I'll take care of everything."

"You'll take care of…?" Sabryna could not believe the audacity of the man. Did he think he could just step in and assume complete control over her life? She continued in utter distaste, "Is that what you do, you just take care of things? What must it be like to be master of the universe? Goodness! Is there anything your money or name can't get you?"

His pointed gaze said it all. "Apparently, there is."

She didn't know what to say to that, didn't think it warranted a response, so she turned her head away, locked her arms in front of her, and stared moodily at the wall.

It was into this tableau that Dr. Simmons entered.

Dr. Simmons was an aging black man with a head of gray hair. He had an engaging bedside manner, and although Sabryna wanted to find fault with him, she couldn't. So she grimaced through the pokes and prods and with growing calm answered his questions.

"Your x-rays came back and it seems you're still in good working order," he informed her at the end of her examination. "You're lucky that bike wasn't going very fast, you didn't break or damage anything. I did see some signs of bruising so you may be a little sore for a couple of days. I'm going to give you a prescription for some Motrin, but I recommend you take a couple of days off work and off your feet. A little rest and you'll be as good as new."

She accepted his prescription and thanked him for coming, then rose to her feet. A surge of nausea assaulted her, but she kept it to herself. There would be time to cry later, when she was alone.

"I'll drive you home." Marcus appeared at her side and took her arm. She was about to argue when she remembered her car was still in the garage at his building. But, then again, hadn't he ridden with her in the ambulance? "I arranged for my car to be brought here while you were getting X-rayed." He somehow followed the direction of her thoughts.

Wanting to get home, she decided she could endure his presence for the next twenty minutes. But after that she was determined that she would never see him again.

By the time Marcus's Lexus pulled up in front of Sabryna's house, her body had started to stiffen up. Therefore, she was grateful when he decided to help her to the door. When she opened the door, he assisted her in and over to the couch. She took the pills the doctor had prescribed out of the bag. They'd stopped by the pharmacy on the way to her house. As soon as he left she was going to take the pill, then take to her bed, and hope by the time she woke up the pain had passed.

She looked up as he handed her a glass of water. Surprised, she hadn't even noticed him retrieving it, she took it from him. Swallowing the medicine, she glanced at him in time to see him shrug his broad shoulders out of his jacket.

"What...what are you doing?" she demanded to know.

"Getting comfortable," he stated as if it should've been obvious.

"What...Why?"

He sat down across from her. "The doctor ordered you to stay in bed."

"I remember. I was there."

"What if you need something?"

"I'll get up and get it."

His lips thinned. "And that's why I'm staying. So you can waste your energy arguing with me or you can accept the inevitable."

Her head was pounding, her nausea was roiling in full force now, and she didn't need this. She needed to be left alone. "I want you to leave."

"And I want you to go to bed. I'll be here when you wake up."

"Don't you get it? I don't want you here." She fisted her hands. "Besides, I believe someone is waiting for you back at your office."

"Sabryna..."

"You better hurry, I wouldn't want her to starve to death," she retorted.

"I'm sure Adrina has left."

She didn't want to hear this. She stood. If he wouldn't leave on his own she would force him too. She walked over to him with the intent to pull him from the chair and send him packing. Perhaps the medicine was making her a little irrational, but she had a right to some level of insanity after almost being plowed down. Yet, as soon as she rose her headache burst through in blinding force and sent her stumbling. Standing, he reached out to her just as her world once again faded to black.

Marcus caught her before she hit the floor and swung her up into his arms. He stood there for a long time holding her against him. Needing the reassurance that she was okay. He was glad she'd fainted, his feisty Angel needed the rest and she appeared to be ready to do battle with him instead. He walked to her bedroom and laid her down on the lilac comforter. She settled into the mattress, her head resting on the pillow.

He wondered was it possible to be envious of a pillow. He noticed a blanket on the edge of her bed and gently spread it over her.

For one moment, he allowed himself to relive the fear he'd experienced when he watched that bike hit her. He should've taken better care of her. He wouldn't make that mistake again. He would stay as long as his Angel needed him. Well, as long as he felt she did, he revised as he recalled her earlier insistence that he leave.

All that fire wrapped up in the body of an enchantress. She was the epitome of a challenge.

He headed for her living room and hoped her couch was as comfortable.

The dream was so familiar that Marcus wasn't sure where it ended and reality began. As usual the two merged together with eerie finesse. Flashes of his memory, depicting scenes from another time, collided with images from the dream world. He was walking with her in the park. She was laughing up at him. He was dancing with her at a party. Her succulent body swayed against his to a hypnotic rhythm. He was holding her in her dorm room, taking her clothes off, words he didn't mean but that she needed to hear falling from his lips.

And then came the sobbing. Once again he was standing on the outside of her door. He could hear her inside crying out her love for him, begging him to love her back.

"Kari, stop crying," he was pleading. "You don't really love me you only think you do."

"Yes, I do," she yelled. "Yes, I do."

And then the sound of the gun shot, it always echoed in his mind. Sending him into that familiar dark place of panic and regret, where he spent so much time when he wasn't dreaming. He banged on the door, begging her to open it. The sobbing had stopped. It was quiet.

The door opened on its own.

She lay on the floor, flat on her back. The gun hung, listless, in her fingers. A pool of red blood collected on the carpet under her head.

He stepped closer. He knew he would see Kari's beautiful face locked in a permanent peaceful slumber. It was a sight that haunted him. He looked down at his victim.

And found it was Sabryna resting in a pool of blood. Her gorgeous eyes captured in death.

"No!" he yelled, anguish threatening to take him under. "No!"

"Marcus?" Her sweet voice, hesitant, unsure, pulled him from his dream. He opened his eyes to find himself sitting straight up, staring face to face with a very alive Sabryna. She was wearing a light blue cotton robe, and her loose hair draped over her back and shoulders.

His hands gripped her upper arms as though she were a lifeline.

She searched his eyes, concern filled her face. "Were you having a bad dream?"

He released her and fell back on the couch raising an arm to drape across his face. "You should be in bed."

"I...I thought I heard something," she told him. Although he had released her she stayed where she was, perched on the edge of the couch at his side.

"I'm sorry I woke you," he told her. "Do you need anything?"

She was quiet for so long that he wondered if she'd heard him. He shifted his arm so that he could see her. "Do you want to talk about it?" she asked.

"It was a dream, just a dream."

"It didn't sound like just a dream," she pointed out. "It must have been intense, you're sweating. If you need to talk about it..."

"I don't want to talk about it," he snapped. "And I don't want a therapy session. I need you to stop bugging me about it. I want you to go back to your room and go to sleep."

She drew back as if she'd been slapped. "I didn't tell you to stay the night on my couch. If you're so irritated then perhaps you should take your nightmares and go home."

She started to stand, but he grabbed her hand. "I'm sorry,"

She nodded, somewhat mollified. He watched as the clouds once again formed in her beautiful brown eyes. He didn't want her anger. "Sabryna, the thing with Adrina this afternoon..."

She stiffened. "It's none of my business."

He continued as if she hadn't spoken, "I didn't have a lunch date with her like you're imagining. The company she works for are customers of ours. Cortland Consulting handles their IT needs and she is their representative. We were meeting to discuss business. Just business. We weren't even going to meet alone, the project manager was also joining us."

He could see in her eyes that she didn't know whether or not to believe him. He continued, "I know the way she made it look, like we have something going on. But, I promise you that is not so. She's a business associate. Nothing more."

Sabryna's turned her face away from him. "I was...jealous," she admitted.

He was touched by her courage. "There was no need for you to be."

"She's very beautiful," Sabryna remarked, looking back at him.

"So are you."

Her head dipped down, a slight smile graced her face. "I'm not beautiful the way she is. It's not that I think I'm ugly, I'm just not like… that."

"I know," he replied and her head popped up. He reached out and fingered a lock of her hair, rolling it in his fingers. "The type of beauty Adrina possesses is superficial and will one day fade. But you, your beauty is so much deeper. It's not just how you look but it's a part of who you are. It shines in your spirit and comes across in the way you care about people. Never mind, that you have the body of a sexual diva or eyes I find myself getting lost in. Your beauty is your heart." His hand moved over her heart. "I'm enchanted by you."

His words were so beautiful Sabryna almost started crying. It was on the tip of her tongue to thank him for his compliments, but she could only think of one way to render a proper thank you for his words.

She leaned down, placed her hands on his chest, and kissed him. He opened for her and she tasted him, gloried in the way he responded to her. His hard body grew aroused beneath her. She was intoxicated with the sensation.

He growled low in his throat and rolled her over. She found herself staring up into dark eyes smoldering with passion. She wondered if they were a reflection of her own.

Trapped as she was beneath him, every inch of her body covered by his, all she could do was feel. Feel and burn. Feel his mouth devour her. Burn as heat spread from her lips to the tips of her toes. Feel the arousal of her own body craving for something she didn't quite understand. Burn as his hand moved from her face and caressed down her body.

He undid the belt tightening her robe and pushed the halves aside to reveal her cotton pajamas, a white spaghetti strap tank and dark blue shorts. He continued to kiss her as one finger hooked under her strap and pulled. Her naked breast sprang free and was immediately covered by his hand.

Every nerve in her body came alive, every ounce of her attention was focused on the point where his warm palm kneaded and caressed her. He freed her other breast and his mouth took possession of her nipple.

She moaned in pleasure, in need, desire. She never imagined it could feel this way. He kissed and sucked, and kissed some more, worshipping her until she thought she would dissolve into a thousand pieces.

Marcus was wild with desire. Her sweet moans in his ear were driving him to the brink. They sounded like the sweetest most hypnotic song ever to grace his ears. She was warm fire beneath him, the most spellbinding woman he'd ever met. He couldn't remember being this aroused, this desperate to strip away both their clothes and slide inside of her. Yet, he sensed if he pushed too hard she would retreat. Fall back behind her inner walls. Perhaps, never to come out again.

It wasn't worth the risk.

So he kept up his gentle torture and kept a tight leash on his control. His hand moved from her breast and made a slow descent to her waist. She flinched but moved to get closer.

Somewhere in Sabryna's passion befuddled mind she realized his fingers were tracing the top of her panty line. Her body raised, wanting more. The sheer force of her desire scared her. If he wanted she would give herself to him right now, right then. Forget the consequences.

But if she did that, gave so much to him, what would be left of her for her?

The thought sent cold panic rushing through, just enough to chill her ardor. She pushed at his chest. "Please...please stop."

"What's wrong, Angel?" he asked, his hands stopped. .

She pushed again and he let her up. She pulled her robe tight around her. "I...I'm still a little sore." It was a shadow of the truth.

He searched her eyes, his breathing harsh and shallow. Then he nodded. "Perhaps you should go back to bed."

Sabryna nodded, unsure, and stood up. She was halfway across the room when she stopped, and faced him. "Will you be here when I wake up?"

His smile contained no humor. "I'll be here as long as you need me."

"Thank you."

He lay back down, flung his arm back across his face. "Get some sleep, Angel. I promise no more bad dreams."

She padded back to her bedroom and wondered if sleep was even a remote possibility when the man she was fast falling in love with was lying aroused with desire in her living room.

CHAPTER ELEVEN

"Where are you taking me?" Sabryna asked from the front seat of Marcus's Lexus. She watched the city disappear outside of her window as they cruised up Interstate 95, headed north out of town.

Marcus smiled. "You don't like surprises very much do you?"

"Not particularly."

"I'll make you a deal," he offered. "If you'll sit back, relax, I promise it won't hurt."

She hmmphed. Yet she did as told. She wasn't ready to confess it to him but she was getting more comfortable with surprises. After all, the past two weeks with him had been a process of surprises on more than just one level. One exceptional date after another.

They maneuvered into a neighborhood and she thought she might be about to at least get the question of their destination answered.

After passing several stately homes, they pulled up to a gate, the home it protected set back from the street, hidden from view by several imposing trees. The guard at the gate touched his cap and let them pass through. Marcus gave a short wave and advanced up the drive, passing perfectly manicured lawns. Sabryna's breath was taken away when she got her first view of the house. Correction, the mansion that lay before her, basking in the Sunday afternoon sun.

She was sure her mouth had dropped open.

Glass panes covered every inch of the large brick mansion. The architecture itself was amazing, reminding her of something out of a Victorian Magazine.

"Welcome to Cortland Chase," Marcus announced.

She turned her wide eyes on him. "This is your home?"

"Technically, no. This is my family's home, but I guess you could say it's mine. I grew up here. I'll one day inherit it."

Parking the car in the drive, they climbed the steps that led up to an impressive entrance. The door opened as if by magic to an even more impressive foyer. A butler greeted them as they stepped through. "Good Afternoon, Mr. Cortland."

"Good afternoon Hinton," Marcus responded. "Is my mother in the Green room already?"

"Yes, sir," Hinton confirmed. "Your brother and sister are with her."

When the butler disappeared down the corridor, Sabryna turned in a semi circle to observe her surroundings. She thought her mouth might be stuck open.

Marcus chuckled at the look on her face, reached out, locked one lazy finger under her jaw and shut it. "There, now I think we're ready."

"Funny, funny," she chided, but his good-natured teasing did help her to feel more at ease in these surroundings. She followed him down a long corridor, noting the large paintings on the wall. One in particular seemed out of place. Compared to the rest, it was awful. She couldn't decide whether it was a tall tree or a fuzzy puppy. It looked almost as if...

"If you're thinking that a child painted that, you're correct," Marcus informed her, following her gaze.

She eyed the hideous picture one more time. One could only wonder at the taste of the rich. "Is it painted by a famous young artist?" she asked helpfully.

"No, just a boy who believed he was important enough to have his artwork hung on the same wall as his mother's favorite Van Gogh."

Her hand flew to her mouth to cover her amusement. "You! You painted that." She burst out laughing. "Wh-What is it? Is it a dog or a tree?"

He pretended to be offended. "It's a bowl of fruit."

She doubled over with mirth, the sound blending with his own. How could she not want this man?

"Well, we were wondering what happened to you," a crisp feminine voice interrupted on the scene. Startled, Sabryna spun to face a handsome older lady who had emerged from a side door.

"Hello, Mother." Marcus moved past her and placed a kiss on his mother's cheek.

Sabryna used the moment to make a quick check of her attire. Marcus had given her little direction on form of dress so she had mirrored his own casual slacks and a polo shirt by wearing a long Khaki skirt, tight fitting violet colored blouse and a short khaki jacket.

It was obvious he held his mother in great affection. For a moment, she wondered if his mother would be as snotty as some of the other women she had met at the club. Marcus introduced her as a friend, and Sabryna noticed his Mother's green eyes grow large with suspicion. Then a smile the size of the Grand Canyon spread across her face.

"I'm very pleased to meet you," Elaine Cortland announced her voice dripping with approval, then before Sabryna could read too much into that statement ,she whisked them both through a door and into an elegant dining room.

In the middle of the room stood a cherry oak table ready to seat eight, detailed carvings etched into the wood. A chandelier held court over head, sending light to refract off the fine china and glass dishes. Large bay windows showcased the expansive lawns. A sense of coziness engulfed her. Elaine Cortland introduced her to the other two family members. Madelyn Cortland was a young, pretty teenage girl, and David Cortland a slimmer mirror image of his older brother. He had a devil may care smile. She sat to the right of Marcus, his mother on his left at the head of the table. His brother and sister sat opposite them.

Had someone told Sabryna she would be having a five-course meal in a mansion and enjoying herself she might have keeled over in laughter. Yet, she was, and she was having the time of her life.

The atmosphere was light. Marcus and his family obviously enjoyed each other's company and liked to engage in good-natured teasing. They all shared little tidbits from their life and everyone seemed to have extensive knowledge of what the others were doing.

This was the type of family she always dreamed of having.

And here she was, for a moment, getting to be a part of it. And a part of it she was. They were very interested in her and asked her a myriad of questions.

Madelyn, whom she was fast learning was not only sassy and spirited, but seemed to enjoy a good dramatic tale, asked, "So, when did you and Marcus start dating?"

Sabryna didn't at first register the stiffening form beside her. She was frozen with a forkful of steamed vegetables halfway to her mouth.

"What?" Madelyn asked in innocent indignation, her curls dancing as she turned her head from her mother to her brother, David. "I just asked what we all want to know."

"Yes, but we were going to use a little tact." David shook his head. "Do you know what that is?"

Madelyn rolled her eyes. "By tact that means they were going to keep asking you random questions until they found out the information they wanted to know."

Marcus narrowed his eyes at his sister who met his gaze with a challenging tilt of her head. "Madelyn." His tone held a firm warning.

"What? I just wanted to know. So does mom."

"Don't bring me into this." Elaine held up a hand.

David mumbled, his mouth full of lobster tail.

"David, don't talk with food in your mouth," Elaine admonished. She looked to Sabryna. "He really does have good manners." Her eyes slid to Madelyn. "All my children do."

David gave a crooked smile. "So, do we get an answer?"

Sabryna panicked. If she answered this question yes, she would be claiming that she and Marcus were dating. She didn't know what they were. She didn't want to commit him to anything that wasn't there, nor did she want to discredit anything that was.

She wondered if anyone would think she was strange if she crawled under the table and waited for them all to disappear. She opened her mouth to answer when a loud thump caught everyone's attention.

Marcus placed his cup down on the table. "Sabryna and I have been seeing each other for almost two weeks now. Now that ya'll have your answer you can stop interrogating her and allow her to enjoy her dinner."

Everyone smiled and resumed eating. Sabryna on the other hand couldn't catch a complete breath. He just told his family they were seeing each other. What did that mean? Did that mean they were just seeing each other as casual friends? Or, were they dating? Sabryna stuck a piece of bread in her mouth to keep from interrogating him.

The dinner plates were cleared away and one of the maids inquired if Mrs. Cortland would like desert brought out, to which she answered yes. "For dessert we're having a seven layer chocolate caked drizzled with raspberry sauce." She directed her prideful statement at Sabryna.

Sabryna smiled at the pleasure on the other woman's face. She truly was a likable lady. "Oh my, that sounds delicious."

David coughed.

"Well, I hope you'll like it. I prepared it myself."

Madelyn groaned.

Elaine shot her children a warning glare.

"Do you enjoy baking?" Sabryna asked.

"Actually." Elaine leaned closer to Sabryna. "I'm just learning. It's a brand new experience for me but I'm enjoying myself immensely."

"She's the only one," muttered Madelyn.

Elaine ignored her daughter. "I like to try new hobbies. I try to teach my children it's always important to expand your horizons."

"Well, I'm sure the cake will be wonderful," Sabryna assured her.

Marcus coughed.

"I sent some cookies to my other son, Alex. He lives in New York," Elaine told Sabryna. "He loved them. Told me they were delicious and asked me to send more."

"Did any one witness Alex eat the cookies?" David inquired in a loud whisper.

"He lives in New York, David," Elaine snapped.

"I think that was his point, mother," Marcus teased.

"I wish you could meet Alex," Elaine spoke to Sabryna but glared at David. "He's a very loving and compassionate son."

"Only because he's not here," Madelyn advised.

Elaine gave a dramatic resigned sigh as she fell back in her chair. "My children like to be mean to me, Sabryna."

"Only because we love you so much," David responded as the dessert was brought to the table. David stood up. "I…ah…I have to call the station." And with those words he left the room.

Madelyn was next. "I forgot to call Christina and get the math homework. I need to do that before she goes to sleep."

Her mother gave her a skeptical look. "It's not even 7:30."

"She goes to sleep early," Madelyn called out as she sailed out of the room.

Marcus began to rise.

"You'll sit and enjoy my cake, young man," his mother instructed in a matron tone. And much to Sabryna's surprise he sat back down with low groan. Apparently, there was a force out there greater than his.

Sabryna was determined to enjoy her dessert. She liked Elaine, hell, she liked the entire family, and she wanted to support her hobby. Besides, it was chocolate cake, how bad could it be, she thought. She took a bite and begin to chew…and chew…and chew. Cake wasn't supposed to be so rubbery. Or crunchy.

Elaine looked at her in clear expectation. "So what do you think?"

Sabryna attempted to smile, but she felt as if her mouth was glued together by chocolate.

"Is it bad?" Elaine inquired, anxious.

Sabryna swallowed. Swallowed again and rinsed her mouth with some wine. "Only if you want to eat it."

Elaine burst out laughing. "Sabryna, I think I love you."

* * *

After dinner, Marcus, Sabryna, and Elaine walked out into the gardens. Engrossed in conversation, Sabryna and Elaine wandered off down the winding paths. Marcus hung back on the deck, tracking his mother's and his Angel's progress as they chatted among the rhodendrums and wondered at the impulse that had driven him to bring her here.

He could admit that wasn't the best decision he'd ever made. He should've foreseen his family's curiosity. Yet, one couldn't blame them. Their curiosity was on high alert because he'd never brought a woman home before. Of course, they'd want to know the nature of the relationship. Based on his uncharacteristic behavior, he was sure his family thought that they had just been introduced to his future wife. But he had no plans to marry anyone.

He hadn't been attempting to send a message or make a statement. And now, he hoped he wasn't sending the wrong signals.

What had inspired him to take Sabryna home? That could be blamed on impulse. A desire for her to experience a real family. Wanted, with a need that was beyond him to understand, to clear away some of the sadness he saw in her eyes whenever she talked about her childhood. So, that one day when she met the man she was going to marry, she would have a clearer view of the type of family life she wanted.

The thought that he was acting now so that she could later find happiness with another man sent a wave of irritation coursing through him.

He allowed the sight of her walking in the gardens on his family's estate to sooth the growling beast within that snarled at the very thought of her being possessed by another.

It was high time he sped along her seduction. Holding himself back was no easy feat when the mere sight of her was enough to make him as hard as stone. Yet, he sensed that intimacy made her nervous. She needed time to relax and get to know him. He didn't wish to lose her because he was trying to rush things.

Any good challenge required patience and strategy.

Over the last two weeks, his endeavors to make her more at ease with him had been rewarded. She welcomed him into her life, a fact he found endearing. And the more he got to know her the more he liked her.

"I like her." David materialized at Marcus's side. "When you get bored with her…"

"Don't finish that sentence," Marcus warned.

David laughed. "Calm down, big brother, I was just suggesting, since you don't like distractions…"

"I like this distraction."

"Yeah, I thought as much."

"Here, I have another kind of distraction for you." Marcus reached into his pocket, pulled out a white card, and handed it to David.

Opening up the card, David read out loud, "Someday, I will make you pay. I have not forgotten, I will never forget." He shook his head. "Your stalker is back."

"It was on my car windshield this morning. I'd ask you to look into it, but what's the point. I'm beginning to think this guy is all talk and no action."

David pocketed the card. "I know I've asked you this before but are you sure you can't remember anything you might've done that pissed someone off."

Marcus shrugged. "I haven't been a saint, but I can't think of anything anyone would want to kill me for." And there were things he couldn't discuss with David.

David mulled some thoughts over. "Why do you think this person wants to kill you? He never actually says he wants to kill you."

"Well when someone leaves you mysterious notes saying they want to cause you pain you just kind of assume death is involved," Marcus remarked dryly. "Though, I'm starting to believe that I'll never know who sent them. It's been over seven years."

"It's never wise to let your guard down," David informed him. "This guy is smart. We've never been able to catch his scent, which means he's patient. Don't underestimate him."

"When he starts doing something more than leaving cards I'll take him more serious." He dismissed his stalker from his mind and joined Sabryna with his mother.

He could be a patient man also.

CHAPTER TWELVE

"Why did you sell your father's company?" Sabryna asked on the ride home. She was dying to know.

Marcus shot her a sideways glance. "Who told you that, my mother?"

"She mentioned it in passing, but that's not the first time I've heard it." Sabryna let out a small yawn.

Marcus's eyes remained on the road. "It was a decision I had to make."

When she let the silence stretch, he added, "It was complicated."

"Was it because you didn't like your father?"

He turned a look of mild surprise on her. "Who said I didn't like my father."

Sabryna shrugged. "It was obvious you were disappointed in him when he died."

"I was," he quietly admitted.

"So, did you do it for revenge?"

"I loved my father." Marcus gripped the steering wheel.

"I never suggested you didn't," Sabryna remarked. "If you don't want to talk about it..."

"I don't want to talk about it," he replied before she could finish her sentence, and she tried to hide her disappointment. Apparently, he preferred to keep his private thoughts locked away. Instead of dwelling on that point she decided to examine his earlier remark to his sister.

She cleared her throat. "I enjoyed spending time with your family."

Marcus flashed a broad grin. "I'm glad." His smile slipped a couple of notches. "That was my reason for bringing you tonight."

"You could've warned me about the questions."

"I'm sorry about that. My sister isn't well known for holding anything back."

"Well, I'm glad you jumped in on that one question," Sabryna told him. "I didn't know what to say."

"With them it's always best to stick to the facts. Madelyn especially has a tendency to over dramatize."

"I see," She said. But she wasn't sure she did. There were still so many unanswered questions.

"What are you doing next Saturday night?"

She did a mental scan of her schedule. "Reading a good book," she teased. "Why do you have a better suggestion?"

"Yes, the African American Culture Museum is having their annual ball. I go every year and I was hoping this year you'd come with me, as my date." He glanced at her. "I hope the grimace on your face isn't because you're thinking of spending the night in my company"

"Spending the night in your company is the only attractive part of that offer," Sabryna admitted. "I don't enjoy going to such parties."

"Didn't we meet at a similar event?"

"Yes, but that was work. I wouldn't have gone if Grant hadn't forced me to."

"I have a hard time believing anyone can force you to do something that you don't want to do." His tone sounded admirable.

She shrugged. "It did take a lot of convincing."

"What is it about these parties you don't like?" he asked.

"It's not so much the event as the people at them."

"People like me?"

"No, not like you, you're not like that," she told him with sincerity. "You're a part of that world but you're not like them, or at least like most of them. They carry around a certain superiority and self importance that I can't tolerate."

"They're not all bad."

She considered his profile. "I know. Your family isn't what I expected. And I have met some nice people. I'm sorry if I offended you. I know these people are your friends."

His smile was grim. "I didn't say your assessment wasn't accurate. And I wouldn't be so quick to call them my friends. We share mutual interests. It's a world built on money and power, and when you are at the top they love you, but when you fall they're waiting to rip you to shreds."

"Are you speaking from experience?"

Marcus shrugged. "Let's just say that it's important to never give them that chance. No matter what the cost."

She was struck by a sense of mystery around him. Was it because he never spoke a lot about himself? She was starting to feel like his life was just one big question. Perhaps, she needed to just let the cards fall where they may. "I'd love to go to the ball with you if you still want me too."

"I would." He reached over and grabbed her hand.

She decided she had all the answers she needed. For now.

"How did you know when you were in love with George?"

At Sabryna's question, Lena's head popped up with interest and her eyes grew wide. Sabryna almost wished she hadn't asked, but she needed to know. Needed to understand if she was confusing sexual attraction with soul-wrenching love. Tonight seemed the perfect time to quiz her friend. They were closing down the center together, cleaning up the common room and no one else was in the building.

Lena, always on the lookout for a dramatic romantic moment dropped onto the couch, pulled her down beside her, and exclaimed, "You are in love with Marcus Cortland, aren't you?"

"I don't know…can't you just answer my question?" she implored.

Lena laughed. "All right, girl. Now keep in mind I've known George for a long time because he was friends with my brother. George always says that the minute he met me he knew that I was going to be his wife, but me, I say I didn't want any machismo telling me what to do. George tried everything. Flowers, candy, gifts, to get me, and I kept saying no. Yet, that didn't stop him. Whenever I needed something George was right there ready to help me, but, I felt that was the kind of things boys do to get their women. Then they change." Her smile grew pleasant as she revisited the past. "Then one day, I went with this guy I had been seeing up to Washington D.C. When we got there he rented a hotel room and tried to make me…well you get the point. I was so angry and scared, I did a little move my brother's taught me, and gave it to him right in the nuts."

Sabryna laughed. "So, what happened?"

"I went running and the only person I could think to call was George. He came immediately. He was going to kill that guy when he saw how upset I was, but he didn't want to leave me alone. He didn't ask questions, didn't get angry at me for going off with this guy, or nothing. He just drove me home, told me to get some rest, and kissed me goodnight. I knew then I would love him forever."

Lena looked at Sabryna a soft smile on her face. "Love is the person you go running to when the rest of world gets too much to handle. The one person you know you can always depend on. For me, that was George."

Sabryna sighed. "You're very lucky."

Lena laid a gentle hand over Sabryna's. "Girl, you can be just as lucky. Marcus Cortland is a good man." Lena rose from the chair to finish shutting down. She winked. "Falling in love with him might be worth the drop."

I've already fallen, thought Sabryna, but how do I know if he's taking the leap with me? One thing was for certain. She was sick of holding back. This might be the closest thing to love she'd ever experienced and she wanted to seize the moment. She wanted to make love to Marcus, listen to his breathing as he slept, and wake up in his arms. He hadn't tried to seduce her in the past couple of weeks. So there was only one thing left for her to do.

Seduce him.

The African American Culture museum was located in a small building downtown. As a result, their annual ball which attracted hundreds of guests each year was held at the Ritz Carlton. Dressed in a strapless dusty rose satin gown she felt like a princess. Her prince was dressed just as elegant in a black tuxedo. Her body grew warm when she remembered the look he'd trained on her when he first saw her that night. His eyes seared through her gown as though he was feasting on her bare skin. There wouldn't be a simple goodnight kiss tonight, she thought slyly. The lady at the store had told her that this dress was meant to bring men to their knees and she was planning to put that theory to the test...soon.

The entrance to the ballroom was located on the second floor. From there a large staircase led down to the main floor. Waiting at the top of the stairs, Sabryna scanned the scene before her. The theme must've been inspired by the spring season now upon them, and golden colored flowers hung in long ropes from the ceiling. The colorful dresses of the women provided a nice contrast to the black tuxedos of the men.

"Usually I'm too busy hating these events to realize how beautiful they can be." She and Marcus descended the stairs.

"It's a shame you don't like them." His voice lowered to those seductive tones she found thrilling. "Because you look breathtaking in a ball gown."

Sabryna decided she liked being thought of as breathtaking.

As soon as they stepped on to the floor they were approached by people wanting to talk with Marcus. Anthony Denton was one of those individuals. He strolled up and greeted them both. "So you must be the reason my friend has been missing these past weeks." He shot her a mischievous wink.

Sabryna laughed. "I'm not sure I should respond to that."

Marcus gave a shadow of a smile. "You shouldn't."

"I'm wounded." He reached out his hand and laughing, she accepted. "Don't worry; you can make it up to me with a dance."

Marcus watched as his best friend led his Angel out on to the dance floor and told himself not to scowl. If there was a beautiful woman in a ten mile radius, Anthony would find her. Anthony was his friend and he wouldn't try anything with a woman that he thought Marcus had an interest in. Yet, he didn't like watching her dance with Anthony. He didn't think he would like seeing her dance with any man.

When had he learned how to be jealous? He experienced that now. He wanted to rush over, snatch her into his arms, take her back to his place, and make sweet love to her. She wasn't just his Angel, she was his obsession. And he didn't want to hurt her. She was sweet and kind and had a certain innocence about her that enchanted him. He was use to women who were selfish, jaded, and vain. Sabryna was none of those things.

He was going to miss her when she was out of his life.

The idea of spending more than just a night in her arms occurred to him. He'd never considered developing a relationship with a woman. He didn't want anyone to start hoping for things that were never going to happen. Yet, Sabryna was practical and sensible. If he explained what he wanted she just might understand. If he was upfront with her from the beginning about not wanting to fall in love and get married, she would not have any illusions about him and they could continue to enjoy each other's company. Why not? They could have fun together and when they grew bored with each other go their separate ways. He could continue with his life of solitude and she could find a husband and have a bunch of babies.

He thought of Sabryna, happy with another man, and his mood darkened. He had to face the truth, he wasn't ready to let go of her yet. One day he would, but for now he would enjoy her company, and find some way to protect her from himself.

"Marcus, I didn't know you were going to be here," a sultry voice said from behind him. He turned around to face Adrina Howell poured into a midnight blue dress.

"Hello, Adrina." He kept his response cool.

"I'm surprised you still remember my name."

The truth was he hadn't thought of her sense the day he'd left her standing in his office. He hadn't appreciated the drama performance that she had delivered in front of Sabryna. After that he had ordered the project lead to consult with her so that he wouldn't have to.

She put her hands on her hips. "I'm going to assume you have a good reason for avoiding my phone calls."

Marcus watched as Anthony twirled Sabryna around the room. "I think you know what that reason is."

She narrowed her eyes and moved closer to him. "Is it because of her?"

"Any business concerns you have can be handled by John Malone, the project lead."

"Not the kind of business I've in mind." She stroked his lapel with a long finger. "I don't know what it is you seem to like about your little charity princess, but she wouldn't know the first thing to do with a man like you. On the other hand, I could rock your world and I guarantee you would be begging me for more."

Angered by her snide remarks about Sabryna, Marcus let his eyes roam with contempt down her body. He couldn't deny Adrina's beauty. He was willing to take a bet that most of the men in the room would be quick to switch places with him. Yet, there was something dark and selfish about her character that made her about as attractive as the bubonic plague. The way she threw herself at him caused his stomach to turn. Unlike Sabryna, she didn't even attempt to be a challenge. "I'd be careful if I were you before you make assumptions about others. You don't have a tenth of what she has."

Anger distorted her features, but before she could respond, Anthony and Sabryna joined them.

"Marcus, I got some bad news for you. Sabryna's decided that I'm ten times more interesting than you and she wants to be my date now," Anthony teased his friend.

"Get your own woman, Anthony." Marcus hooked his arm around Sabryna's waist and drew her close to his side.

Adrina was more than primed to release some of her venom. She gave Sabryna the once over and declared, "What an interesting dress you're wearing. That color isn't always the best combination for your type of skin, but I admire you for being willing to take a risk."

Sabryna leaned further into Marcus, placing a hand on his chest. "Thank you. I like your dress, also. Tell me, are you here alone?"

Adrina got the point, and sending the couple a disgusted sneer, left.

"She didn't answer my question." Sabryna pretended innocence.

Anthony chuckled. "I think it's safe to say you put her in her place."

Sabryna lifted her shoulders in a dainty shrug. "Well, you don't spend your days with teenage girls and not learn how to be catty. I can give as good as I get."

Marcus laughed, pulling her closer. "Angel, there isn't a single doubt in my mind."

Neither Marcus nor Sabryna wanted the night to end so they decided to have a nightcap at her place. He took a seat on the couch and she went into the kitchen to start the coffee maker perking. Joining him in the living room, she commented, "I must admit, after always having to dress for comfort at work, my favorite part of the night was getting to wear this dress." Standing in front of him, she did a quick turn.

"Come here," he pulled her onto his lap. He rained butterfly kisses along her slender neck. "I love this dress."

"Even if it's the wrong color," she quipped, angling her neck for better access. She'd been waiting for this moment all night.

"You're gorgeous in this dress." His hand ran up her back and located the zipper. Pulling it down he lowered the front part of her dress exposing her strapless black lace bra. "You're gorgeous out of this dress."

Sabryna moaned as his other hand caressed her breast. She was thankful for his strong arm supporting her, without which she would have slid to the floor.

Marcus's fingers unsnapped her bra and it fell away from her, leaving her breast exposed to his heated gaze. "I've been dreaming of doing that all night." His mouth found her nipple and began to suckle. Pleasure spread through her body. She reached up and pulled his head closer, craving his touch.

Raising his mouth from her breast, he found her lips and kissed her deeply, exploring the recesses of her mouth. Their tongues dueled, mingled, explored. Answering his hungering need with her own. His arousal hard and compelling, beneath her. He tasted of the wine they'd shared earlier, it made her dizzy with excitement and something else she couldn't put a name to. She only knew one thing for certain. She wanted him and she wanted him right now.

He pulled back from the kiss. She tried to reclaim his lips, but he resisted. "I should go."

"I don't want you to." She locked her arms around his neck and placed a soft kiss on his mouth.

"Angel, if I stay..."

"Stay."

"If I stay we both know what will happen."

She rose from his lap and reached behind her to finish unzipping her dress, letting it fall in a pool of satin at her feet. "I know what will happen. I want you." Sabryna stood before him, bold in nothing but a pair of lacy black panties. "I want you to make love to me."

CHAPTER THIRTEEN

Marcus hesitated for the barest of seconds. Then he stood and scooped Sabryna up in his arms. He kissed her hard on the lips. "Are you sure?"

"I've never been more sure about anything in my life," she told him and he carried her to the bedroom.

He laid her down on the bed. "You are so damn beautiful."

She smiled a sirens smile. "When you look at me like, that I feel beautiful."

How she could seduce him with mere words he'd never understand. He removed his clothes, dropping each piece to the floor. Silent, her liquid brown eyes drank in the sight, and he realized when she looked at him like that he felt invincible.

Naked, he joined her on the bed. She turned toward him offering her mouth for his pleasure. He took, drank all she had to offer and more. Her taste was intoxicating. Running his hands up and down her body, learning her curves, exploring each one, his body ached to be inside her. Marcus made himself go slow, to make her burn to match his need, want, desire. Holding tight to the reins of his control, he feasted on her breast.

Sabryna thought she would turn into a ball of flame at any second. His body was so hard against her softness. Everywhere his hand touched, warmth infused that spot. It was as though she was being licked by the sun.

She had no idea what she was doing, but she decided instinct was a beautiful thing and she let her hands roam over his body. He groaned and squeezed her. Sensing she had pleased him, marveling at her ability to do so, she decided to explore further. Her hand wrapped around his erection and he shuddered. She felt emboldened, as though she held his power in the palm of her hand. He had such a magnificent body. Every chocolate inch of him was well toned and rock hard. Including his well-endowed manhood.

Marcus pulled her panties off, almost ripping them in his urgency to do so. He spread her legs and closed his palm over her most intimate place. Feeling drunk on pleasure, she pushed up against him, begging for more. She was rewarded when he slipped a finger into her tight, wet passage. For a moment her world fractured in a dizzying release of pleasure. Every nerve in her body sang with his touch as he explored her. He inserted another finger, pushing her wider. "Oh sweet Angel, you are so tight, so hot."

For a brief moment he separated from her and rose from the bed. She almost cried out at the loss of his heat. Realized he was taking measures to protect them both.

Marcus looked down at her luscious body writhing in ecstasy for him. His wildest dreams could never have prepared him for this moment. When he rejoined her he positioned himself between her legs and setting his lips to hers he entered her, sliding deep into her warm passage and met resistance.

He froze.

"Marcus?" He glanced down into her beautiful tense face. Her furrowed eyebrows and strained expression attested to the level of discomfort she was experiencing.

Marcus reeled in astonishment. She was a virgin. How could that be possible? She was twenty-seven. She was sexy as hell. Was every man but him blind and stupid? He told himself not to move, not to cause her any unnecessary pain.

She seemed to undermine his self-control. She raised her hips toward him in a silent plea he was helpless to resist. She was so vulnerable in her need, he could do nothing but fulfill it. His own body wouldn't have it any other way.

"Please don't stop," she pleaded.

He could deny her nothing. "Ssh, Angel," he soothed and eased deeper into her.

"I should've told you but I wanted you so bad--" her words broke off on a moan of pleasure as he repeated his action.

"I want you too," he whispered. "I want you so damn bad."

He glided into her again and again establishing a rhythm that caused her to scream out his name. She answered each thrust with her own, her hands gripped his shoulders.

Marcus felt her tense beneath him and then shatter. Watching her climax, Marcus found his own. Groaning he drove into her one last time and released himself. He collapsed on top of her, skin to skin, still buried deep inside of her heat.

When the last of her shudders subsided, he rolled next to her. They both lay on their backs.

"I never knew. I never knew it could be like that."

Marcus could hear the wonder in her voice. He'd never known either. How could the most satisfying sexual experience he'd ever had be with a virgin? How was she a virgin?

He needed answers and would demand some just as soon as his mind stopped reeling.

Sabryna rolled to her side and observed his profile. Thinking it was anger that had him in its grip, she said quietly, "I'm sorry I didn't tell you."

He turned his face toward her. His eyes burned into hers. "You were a virgin."

"Yes, I was."

"You're not anymore."

Her lips edged upwards. "No, I'm not."

"Did I…" he had to ask but couldn't force himself to say the words.

Sabryna placed her fingertips over his mouth. "You didn't hurt me and you didn't force me. I wanted this, I wanted you."

His eyes searched hers and in them he saw the truth. "I don't understand. Why me?"

With tenderness, she stroked the side of his face. "I never wanted anyone until you."

Humbled by her words, he kissed her. The kiss served to reawaken their passion and once again he made slow sweet love to her, showing her how much he appreciated her gift.

Sabryna was awakened by an unfamiliar bulk in bed with her. Her eyes opened and reality came crashing back. She lay in her bed, still naked, with an equally naked hard male body next to her. After they'd made love again, Marcus had pulled her into his arms and she'd fallen asleep with her head resting on his chest. Her limbs intertwined with his. At some point he must have covered their bodies and shut off all the lights.

Never had she felt so protected, sated, and cherished in all of her life. Or so connected to another soul. This was what women went crazy over. It was a feeling she could now fully comprehend. It had been magnificent.

All doubts she harbored about loving this man disappeared the moment he took her in his arms. How could she doubt anything when every second had been so right? Her future, their future, spread out before her. Oh, all the nights they would enjoy like this one. She was going to spend the rest of her life loving him. And no matter what it took she would get him to love her back. That was, if he didn't already. Hope swelled in her chest at the thought. He had touched her with such tenderness, loved her with such thoroughness, was that his way of confessing?

She snuggled closer to him. Her fingers played with the hairs on his chest.

"Why aren't you sleeping?" he asked, startling her from her thoughts.

"I was just thinking."

"About?"

She rose up on her elbow and looked down at him. "I love you." Those three words now seemed so simple.

His dark eyes clouded over and his face went unreadable. Then he pulled her head down for a kiss. She wanted to hear him say the words back, but her thoughts went flying out of her mind as his touch turned more intimate. She let him show her instead.

It wasn't the dream that woke Marcus this time. No screams from his past awakened him. Only the screams of his conscious cut through his slumber. Or perhaps, it was the deadening sensation creeping up from the pit of his gut

What had he done? How had he let it go so far? Why hadn't he stopped her, pulled back, explained things? Why was he so weak where she was concerned?

For just a moment, he pushed all those questions aside and held her closer to him. Nothing compared to the feeling of her lying naked in his arms. The knowledge that no other man had ever touched her this way, been deep inside of her, or heard her call his name in a passionate plea sent a bolt of possessiveness coursing through him. There was infinite satisfaction in knowing he'd been her first. She'd been so giving in her love, so passionate, so his. She had chosen to bestow her most precious gift on him and for that he was humbled.

And, so utterly unworthy.

He had nothing to offer her. He couldn't give her the life she was entitled too. He was incapable of loving her the way she deserved to be loved. He knew his love was toxic. Something that destroyed people from the inside out. All he wanted to do was protect her from that truth. Had hoped he could keep things casual between them.

And yet, she was in love with him.

Her confession had aroused him and terrified him at the same time. Perhaps it hadn't been the best move to make love to her again, but he'd been helpless to resist when she looked at him. In that moment he wanted to be the man that she saw in him. But he wasn't, could never be. In time the reality of that would disillusion her, destroy her. The innocence she carried with her would be crushed. The light that shimmered in her eyes would dim and then disappear.

He'd rather die than let that happen.

She needed to be protected from him and the hurt that he would cause her. How ironic that the only person capable of protecting her from him was himself. He needed to leave. If he stayed, she'd continue to believe that she was in love with him. She would cling to hopes that he had no intention of ever fulfilling. Each day would bring a new disappointment for her until eventually she would hate him, or herself, for loving him. There was also the possibility that he was wrong, that she was stronger than that. But, it wasn't worth the risk to find out. He had taken that risk before and the consequences had been fatal.

Keeping quiet, he separated from her and rose out of the bed. He put his clothes back on, unable to take his eyes from the sleeping figure in the bed. When he was dressed, he leaned down and brushed a curl back from her face. "Angel, you're going to hate me in the morning. But one day you'll understand this was for the best."

He placed a gentle kiss on her lips. She smiled in her sleep and snuggled further under the covers. He forced himself to turn away. And walk out of her room and out of her life.

CHAPTER FOURTEEN

Seated at the desk in her office, Sabryna checked and double checked her lists. She wanted to make sure everything was perfect for the basketball tournament the next morning. The past two weeks she'd spent every possible waking moment preparing for the tournament. Between her other responsibilities at the center and getting ready for this huge fundraising event she hadn't had even a second to breathe. No time to think about the pain that was threatening to take her under. No time to think about the man who had used her body and walked out of her life without a goodbye. No time to think about what a fool she had made of herself.

No time to think about how much she missed him.

Marcus hadn't even sent a note. At first, she'd been in a daze. The morning after that eventful night she woke alone in bed. She half expected him to walk back through her bedroom door carrying a plate of bagels and a smile. Disappointed when this didn't happen, she rose from bed and discovered he wasn't in the apartment. She called his cell phone, wanting to say good morning, wanting to hear his voice. She was greeted by the voice mail. She left a message asking him to give her a call back. He never did.

On Monday, she called him at work. Perhaps he hadn't received her message. Maybe he was worried about how she might be feeling and wanted to give her some space. Or maybe the fact that she was a virgin had scared him off. She decided to think positive, he was a good guy, and he hadn't shown signs of anger when he learned she was a virgin. However, when she called him at work his secretary informed her he was in a meeting. When he was in a meeting the next three times she called she started to feel like a stalker. Uncomfortable, she left a message for him to call her back.

And she waited.

Every time the phone rang her heart beat just a little faster. Every time the door to the center opened she broke her neck trying to see who came through it. She looked for him everywhere, hoping he might surprise her and just pop up.

Two weeks later she was still waiting.

And dying a little more inside with each second that passed and he didn't call.

Grant and Lena had been curious. Yet, no one approached her or asked her any questions. She knew if she discussed it, she would break down. There had been one scary moment where she almost did crack. It occurred earlier that week, on Tuesday. Three kids cornered her in the common room, enthusiasm dancing on their faces.

"It's Mr. Cortland," Latisha told her, excitement ringing in her tone. Sabryna's heart sped up and her stomach dropped to the floor, as she looked to the door, in dread, in hope.

Latisha thrust the newspaper at Sabryna. "Here in the paper, there's an article about him." Numb, Sabryna took the paper from her and the face that haunted her dreams stared back at her. He was smiling and her heart lurched at the sight. He was dressed in a sharp black tuxedo, his mother stood next to him. The caption read: "Marcus Cortland, Jr. attends opening night at the opera with his mother, socialite Elaine Cortland."

The truth came crashing in on her at once and if Latisha hadn't reached for the paper it would have fallen out of her hands. He wasn't at home thinking about her, missing her. He was attending opening night at the Opera. Living the life of a rich playboy.

"Were you there too?" Latisha wanted to know, her large eyes full of awe.

"No, I wasn't there." It was amazing how much that hurt just to say.

"Can we hang it up on the wall?"

Panic seized her. It was a horrible idea, but Marcus had become their hero. What could she say? No, because having to see his gorgeous face every day would tear me apart.

Grant materialized from nowhere. "I don't think we can do that. It wouldn't be fair to our other sponsors. And besides, it has nothing to do with the center. If you want, Latisha, you can take the picture home."

Satisfied, Latisha thanked him and skipped away to show off her new picture.

Sabryna was afraid to meet Grant's eyes, worried he would see her telling appreciation in them. But Grant only placed a comforting hand on her shoulder and asked her to check on things upstairs. The fact that neither Grant nor Lena chose to meddle in her life, told her without a doubt her pain wasn't as well hidden as she would like it to be.

However, within the black hole of hurt she lived in, a bright light showed through. That light was Damon. He hadn't just taken his job serious, he excelled at it. He was at work every day on time and he left when she did, despite her urgings for him to take off sooner. Any task she gave him he completed it as though it was his life's mission. He even developed a relationship with the younger kids. He would sit with them in the afternoon and do his homework, which inspired them to do the same. He organized games for them, mediated fights, and listened to their stories. Whatever problems he had with the older boys seemed to have faded to the background and the other teens started to view him as Sabryna's right hand man.

At first, Sabryna was shocked by the level of commitment and effort he put forth. She expected he would do the work, she hadn't expected him to love it. However, as they got closer she realized that Damon needed the Center just as much if not more than the Center needed him. He didn't become an open book, but the few glimpses he gave her into his personal life clued her in. Quite simply, he was lonely. He was an extraordinary and bright kid, born to a crack addicted mother. An only child, he and his mother had moved here from Philadelphia to live with relatives. It was that or become homeless. Damon had been on the fast track to juvenile detention. Circumstances had forced him to learn how to fend for himself and the streets gave him that opportunity. She could relate with ease.

Sometimes she would sense Damon watching her, as if there was something he wanted to say. She guessed it was thank you. Damon had found a place where he could feel safe and wanted. He couldn't say the words so he thanked her by putting everything he had into the job she'd given him. As a result a strange relationship of mutual respect and understanding developed between them.

Lena stuck her head in the door. "Is everything ready for tomorrow?"

Sabryna took a deep breath. "I think so."

Lena came in and sat down. "Good. Then I think it's time we talk."

"About?"

"Marcus Cortland."

Sabryna stood up, almost overturning her chair. "I don't want to talk about him."

"He is going to be there tomorrow."

Stunned, Sabryna sat. How had she overlooked that detail? Of course, he would be there. He signed up a team weeks ago.

"I can tell you forgot." Lena's voice was soft with understanding.

"Lena, I…" Sabryna knew she should say something, but she didn't know what.

Lena placed her hand over Sabryna's. "I don't know what happened between you and Marcus. I've respected your privacy because I got the idea that whatever it was, it was very painful for you. But honey, you have to know, you're not the first woman who has had her heart broken and you'll survive this."

"How will I survive this?" A tear slid down her cheeks. She was afraid she wouldn't be able to stop crying, like all those nights she'd lain alone, knowing he wasn't going to call her again.

"Oh, honey I don't know." Lena pulled her chair over so she could wrap her arm around Sabryna. "I just know you will."

"He hurt me. He hurt me more than I can even say," Sabryna told her friend. "I loved him and he made a fool out of me."

"Sabryna, did you…did he…force you?"

Sabryna shook her head. "No, he didn't take anything from me that I wasn't willing to give. God, how could I have been so stupid? I should've known better. He didn't make me any promises, any claims to love. He told me from day one what he wanted and like an idiot I believed that he might've changed. That he might be feeling the same thing I was feeling."

"It's not wrong to fall in love, Sabryna." Lena rubbed her back.

"It is when you fall in love with someone who doesn't love you back." Sabryna buried her face in her hands. "I swear I'll never fall in love again."

"Don't say that. Look at me and George and Grant and his wife Grace and…"

"I do…I did. You all were my love role models." Sabryna's laugh was self-deprecating. "But that won't work for me. Love is not in the cards, not for me. I have this Center, and my friends, and that's all I need."

A sad smile graced Lena's face. "Love isn't something you can just toss away, Sabryna. Love comes when you least expect it, when you think it never will. Maybe, this wasn't the real deal, but that…"

Lena was interrupted when the door to her office burst open and Damon stepped in. "I have everything packed up for tomorrow." His eyes narrowed on the scene before him. "You're crying?" It sounded like an accusation.

Sabryna swiped a hand over her eyes. "No, something was in my eye."

Damon's perceptive gaze swept Lena's position beside her and then

112

back to her face. "You told me there is never an excuse for lying."

He had her there. "Yes, Damon, I was…tearing up, but I'm fine now."

"Is it because of that dude?"

"Damon, if you don't have anything left to do you can go ahead home. We have an early day tomorrow."

Damon looked as though he was going to argue but after a moment he left. Sabryna threw up her hands. "Great, just what I need, another meddling someone in my life."

Lena laughed. "I'm going to pretend I didn't hear that."

Realizing how her comment must sound, Sabryna broke into shaky laughter. Giving her friend a hug, she told her, "Lena, it's so good to laugh. I feel I haven't done that in a long time. Don't worry about me. I'm going to be okay. To prove it, tomorrow I will be the consummate professional. Ten million Marcus Cortlands' can show up and I won't bat an eye."

That night she prayed for strength.

The next morning dawned clear and bright. The rain clouds they had suffered through earlier that week had beat a hasty retreat and a sunny April day was predicted on all three news channels that Sabryna checked. She had enough to concern her without worrying about being rained out. The tournament was to take place in West Area City Park, which was located in the heart of a large middle class community in Richmont. The park boasted of five large blacktops, in close proximity, which would allow ten basketball games to go on at once.

Damon had been in quiet awe since stepping out of her car at seven that morning. He turned in a full circle taking in the scenery. "We gonna be here?" He sounded as though he was sure she'd driven to the wrong place.

"Yes, we gonna be here." Sabryna laughed. "Now let's get going. The staff will be here with the vans in a few minutes and I want to be able to tell them where to set up." Taking Damon by the shoulders she directed him toward the blacktops. She wondered if he'd ever seen a city park that wasn't colored in graffiti, dressed in litter, and haunted by drug dealers.

The vans from the center arrived loaded with kids, materials, and supplies and the rush of the morning kept everyone absorbed. At 9:00 a.m. the registrants and spectators arrived. One of the first registrants was Steven Barclay and his team. Spotting her, he separated himself from a group of guys, and headed her way. He looked handsome dressed in a red and gray jogging suit that accented his slender, muscular frame. Dressed in a similar pink and gray jogging suit, Sabryna watched as Steven approached her with his usual devil-may-care smile on his face.

Happy to see a friend, considering who else she would have to face that day, Sabryna greeted him with a warm smile and hug. "I'm glad you're here."

"I should be the one thanking you," Steven responded. He gestured toward the group of guys he'd just left. "I got some of my old high school buddies together. They jumped at the chance to relive some of our glory days."

Sabryna laughed. "I'm sure you'll do just fine."

"You do have 911 on standby, don't you?"

"Steven, ya'll are not that old, and you're in great shape." Glancing at his team, she added, "It looks to me like you all are."

"See anything interesting?" Steven teased.

"Steven, no! I was just taking a peep at who you're playing with today. Trust me when I say that is the farthest thing from my mind."

Steven's smile slipped a few notches and his eyes grew more intent. "I wouldn't have thought so from the picture I saw in the paper."

She let her confusion show. "I'm not sure what you're talking about."

"Your picture was in the paper a few weeks ago. Didn't you see it?"

She thought back. Three weeks ago was around the time that…she swallowed and raised wide brown eyes to Steven.

"I guess you didn't know," he remarked studying her face. "It was a picture of you and Marcus Cortland at the museum's annual ball. I can't tell you how surprised I was to see it, considering you told me there wasn't anything between you and him."

She couldn't meet his eyes, so she glanced down at the clipboard in her hands. "There's nothing going on between us."

"That's not what the picture suggested."

"We were…friends, but that has since changed."

"Can I ask what happened?"

She Shrugged. "There's nothing to tell. We were friends and now we're not."

"Sabryna, you're not being honest with me."

"It's not the kind of thing I want to talk about, now, or ever," Sabryna insisted.

Steven put his hand on her shoulder and pulled her closer. "Sabryna, you and I may not be the best of friends, but we have never held back with each other."

"I know. But, please let this go. I have to be one hundred percent about my job today," she pleaded.

"Damn it Sabryna." Frustration edged his tone.

Shocked at his quiet outburst, Sabryna stepped back. "That's not fair."

"Isn't it? I have known you for how long and you have always been the same. In college you were all about the books and now you're all about the job. Whenever it comes to something personal you back off, shy away."

Sabryna met his eyes. "I made it about me and I got burnt. Is that what you wanted to hear me say?"

Steven stared at her for a long minute. "Was it Marcus?"

"Steven!"

"Answer me, was it Marcus?" he demanded.

"Yes, it was." She held up a hand when he opened his mouth to speak. "Before you say anything, just know that it's over with."

Steven's grip on her arm tightened. "It's the best thing. I don't want you to get hurt."

Too late for that, thought Sabryna as she placed her hand over Steven's.

He gave her a gentle squeeze. "I'm sorry I made you bring up something painful, but its better things ended now before it's too late."

Her smile was forced. For her, it already was.

CHAPTER FIFTEEN

From a short distance away, shielded by the shifting bodies of the crowd, Marcus observed the scene in front of him. Sabryna stood, wearing a stylish suit that hugged every curve to perfection, her hair pulled back in a pony tail and the curls flirted with her shoulders. She was more beautiful than he remembered. His eyes had ached for the sight of her. That was part of the madness that had inspired him to come today, to an event he knew she would be at. Yet, this was not the sight he wanted to see, Steven Barclay standing so close to her they could touch. Narrowing his eyes, he watched as Steven reached out and placed a hand on Sabryna's shoulder, pulling her closer to him for an intimate conversation. He wanted to race over, punch Barclay in the face, twice, and take her into his arms.

He killed any chance of being with her when he disappeared from her life. But it had to be done.

Yet, his noble gesture had done little to alleviate the numbness that settled into his body the minute he left her bed. The last few weeks he existed in a fog, not knowing how to regain his equilibrium. He expected to employ his usual ability to turn his emotions on and off to erase her from his mind. Sure she was unique, different from any woman he'd ever been involved with, but she was still a woman. Sure she had touched a part of him he hadn't known existed, had him for a minute considering a relationship, no matter how temporary. It was a thought he never contemplated before, yet with her, it seemed so effortless. Still, when the time came for him to walk away, he had expected to be able to do it with relative ease.

And then the time came to walk away from her and easy wasn't a word he would associate with that action.

His mind was obsessed with thoughts of her. How she responded, so passionate and feminine. How she looked at the moment her pleasure overtook her. The way her eyes danced when she laughed, how caring and compassionate she could be, the way she made an utter mockery out of the game of golf. The way she stood up for herself when Adrina tried to make her feel inferior.

How beautiful her eyes had shone when she said she loved him.

Those were words he replayed in his mind a hundred times a day. In part to torture himself, for he knew he was hurting her with his absence, and because he needed to prove that for just one night he was worthy of her.

Ignoring the impulse to call her, he stuck to his plan to eradicate her from his life. He threw himself into his work and the social whirl. He often limited his number of social events, but for the past three weeks he had accepted almost every invitation, desperate for the distraction. Night after night he stood in a sea of people, surrounded by individuals demanding his attention. And he'd never felt more alone his life.

He didn't want their attention, he wanted hers.

His eyes locked on where she and Barclay were still talking. Why couldn't she see Barclay for the pompous jerk that he was? Now that she'd been sexually awakened would she turn to Barclay? That thought alone ate him like acid.

"Why are you here?" He turned at the sound of Grant's harsh voice.

"Hello, Grant. How are you?" Marcus had to look up at Grant. It wasn't a feeling he was used to.

Grant studied him, his expression unreadable. "Why are you here?"

"I'm sponsoring two teams." A shadow of the truth. What drove him today had been a simple question. How was she? He envisioned her being angry, hating him, and burying herself in her work until the wound wasn't so fresh. Sabryna possessed a strength that wouldn't allow him to break her. He was depending on that strength. But, what if he miscalculated, as he so often did with her? After all, he hadn't expected her to be a virgin. What if, in her innocence, she wasn't able to cope? What if she crumbled the way Kari had?

"Are you playing?" Grant folded his arms across his chest.

Marcus grew uncomfortable under Grant's steady stare. He was the CEO of a multimillion dollar company, not an errant teenager. He shifted. "No, both teams are registered in the adolescent category."

"So you're not playing," Grant concluded. "Then why are you here?"

"I did sponsor the teams." Marcus attempted to keep his tone even.

"She doesn't need you here." Grant's low voice rumbled.

He knew he should leave, but he swallowed his pride. "How is she?"

Grant stared at him for a long time. "Sabryna's father lives out of state. She doesn't see him often."

"I know that." Marcus wondered at this direction.

"Sabryna's like a daughter to me, there's nothing I wouldn't do for her." Grant's spoke in a controlled tone. "That's why I regret ever encouraging her to give you the time of day."

Marcus deserved the insult. "Grant, I ..."

"I don't need your excuses young man," Grant interrupted. "I don't care who you are, I don't care who your parents are. Nothing gives you the right to treat people like meaningless objects you can play with when the mood strikes you. Did you think because she didn't have as much money as you that she wasn't worthy of your respect?"

"Absolutely not," Marcus answered without delay.

"Well, if you have any respect for her, leave. You're not wanted here." Leaning closer, Grant's eyes glowed with animosity. "Your gifts were nice. They blinded us to who you truly are. But anyone who can crush the spirit of a kind-hearted person with such ease deserves anything he's got coming to him."

His words were so close to how Marcus was feeling that it overwhelmed him in guilt. "What happened between Sabryna and I is none of your business." He knew he shouldn't say anything but he didn't need the reminder of how much of a bastard he was.

Grant took a threatening step closer. "That's where you're wrong. Unlike you, I care about her. I care when she comes to work looking like someone's hollowed out her heart. I care when she spends the bulk of her day trying to hide from the rest of us how much pain she's in. I care when the man who used her thinks he can come back for another try."

"I didn't come here today for that," Marcus defended.

"Then why are you here? You aren't playing. You aren't necessary."

"I wanted to know how she was."

"She's fine. And when you leave she'll be better," Grant bit out, stepping back from Marcus. "Now leave."

With a curt nod, Marcus headed for his car.

From a distance, Sabryna watched Grant talking to Marcus. She didn't have to hear the words to know who was being discussed. Both Grant and Marcus's postures were stiff, tense. Grant's body language radiated suppressed anger. He seldom showed his temper, but when he did...

Her eyes followed Marcus as he walked off. He didn't glance her way.

"It's about time he dipped." Damon's hostility was apparent.

Sabryna turned inquiring eyes on him. "Who?"

Damon rolled his eyes. "That punk over there." He gestured toward Marcus's retreating back.

"Damon, he has teams signed up today," she insisted.

"He came here to try to get at you." Damon spat the words out as if he had a bad taste in his mouth. "He can't be a man about it so he's trying to do it on the low."

"I don't think that's the case." Marcus proved in the past weeks that she was the farthest thing from his mind. "Any way, we have too much work to do to worry about anyone else."

Damon wasn't quite ready to let the subject drop. "Why do you act like you ain't pissed off? I know what he did."

"Really?" Sabryna infused her voice with ice. She was not in the mood to have her life examined by a kid. "What did he do?"

Damon reached down and hauled a bag of basketballs over his shoulder. Sabryna caught the strange expression that crossed his face. "What all those punk bastards want. When they get it, that's it."

Sabryna couldn't argue. She was walking evidence. However, something lurked in Damon's voice that cut past her pain and made his more visible. Placing a gentle hand on his shoulder, she asked, "Are you thinking about your father?"

"I don't have a dad." He knocked her hand off his shoulder.

"Damon…"

"Don't we have stuff to do?" Damon interrupted.

Sabryna decided that the tournament wasn't the time or place for anyone to deal with their issues. "Maybe it would be best if we agreed that certain subjects are off limits."

He nodded stiffly.

After wrapping up the first successful day of the two-day tournament, Sabryna knew a calming sense of accomplishment. Damon elected to ride back in one of the vans to help with unloading, but Sabryna guessed he was avoiding the chance that she might bring up his dad. After seeing the last van off, she headed back to her car.

There stood Marcus leaning, assured, heartbreakingly handsome, against the drivers' side of her car. His expression hidden by the dimming light of dusk.

Her heart skipped several beats and she almost tripped over nothing. Taking a deep breath she kept walking straight for her car, ignoring him.

He waited until she was almost upon him to speak. "Hi, Sabryna."

She ignored him.

"Sabryna?"

She walked around to the trunk and placed the items she was carrying inside. Screened by the open trunk she took more calming breaths. She hadn't anticipated being trapped alone with him.

He called her name again.

She slammed the trunk closed. "I thought you left."

"I came back."

"Well, I'm leaving. So get off my car." Her icy tones were clipped and angry.

"I came back to see you."

"I don't care." She stopped in front of him because he hadn't moved away from her car. She waited, with obvious impatience, her eyes looking everywhere but at him.

Marcus was ready to take on her anger if it meant hearing her say she was okay. "You shouldn't be out here alone."

"I'm fine," she snapped. "Now move."

"Do you think we could talk for a minute?"

Sabryna looked at him as though he suggested they jump into a vat of boiling oil. A slight sneer turned her lips up. "I'm in a meeting."

He stepped back. Her pain washed over him, leaving his world in a red haze. He heard more than saw her get in her car. The car sped off. A tear dropped from his eye, unbidden.

CHAPTER SIXTEEN

Marcus wanted to turn her against him. He knew she would hate him. Like all other goals Marcus set for himself, this one had been a success.

A victory which left him hollow.

The next day he took refuge at his family's home. The quiet serenity of the estate never failed to soothe his inner turmoil. On arrival, he opted to walk in the solitude of the gardens. The day was clear, perfect weather for day two of the tournament that was taking place at West Area Park.

"I thought I might find you out here." His mother's voice broke into his thoughts. She strolled toward him, pulling a lavender shawl around her to ward off the slight chill in the air. Reaching his side she held her cheek up for a kiss, and he placed one there.

"Did you come for dinner? It's not until six." She sat down on one of the white garden benches.

"I know." Marcus lowered his large frame next to her. "I just came to visit."

His mother's perceptive gaze studied him. Marcus laughed, uncomfortable. "When you look at me like that you remind me of David."

She shrugged. "What's wrong?"

Marcus forced a smile. "Can't I just come to see my family? Does there have to be an ulterior motive?"

"Of course you can," Elaine assured her son. "But give your mother some credit, I can tell when one of my children is bothered by something."

Marcus leaned back on the bench and surveyed the roses. He wondered if the petals were as soft as Sabryna's skin. Fantasies of making love to her on a bed of roses flashed through his mind. He shook his head to clear the maddening thought.

His mother let out a resigned sigh. "You were always my silent one. The world could be crashing down around you, and the rest of us would never know. You'd sweep in like a black knight and shoulder the burden all on your own. But I wonder son, who do you share your problems with?"

There was something about her wording that had him shooting her a sharp glance. She faced forward, her face etched with concern. "I'm not that secretive." He spoke carefully, unsure of her intention. "I tell you what's going on with me"

His mother humphed. "You tell me what you want me to know." She waved her hand. "But I understand and I've gotten used to it. For example, when you made the choice to sell your father's company, without explanation might I add, your family understood and we stood by you."

Marcus studied his hands. Back to that long ago night, when he sat his family down in the study, two days after his father's funeral and explained his plans for the company. His mother was right, they hadn't asked too many questions. Simply accepted his reason that it was the best thing for everyone involved. He assumed that since he inherited the bulk of the company and was the head of the family, they just fell in line with his plans. He took their easy acceptance for granted. Perhaps, he did owe his mother an explanation. "You want me to tell you why I made that decision?"

She held up her hand to silence him. "I don't need to know. The past is the past." His mother pulled her shawl closer to her body. "I loved your father. He was a good husband and father. I know he wasn't perfect, but I cherish my memories of our marriage and our life together. I don't want to know anything that will tarnish that. Your father placed you in charge because he trusted you to do the right thing. Even if it's not the easy thing, even if it's not what he himself would've done. I trust you. And that's all I need to know."

Relieved, Marcus never loved his mother more than he did at that moment. "Thank you."

She smiled. "Honey, I know my children. And I know that something's been bothering you. Something that has nothing at all to do with your father's company. You haven't been yourself. It's almost as if some part of you is…disconnected."

"Mom, I…" So she knew he was throwing her a bone.

"Don't try to tell me its nothing. I've been watching you these past couple of weeks. At all these events that we've been attending, where these women throw themselves at you, and you pretend they don't exist. And furthermore, where did your smile go?"

He smiled to show her it was there, but even to him it felt brittle.

"Didn't you say I was the more serious son?"

Her lips curved in amusement. "Just like your father. But it's not that. It's something more." She hesitated. "Does it have something to do with Sabryna?"

Hearing her name made him miss her more. He looked away. "She and I are just friends." Actually, we're not even that.

Elaine raised her eyebrows. "A friend you bring home to meet your family?"

"Exactly."

"And here I thought I was meeting my future daughter-in-law."

They locked eyes. "Mom, I think it's time I tell you something. I have no intention of getting married."

He expected his mother to go into hysterics.

She lifted her eyebrows even higher. "What kind of foolish notion have you gotten into your head?"

"The notion that marriage...love is not for me."

"Why not?"

Marcus searched for the right words. "I don't have a very high opinion of love. I don't understand what all the hype is about."

"Weren't you loved as a child?" His mother challenged.

"That isn't the type of love I'm talking about."

She sighed "You're talking about the love between a man and a woman."

He nodded. "Love is toxic. It destroys those who believe in it."

"Have you ever been in love before?" Elaine asked.

"No."

"Then how would you know?"

Marcus didn't want to answer that. "It's a convenient excuse for people to do or get what they want."

Elaine shook her head is disbelief. "How did I raise such a cynical son?"

"I would say I'm practical."

"Well, I would say you're wrong." His mother gave him a half hug to minimize the sting of her words. "Marcus you can't spend the rest of your life being afraid of getting close to someone, or being scared of what will happen when you do."

"I'm not afraid of love."

"Then what would you call it?" she asked.

Marcus didn't respond.

Elaine let out a tiny sigh. "You know there were days when I was married to your father that I wanted to strangle him in his sleep. And then there were the nights that I would wake him up just to talk to him, because I missed the sound of his voice. That's love Marcus. It's not easy, it's not simple, it just is. But when it's real and true it can be the most powerful force in your life.

"If you want to spend the rest of your life as a bachelor that's your decision. I won't like it, but I'll accept it. However, before you do that, ask yourself this. When you want to share your thoughts, who will be there to listen? When you come home from a long day of work, who will fill the silence? When you need a confidante, who will keep your secrets? When you need a smile, who will make you laugh? When you feel like the world is turning against you, who will have your back no matter what comes? And before you say your family can, keep this in mind, we won't always be there. Someday I'll be gone and your siblings will have families of their own. Where, my son, does that leave you?"

Who would be there? The thought, one he hadn't considered before his talk with his mother, haunted him long after he left the estate. Could she be right? He rejected the notion before it took root. There was still so much about him his mother didn't know. She could make him think, but she couldn't give him absolution for past misdeeds. Could anyone?

Friday morning brought some wonderful news to Cortland Consulting. They landed a multi-million dollar contract. As a result, everyone was in a celebratory mood. Marcus released his employees an hour early from work.

Marcus sat in his office alone.

"Who will be there?" His mother's words played over and over in his mind.

He knew he shouldn't, but he wondered how it would be to share his exciting news with Sabryna. She would think it was wonderful. She'd smile at him in that easy way of hers, while she listened to him explain. Then they'd make love all night.

He shifted, uncomfortable in his chair.

This obsession with her was starting to border on the ridiculous. She was just a woman, and, if he repeated that enough he would start to believe it. It wasn't in his nature to sulk over a woman he couldn't have. He was a man of action and it was time he started acting like one.

It was time to reclaim his life. Reclaim his mind. Reclaim his concentration. Wipe Sabryna Givens from his thoughts. She was just a woman and there were millions like her. Some who were more beautiful, more ready and willing to please him.

He stood up and headed for the door. By tonight he would back on his groove and Sabryna Givens would be a long lost memory.

Theory was never the same as practice. Marcus mulled over this thought as he stared into his vodka. He sat in the V.I.P section at Plush, one of his favorite night clubs. In the past it had been the perfect spot to blow off steam. Tonight shouldn't have been any different. The music was hot. The club was crowded, but not the V.I.P room which was known for its exclusivity. There were plenty of gorgeous women in come-and-get-me outfits.

But he sat at the small bar...alone. He'd already run off two women. The first girl had thrown herself at him the minute she sat down. She wore a black tank top with cleavage deeper than certain parts of the ocean. She purposefully leaned over to show him all that she was offering. He turned up his nose at her brazen behavior and told her he wasn't interested. She rolled her eyes and left.

The second one had been a little more subtle. She walked over in her skintight red dress and asked if he was waiting for someone. Forcing himself to flirt he responded, "Only you." With an encouraging smile, she sat and managed to engage him in an interesting conversation. He spent the time checking her out. Her brown eyes disturbed him. They didn't light up when she talked. They didn't shimmer when she laughed. They didn't have any golden sparkles that mesmerized him. Fortunate for her, she did have enough self-respect to tell he wasn't interested. When his attention drifted she wished him a crisp goodnight and left.

Alone, with a drink and his questionable mood, Marcus wondered how a well laid plan to erase an Angel from his mind was going so poorly.

David slid onto the stool next to him. "I had a feeling you'd be here."

Marcus straightened, not wanting his brother to notice something was wrong and start asking questions. He wasn't surprised to see David, Plush was one of his favorite spots as well. "Here I am. Do you want me to get you a drink?" He started to signal the bar tender.

David stopped him with a hand on his arm. "No, my plans for tonight don't include getting drunk with my brother."

Marcus laughed. "I can't remember the last time I was drunk."

"You really should loosen up more."

Marcus held up his glass. "Good advice." He swallowed the remaining Vodka in one gulp. "Anymore where that came from?"

David's eyes locked with his brothers, his voice turned serious. "Yeah, call Sabryna."

Marcus signaled for a refill. "Stay out of it, David."

"I should. Normally, I would. I don't know what happened between the two of you. Like everyone else, I would be inclined to think that she's no different from any other woman you dated. But there is something different about her."

"Talked to your mother lately?" Marcus asked, not bothering to hide his facetiousness.

"I've talked to Sabryna."

Marcus turned to look at his brother. "You talked to her? When?"

"Yesterday, at an Eckerd drug store on 43rd Street."

"How...how did she look?" Marcus didn't want to reveal too much but he needed to know how she was.

David seemed to consider his words then went on as though he was idly discussing the weather. "Same as you. Miserable. Only difference was, she was carrying a pregnancy test." He motioned to the bartender. "You know, I think I will take that drink after all."

Marcus froze. "What did you say?" he whispered.

"I said I'd take that drink."

"Before that. What did you say about Sabryna having a pregnancy test?"

"I believe you just said it."

Marcus's heart slowed to one beat per hour. Every thing moved in slow motion. "Is she--? Did she say--? How do you--?"

"You do realize none of those were complete sentences, right?"

Marcus stood and threw some money on the bar. "I have to go."

David smiled. "I thought you might."

CHAPTER SEVENTEEN

Marcus broke all kinds of speeding records driving to Sabryna's apartment. He made the twenty five minute trip in half the time, but hadn't taken a single moment to think of what he was going to say once he got there. Assuming she answered the door. That thought was the only one on his mind as he stared at her apartment from the driver's seat of his car. The apartment was dark, more than likely she was sleeping. After all, it was almost two in the morning.

Praying the words would come, he exited his car and climbed the steps up to her door. He rang the bell. He pushed the button again and again.

"Who is it?" Sabryna yelled. She sounded sleepy, confused, and worried.

"Marcus."

The silence stretched for a full minute. "What are you doing here?"

"I need to talk to you."

"It's two in the morning."

"I know, please open the door." He felt silly yelling through it.

"Go home."

"Sabryna?" He waited a moment then he rang the bell again. And again.

The door opened a crack. The chain lock was still on. His eyes locked on the portion of her he could see. In the weak light he couldn't quite make out her expression. He moved closer to the door. "I need to talk to you."

She shook her head. "Have you lost your mind?"

"Just give me five minutes."

She was quiet. Then she shut the door. For another long minute there was no movement. He was about to ring the doorbell again when he heard the chain lock slide. The door opened.

Sabryna didn't step back and wait for him to come in. After opening the door she walked into the living room leaving it to him to shut. Stopping in the middle of the room she turned to face him, and drank in his muscular frame. She pulled her robe tight about her.

His presence made her apartment so much smaller.

Why had she thought it was a good idea to open that door? She could tell herself it was because he would stand out there and ring the doorbell keeping her awake, as well as her neighbors. However, the despicable truth was there was a part of her that couldn't resist him. No matter that she fought it with every ounce of her being, when it came to Marcus Cortland her heart and mind waged constant war in her soul. She hated him. She missed him. She hated what he had done to her. She wished he could love her the way she loved him. It was a vicious cycle she grew tired of fighting. In the morning she would throw back up her guard, but for tonight, she would let him have his time, while she indulged her senses with his presence.

He walked in the room but stopped a small distance from her. For a moment, they just stared at each other.

"You needed to talk to me."

Marcus released a breath. "I, uh, I wanted to know how you were doing."

She put up her hands as if warding him off. "I wish you'd stop asking me that question. If you really wanted to know if I was okay you would've called me weeks ago, or returned one of my phone calls. Did you come here tonight to relieve a sense of guilt? Well, let me put you at ease and save us both some time." She sat on the couch. "I'm fine. I'm going to be fine."

He put his hands in his pockets. "I want you to understand why I did what I did."

Her derisive laugh interrupted him. "Oh, I understand. Just because I was a virgin doesn't mean I'm stupid. I was a challenge. Something to be conquered. You intended for us to be temporary lovers. Unfortunately, I wasn't smart enough not to fall in love with you. I believed what was happening between us was real. Mission accomplished. Have I covered everything? Now, can you leave?"

His eyes searched hers. "Your virginity was not something I took lightly. If I'd known I would never have let things go so far."

She waved his comment aside. "I had to lose it some time, right?" She stood up and started walking to the door. "Your five minutes are up."

"Are you pregnant?"

She stopped dead in her tracks and slowly turned to face him. "What?"

"Are you pregnant?" he repeated with more force.

"Why would you ask me that question?" Sabryna wondered where that had come from. Then she remembered. "Your brother."

"He told me he saw you with the test."

"It was none of his business. It's none of your business." All the pieces of the puzzle clicked together. He wasn't here because he missed her. He wasn't here because he cared how she was doing. "Oh, I get it now. That's why you're here. Your brother told you he saw me with a pregnancy test and you rushed right over to make sure the baby isn't yours. Let me assure you then…it's not."

For a moment he looked as though he'd just been hit and then he straightened. "Don't play games with me. I have a right to know if you're pregnant."

"You have no rights as far as I'm concerned," she thundered back at him. "You come into my apartment, demanding information, expecting me to up and obey you. I suggest you go play king of the world on one of your rooftops and leave me the hell alone."

She tried to turn away but he reached out and grabbed her hand. "Are you pregnant?"

Startled by his touch, she struggled not show any reaction to it. "No… No."

"You took the test already?"

Pulling her hand free she rubbed it trying to erase his touch. Wanting him to leave so she could get back her equilibrium, she gave him the truth. "The test wasn't for me."

She wasn't pregnant. Marcus waited for the relief to overtake him. Sabryna stood there and stared at him. He, in turn, stared back at her. She was probably waiting for his sigh of relief. He waited to feel it.

They were both disappointed.

Breaking her gaze he searched the room as if the explanation to the strange feelings twirling inside of him was lurking in her living room. His emotions began to take shape with gradual clarity. Was that disappointment? Unsure, he sat back down on the couch.

"You're not pregnant." He sounded as if he was testing the words.

"No. So, you have nothing to worry about."

Worry? That was the least of what had overcome him since his brother had first dropped his bomb. His only worry had been that she would be pregnant and shut him out of it. But if she carried his child he would have to stay close to her. A relationship would be necessary.

He wanted to be with her.

The truth hit him so hard he almost stood up and shouted it out. He wanted her to be pregnant because it would be a wonderful excuse for him to be around her. He wouldn't have to be noble anymore, the choice would be out of his hands. A horrible reason to want a child, but he was a man grasping at straws.

He was a man in love.

It was time he admitted the truth to himself. The one thing he spent most of his adult life avoiding had caught up with him.

He didn't even know when it happened. Maybe it had been the night she shared herself with him. Yet, his mind, the part that was still capable of rational thought, was telling him that he loved her long before that.

How could this happen to him? He knew love was a toxic force waiting to destroy those who trusted in it. Look at how much he had already hurt her.

Marcus looked at her. She was still standing in front of him, looking pale and withdrawn. She also looked a little too skinny, as though she hadn't eaten a decent meal in weeks. He'd done this to her.

He couldn't change the past and he couldn't promise her a future. But he did have the ability to give her the one thing that might help her understand and move on.

The truth.

He cleared his throat. "Can I have a glass of water?"

Sabryna looked at him as if he had just grown an extra head. "You want a glass of water?" she asked, incredulity evident in her expression.

"Yes, please."

For a long moment she didn't move. "One glass, then you have to go."

Marcus tracked her as she walked into the kitchen. She was mumbling something under her breath and when she reappeared she thrust a glass at him. The glass was half full. He cracked a smile.

How could he not love this woman?

Taking the glass, he took a tiny sip. She scowled but she didn't say anything, sitting on the chair across from him, stiff as a board.

He finished his measly drops of water and sat the glass down on the table. "There are some things that I need to talk to you about."

In a blink, Sabryna stood up and gestured to the door. "I don't want to have the same conversation twice. I think it's time for you to- -"

Her words died on an abrupt shriek when Marcus sprang from the couch and grabbed both of her arms. He pulled her against him and settled his mouth on hers.

Her sweetness was a like a cool glass of sweet ice tea on a summer day. Black Pekoe Tea, with just the right mixture of honey. He drank from her as though he was a man starving. And he was, had been, ever since he'd met her.

She stiffened as his lips moved on hers, but her resistance gave away and she opened her mouth and let him in. His body rejoiced in the sensation of her warm and feminine form against him. He pulled her tighter, wanting to absorb her, wanting to imprint the feel of her on his body so that in the future he could always remember how it was to hold her.

Knowing the kiss was going too far, sensing his own body's violent reaction to her, he raised his head, breaking the kiss.

She stared up at him with wide dazed brown eyes.

Smiling, he confessed, "I just needed to shut you up." He placed a thumb on her lips when she opened her mouth to protest. That garnered another scowl but she remained quiet. "Now, where was I? Oh yes, I'm a bastard."

CHAPTER EIGHTEEN

Locked in Marcus's embrace, his finger lying gently on her lips, Sabryna didn't dare speak. Besides, she had no desire to argue with his last statement.

A brief, self-deprecating smile touched his face. "I see you agree. And not only am I a bastard, I'm a stupid selfish jerk."

"You regret that we slept together?" Chiding herself at the hurt she heard in her voice she waited for his response.

He shook his head. "No."

His hands rubbed her arms and her body came alive with unwanted desire.

"I could never regret that. That one night with you was…" He experienced a visible struggle for the words, and then replied, "indescribable."

"That's an easy out," Sabryna accused. She tried to ignore the pleasure that shot through her at his words and failed. Would he always have the power to affect her emotions, even when she wished to remain indifferent to him?

"That night will always have a special place in my memory."

What she wanted was a special place in his heart. "I'm glad you don't regret it."

"I don't want you to either."

She looked away. How could she explain that it wasn't that night that she regretted? Deep inside she was still happy it had been him. No matter how angry she was, her love for him still burned.

"Sabryna, what I regret is how I handled things. How I treated you. I need to explain some things to you."

Sabryna wondered what he could tell her to justify how he behaved. But she couldn't deny that part of her that needed answers. "You will let go of me."

"Will you promise not to go into another rant about me leaving?"

"I don't rant."

He raised a skeptical eyebrow but released her. She rubbed her arms.

Without a word she walked over and settled in a chair. "You want to talk. I'll listen. But don't expect me to suddenly see things the way you do. I'm not that noble."

Lowering his frame on the couch opposite her, he rested his elbows on his knees and stared into his hands. For a long time he was quiet. "I'm not sure where to start."

Sabryna crossed her arms in front of her. She agreed to listen, she didn't agree to help. Besides, she still had no idea what he planned to say.

His eyes appeared vacant. He was staring at her but not seeing her. Whatever he wanted to say had its roots in some deep part of him.

"I think to explain I would have to start with my father."

Now she was intrigued, remembering when he rebuffed her attempts to discuss his father.

He continued, "You once asked me about him, I believe you wanted to know if I was angry at him and sold his company for revenge. The truth is, I loved him." Marcus shook his head. "I worshipped him. He was my entire world. I remember watching him when I was a young and thinking he was something like a superhero. There wasn't a Batman invented that could out shine him. He was large and powerful and when he was around things just seemed to happen."

They had that in common, Sabryna thought. Marcus was his own force.

Marcus continued, the words tumbling from his mouth. "People respected him. When my father spoke, people listened. When he gave compliments, which weren't many, people puffed up with pride. I could never understand the affect he had on others, but I was mesmerized by it. Lucky for me, my father returned my adoration with some of his own. I was his heir and he took great pride in that fact. He took me everywhere. This was fine with me, as there was nowhere I would rather be than with him. My mother used to tease that if I could climb into his pocket I would. And she was right."

"Was it the same for your brothers?"

He shook his head. "No. I guess because I was the eldest my father put all of his energy into me. David and Alex didn't seem to mind. He still spent time with them, just not to the level that he did with me. And besides, they never seemed to be interested in the same things."

"Such as?"

"His company, mostly. He loved golf. And he was obsessed with the stock market. Not their thing, but it was mine. I wanted to please my father. He had plans for me and I was content to follow in his footsteps.

I went to Harvard, his alma mater, because he wanted me to. I declared a major in Business because it was what he wanted. I interned at his company at his command. He had my entire life mapped out, ending with me working with him in his company and eventually taking it over, and I fell in line. Looking back, that was my first mistake. I allowed my life to become so wrapped up in his wishes that I had no identity of my own. "The summer after my junior year of college I interned with my father, as usual. One night I was working late, we had an audit coming and my father asked me to help out. George McKinley was the senior accountant at that time, and to be honest I didn't like the man. He was an arrogant jerk and I could never understand why my father put so much trust in him. I decided to double check him, hoping to find some mistake to rub in his face. Had I not been so intent on making a fool out of him I would never had made one out of me. I'll spare you the details, it's enough to say I noticed some serious discrepancies."

"George had made a lot of mistakes?"

"George had made so many mistakes that he was covering something up. On further inspection, I realized that he was covering up an embezzlement ring. I went straight to my father. I showed him everything I'd uncovered and all of the evidence. I waited for the explosion."

"What did your father do?" Sabryna had a creepy inclination she knew the answer.

Marcus took a deep breath. "My father looked at me in a way that made the hair on the back of my neck stand up. I'll never forget that moment. I knew even before he opened his mouth that he was going to tell me he'd known all along and he was a part of it."

Sabryna's hand flew to her mouth. Her sympathy for him welled until it was an almost ungovernable flood. How horrible it must've been for a young man who worshiped his father to realize he wasn't a hero. "I'm sorry."

"It was his idea from the beginning. When he started the company it had been an almost overnight success, but over time that success began to fade, so he and a few select other's developed a scheme that paid off and tripled their worth. He told me that it was time I understood how he provided for our family. That his actions were those of a man who loved his family and was determined to protect and provide for them in the manner they deserved. He said I would have to carry on if I were to keep his legacy alive. I told him that I didn't want a legacy that involved cheating, lying, and betraying innocent people."

Marcus rubbed his forehead and Sabryna resisted the urge to smooth away the lines of pain that had gathered there.

Marcus's body shook as he continued, "I told him I wanted no part of his life. I walked out on my father, and the only life I ever knew." Marcus paused for a breath. "My father suffered a heart attack that night."

"Oh, Marcus." Unable to hold back any longer, a tear slipped down Sabryna's cheek.

"I'm not telling you this to make you sad." His eyes followed the path of that tear. "I need you to understand. I need…"

She reached out and grabbed his hand. "Please continue."

He gripped her hand as though it were a lifeline. "It took my mother almost two days to find me and tell me what happened, after I had taken off. David managed to locate me. The Doctor's said he died of a stress induced heart attack. I didn't need a medical report to know that I was responsible for my father's death."

"You did not cause your father's heart attack." Her words were forceful, vehement.

He emitted a sardonic laugh. "My father was a healthy, active man."

"Who was carrying around a lot of secrets. That would put strain on anyone."

He shrugged. "Maybe. But none of that mattered at the time. My family was now my responsibility and I could no longer allow their reputations and future to be part of a lie. When I saw how my family grieved, I knew I couldn't ruin their image of my father, so I kept the secret and closed up shop on the company. My father's associates were infuriated, but when I threatened to expose them they fell in line. After all, when I sold the company I made them even richer."

The strength he possessed to carry the burden and be his family's rock amazed Sabryna. "What did you do?"

"I went back to school and for awhile I floundered. I'd never been in a position where my future was mine to command. I took a class in IT, loved it, and the rest is history."

What she did know what that he was brave and strong.

"Professionally, I bounced back quickly. Personally, I was still at sea. Whatever sense of integrity my father had taught me went right out the window with the rest of his lies. I was angry and reckless and I wanted to inflict my pain on others. I sought…comfort in the arms of women. Telling them whatever they needed to hear to let me get close to them. I knew I was playing with their emotions and I didn't care. Until Kari.

"She was beautiful. The minute I saw her I wanted her. The

attraction was mutual. It was senior year we were all looking to the future, especially Kari. Kari had a selfish streak, but she was fun and I enjoyed her company. I thought she understood the rules, but she wanted love and I let her believe I did. I made promises I had no intention of keeping. Kari was possessive and clingy and when she began to bore me I ended things. That was when things took a turn for the worse. Kari claimed that she loved me and that she would die loving me. She called so much I had to switch my number. She stalked me. One night she left a letter at my dorm. In it she wrote about how much she loved me, how she couldn't live without me. How if she was forced to live life without me she'd rather be dead. She wrote to say goodbye."

"Goodbye?"

He nodded. "It took me a moment to realize and when I did I ran as fast as I could to her dorm. I called every number I had for her. It was too late. I found her body. The coroner report stated she had shot herself in the head. Death on impact."

He focused on her. His brown eyes burned into her. "There is a scary trend that seems to occur with people who love me."

Something inside of Sabryna snapped. Tears poured like rivers from her eyes. The wealth of her pain disappeared, buried beneath the weight of his. He was so strong, so proud and arrogant. He'd endured the betrayal and deceit of a father. He'd taken on a burden at a young age that would have destroyed lesser men. Seen the darker side of love and now here he was barring his soul to her so that she could understand he hadn't wanted to hurt her. He was exposing his wounds to heal her own.

Any doubt she ever had disappeared. This was love.

Her hurtful words hadn't pushed him away. After venting her pain and her anger on him, he'd come to reveal his own secrets. This was love and she wasn't going to run from it. Nor allow him to run from it either. She acted on impulse, driven by her overwhelming love for him. Reaching out, she touched his cheek, a gentle caress. Noted the contrast of rough skin against her smooth palm. "Why did you tell me this?" The question was soft. There was no challenge in her voice.

His eyes searched hers. "I told you why. I wanted you to understand why I left like that. Why I can't, couldn't be with you."

"Yes, but why?"

"I don't understand what you're asking for."

She held his gaze. "I want to know why you came here tonight and told me your secrets. Why did you need me to understand? Why didn't you just treat me as you have everyone else in your life?"

Marcus shifted, uncomfortable. "I came because I thought you were pregnant."

"I want to know if you love me." Only her mouth moved. Her body stilled, afraid of what he might say.

On her question his eyes closed. When he opened them the truth was there swimming in the brown depths. "It doesn't matter."

Consuming relief swept through Sabryna. "It matters to me."

"Sabryna, you and I are not possible. It can't happen."

"Why? Because you've decided that you're not good enough."

He stood up and began to pace like a caged tiger. "I told you all the reasons why. When people love me they get hurt. If you put your faith in me you'll regret it."

"Now you can prdict the future?" she asked, watching him pace her carpet.

"A psychology professor once told me the best predictor of future behavior is past behavior."

"You're not responsible for what happened to your father or Kari," she insisted.

He stopped. Faced her. Simply looked at her. "My father was healthy and alive before I ripped into him. Do you know how much he loved me?"

"You didn't tell your father to involve himself in illegal dealings. What were you supposed to do? Throw away your values, your integrity for what he believed was right? He had no right to expect that from you." Sabryna's voiced raised at the injustice to him.

"I could've helped him."

"You were young and you had just learned the father you adored was a thief. You dealt with that shock the only way you knew how."

"I acted like a spoiled child."

"You were a child," she pointed out.

He lifted an eyebrow at her raised voice. "And what are you going to say to excuse my actions with Kari?"

She walked over until she was standing so close to him her breast brushed his chest. He tensed but didn't step away. "I'm sorry. I'm sorry your father lied to you. I'm sorry you've carried that burden alone all these years. I'm sorry that Kari died. I'm sorry that you seem to think love is some destructive force that ruins peoples' lives. I'm sorry that you want me to stop loving you. But mostly, I'm sorry to disappoint you, because I won't, can't stop."

Marcus went to speak but his words choked in his throat. He didn't deserve her. He didn't deserve her forgiveness or her compassion. And yet, here she was, so close his skin was tingling with the need to connect with hers. And she loved him. Despite all he had said, all he had done, his beautiful Angel loved him.

"Do you love me?" she asked again.

"Sabryna —"

"Do you love me?"

"I don't know if I know how to love."

She reached out and caressed his cheek. Wrapped her arms around his neck and brought his head down for a lingering kiss. When there lips were seconds apart, she whispered, "We can figure it out together. Just take a chance. Take a chance on me, on us."

"I don't know if I can. I don't know how."

"Yes you do. You took the first step when you came here." She searched and found his hands lying at his side. Gripped them in hers. "Whatever brought you here tonight will take you the rest of the way there. Just say you love me."

For a second he hesitated, then he locked her in his arms, hugging her so tight she thought her bones would snap. "I love you." His fervent whisper brushed through her hair. "I love you so damn much."

CHAPTER NINETEEN

When Marcus kissed her, there was no gentleness in it. Sabryna felt the need in him and was ready to answer it. His tongue dueled, mated with hers. He took her breath and replaced it with his own. She clung to him as arousal began to spread throughout her body. His hands roamed up and down her as if to reassure himself she was still there. Everywhere his hands touched her skin came alive.

All of a sudden she was placed on the chair. He dropped to his knees in front of her. Parting her legs, he positioned himself between her thighs. He undid the knot on her robe, his eyes never once leaving hers. She relaxed back into the chair allowed him to bare her to his eyes. Willed him to take whatever he needed from her.

He pushed back the folds of her gown. Relaxing into the couch she waited in aroused anticipation for whatever would come next.

She was wearing a pair of pink night shorts and a pink tank top. Under his hungry stare, her nipples hardened. Noticing the change his eyes darkened. His hands once again gripped her thighs then made a slow trek up her legs, spreading heat throughout her body, until they reached her shorts. He tugged. Obedient, she lifted her lower body and allowed him to slide the shorts from her. Her panties followed and then her tank top, leaving her exposed to his gaze. He shifted closer, ran a possessive hand down her body, then cupped one breast, squeezed and then gently fondled. Sinking further into the couch, lost in his sensual caresses she moaned. It brought his attention back to her lips and he began kissing her again. From her lips he moved to her breast, sucking one as he caressed the other. He rained kisses on her neck before sliding his mouth in a down ward trail along the curves of her body.

She was so far gone she didn't at first register when he parted her legs further and begin to kiss her thighs. His gentle mouth kissed her most intimate region.

She almost came off the couch. "Marcus!" His name strangled in her throat.

He quieted her with a hush. "Let me love you." His hands, which gripped her thigh came up and cupped both her breasts. A possessive anchor keeping her physical self in this world, while her soul soared, existing on some foreign plane where only need, his and hers, reigned. Sensation welled inside of her as his tongue devoured her. Gripping his shoulders she felt the beginning of her climax hove onto the horizon. The world exploded into brilliant bits of light.

Still he continued, as though he could drink her ecstasy from her. Tremors quaked throughout her body, then ebbed. He raised his head, his eyes ablaze with desire, and shifted back onto his heels. Realization came swift. He wanted to satisfy her, was content with the knowledge that he had. However, she was not. She could only truly be content when he had reached the same dizzying heights she just been privileged to experience.

"I want you inside of me." Her voice was low, sultry. Foreign to her own ears, but there was something about this man that made her act in ways she never had before. The very essence of him appealed to something deep within her that had been buried for far too many years. When she was with him she felt like a beautiful, sensual creature. She knew he recognized the new spark in her and that he liked it. The fire in his eyes flared.

She knew she wouldn't have to ask him twice.

His fingers made quick work of the buttons and zipper, freeing his erection. His manhood rose proud, hard and ready for her. She wasted no time, moving toward him as he reached for her, she impaled herself on him, sliding down, her breast resting against the fabric of his shirt. His hands gripped her buttocks and squeezed as he worked her over him.

The sensation of him deep inside of her sent sheer joy pumping through her veins. She wanted him to burn the way she did.

Lifting up until he was almost out of her, she paused then sank back down.

"Sweet Angel," he growled. She repeated the action again and again. The muscles in his arm and chest tensed with each stroke. Her lips nipped at his neck, kissed, licked. He moaned again.

His hands clutched her sides so tight, the thought of bruises drifted through her mind, only to be discarded. There was no pain in the pleasure of loving him. With her naked skin draped over his still clothed body, she had never felt more vulnerable. However, this elicited no fear or unease. He was her man and he would take care of her. She relaxed, let go her control, and allowed their love to take over.

Her second climax was more powerful than the first. A feeling intensified when he joined her, locked in each others embrace, as they sailed together to heights of amazing ecstasy.

Sometime later, they made it from her living room to her bedroom. Boneless, Sabryna had no inclination to argue when Marcus picked her up and carried her to the room, laying her on the bed. She snuggled under the covers, enjoying the sight of him getting undressed. His body was so perfect, with his broad shoulders and muscular chest. Every chocolate inch of him looked delicious. And she thought with wicked delight, tasted delicious.

Naked, he joined her under the covers. Still breathing heavy, he sprawled on his back. She followed, resting her head on his chest, her own breath ragged. She was so happy her joy felt as though it came from the depths of her soul. She giggled.

"There's a sound a man wants to hear when he gets done making love to his woman," he teased.

Intrigued by his words she lifted up to meet his eyes. "Your woman," she tested the words. "I like the sound of that."

Marcus tucked a strand of hair behind her ear. Marveled at her beauty. "So do I."

She snuggled into his arms. "I've never been anybody's woman before."

"Well you're mine now."

Rising up on her elbow, she looked at him. Her expression grew serious. "Are you sure?"

"Of course." Tracing a finger around a nipple now exposed by her pose he watched as it hardened. "You have such beautiful breasts."

"I'm serious." She raised all the way up, drawing the sheet up to conceal her.

"So am I." He tugged at the sheet. "I think your breasts are gorgeous."

"I meant about us. About you being here. You aren't just going to disappear again?"

Realizing the lightness of the moment had faded, Marcus lifted up until his back rested against the backboard. "I though I was the doubting Thomas."

Her smile was brief. "I know you are…uneasy with this, with what is happening between us. I just don't think that I could handle it if you disappeared again."

Reaching out, he caressed her arm. "I didn't want to disappear the first time."

"I understand. Well, at least I do now." She thought for a minute. "When my mother died my father checked out on me. He couldn't handle her death, he couldn't handle his life, and he couldn't deal with me being a constant reminder of what he lost. We lived in the same house, but emotionally, he just shut me out."

Understanding dawned on him. "I couldn't handle my fear and I did the same."

She nodded. "I understand, at least, now that you've explained. But whatever the future holds for us I need to know that you're one hundred percent committed to us facing it together."

Marcus pulled her into his arms. The hurt he read in her eyes as she talked about her father was too much for him to see. The knowledge that he awakened that pain in his own actions stung even more. "I wish your life had been different growing up."

"Well, I'm the better for it."

"I wish I'd handled myself different." When she remained suspiciously silent, he teased, "What? You aren't the better for it?"

Laughing, she slid down. He followed until he was looming over her now flat on her back. His eyes searched hers. "I can't predict the future. But being here with you, like this, feels right. I wasn't expecting it. I sure wasn't looking for it. I fought and fought against it. Lord knows there is still a part of me that believes I might be the worse thing that happened to you. But I can't let you go. I need you. I love you."

Tears welled in her eyes and fell down her cheeks.

He kissed them away. "Don't cry sweet Angel."

A teary smile touched her lips. "I'm sorry, it's just that I love you so much."

Reaching her arms around his neck, Sabryna stretched her body beneath his, signaling her desire for him. He hugged her close, entering her body in one sure thrust. Already hot and wet for him, she moaned in pleasure as he slid into her again and again. A gentle benediction that chased away all her sadness and fear and left the wonder of his love in its wake.

The next morning she woke up alone.

Rolling over, Sabryna squinted against the bright shaft of sun that poured in despite the closed blinds. She was warm deep within the marrow of her bones, complete in places she didn't even know were empty.

And she was alone.

Not again. Her eyes searched her room looking for proof that he'd been there, that last night hadn't been a part of her over active imagination.

Bolting up, she told herself not to jump to conclusions. History couldn't repeat itself. A cold knot of dread formed in the pit of her stomach.

Had she been twice the fool?

The smell of bacon frying reached her nostrils. The walls of her apartment were thin, but not that thin. Someone was cooking in her kitchen.

Relief spread throughout and she jumped up, grabbed her robe, and wrapping it tight around herself she headed for the kitchen.

Marcus stood at the stove, his back to her. He was dressed, and true to her senses, frying bacon. A plate of eggs rested on the counter next to him.

"Are my eye's playing tricks on me?" she teased, leaning against the entranceway.

He turned around. "Good morning Angel. Do you want some juice?"

"Don't worry, I'll get it." She walked over to the fridge and got the juice out, poured a cup for both of them. "I can't believe you cook."

"It's a little skill I picked up."

"Not from your mother, I hope," she joked.

He laughed. "No. You can eat my food without your doctor on speed dial."

She leaned against the counter and studied him as he flipped the bacon in the pan. Two pieces of toast popped out of the toaster and he reached over and dropped them on the plate. She watched as he prepared her breakfast, and wondered should she be so turned on by such a domesticated sight.

It wasn't just arousal that she experienced. Although, with the thoughts of the previous night still burning in her memory, there was a healthy amount of that. But along side it was a sense of calm. A sense of peace. It seemed so normal to wake up to him cooking her breakfast, after spending the night in his arms.

After weeks of living with the pain, of crying herself to sleep at night, here she was standing in her kitchen while the man she loved cooked her eggs. He'd come to her and confessed his love to her and accepted her own. Branded her with that love, possessed her, and allowed her to posses him.

"I hope I have something to do with that smile."

He was standing in front of her, close enough to touch. She couldn't resist. Winding her arms around his neck, she pulled him close for a warm kiss. When there lips were mere inches apart she replied, "This smile has everything to do with you."

CHAPTER TWENTY

Over the course of the next few weeks, Sabryna existed in a dream world. Although, no dream could ever be this wonderful. Yet, the perpetual grin on her face told a different story. If she was in the middle of a dream she'd no intention of ever waking up from.

Of late, she was more in tune with Lena's overt romantic nature.

She and Marcus settled into a comfortable routine. One that involved them being as much in each other's company as possible. No small feat considering the demands of his job and hers. Although, as she soon discovered, being the CEO of your own company meant a more flexible schedule, a fact which left a lot of room for Marcus to coerce her into long lunches and not so short breaks. Not that he had to exert too much coercion. When it came to him, she was an addict always looking forward to her next fix. Unfortunately, she didn't have a job that was amenable to such an open schedule. Plus she figured Marcus's image with Grant wasn't earning any points when it started to affect the center. Grant had already voiced concern about Sabryna's forgiving Marcus. He wasn't quite ready to believe a leopard, even a rich one, could change his spots. However, when she tried to explain this to Marcus, she was met with resistance.

"You spend your entire life in that building. I don't think Grant should begrudge you some extra time." Marcus gave her this observation from her bed as he observed her rush to get ready to leave for work.

She laughed. "Since we've been together I've been late to work more times than I have in the past five years."

He flashed a devil-may-care smile. Folding his arms behind his head as he rested his back against the headboard. "Which makes my point. If you're going to be late you might as well just stay home with me."

"Stay home and do what?"

His grin was sinful. "You have to ask?"

That thought was tempting. "If you'd stop making me late I wouldn't have that problem."

"You enjoy it."

She couldn't deny it. Marcus was enamored of waking her up by making love to her. It didn't take much convincing to fall in with plans. One particular morning, determined to make it to work on time, she woke up before him and quietly snuck into the shower. He found her, and proved his morning lovemaking didn't have to be confined to the bed.

She held a new appreciation for her shower.

"Regardless of whether or not I enjoy it, I have a job."

"So do I," he pointed out.

"Yes, but you can't get fired from yours."

That sealed that particular argument in her favor. Marcus possessed a strong work ethic and respected that she took her career serious. Yet, for all his down to earth ways, he did come from a very privileged background. He wasn't a fan of being denied anything he wanted.

And he wanted her.

The next day following their discussion he showed up at the center. It was a little after five and she planned to stay late to keep the center open that night. Marcus arrived, laptop in hand. Suspecting he was there to whisk her away she prepared to send him on his way, alone. Ignoring her warning stare, he set up shop at her desk.

She looked her question.

"Well, if you're going to work late tonight then so am I." He waved her back to what she was doing. "I promise not to distract you."

Fat chance of that, she thought. However, Marcus remained true to his word. He sat at her desk and worked. Out of the room most of the time working with the kids, she sent an occasional glance into her office and noted his handsome head bowed toward his laptop.

Despite the kinks that revolved around their careers, the rest of their schedule fell together with ease. Each night ended with a new delight in their sensual journey. Sabryna never failed to look forward to this, always curious about what path her lover would lead her down next. At times he was playful, teasing her until she writhed in pleasure beneath him. Other times he took her fast and hard, making her scream his name. Sometimes he lingered over her, like fine wine to be savored, until she was aching in her need and begging for release. Whatever his mood, Sabryna enjoyed every second spent in his arms. She discovered her own inner sexual Goddess. With no other man could she be so free, but Marcus didn't allow her to hold back. With him she felt safe. Safe to explore a temptation she denied herself for far too long.

Settling into his assigned seat at a luncheon hosted by the local chapter of the Virginia Society of Black Businessman, Marcus experienced mild annoyance at discovering Steven Barclay sitting one seat over from him at the same table. These days his spirits were so high that it would take a lot more than Steven's irritating presence to deflate them.

"Barclay." He nodded in greeting.

"Cortland." Steven acknowledge back. He glanced around the table that seated seven but now remained empty, save for the two of them. "I guess we're early."

"Guess so."

Both looked around, neither interested in engaging in conversation with each other. Marcus wondered why he and Barclay always seemed to clash. As boys they'd played together. However, as they grew, Barclay cast Marcus in the role of his rival. For Marcus, Barclay didn't even rate as a blimp on his radar. Aside from being pompous, Barclay tended to be conceited and selfish. He represented all the qualities that Marcus hated about his world. How Barclay managed to befriend someone as kind and selfless as Sabryna, Marcus would never understand.

With thoughts of his Angel, he turned to more pleasurable contemplations. Sabryna was never far from his mind. Not since the day her laughter chased away the demons in his soul. But now he could think of her, knowing he would be able to assuage his need to for her.

Visited by a ferocious need to see her, he glanced around the almost empty room, impatient. When would this thing start? Of late, he never felt whole unless she was somewhere close. He wondered if this compulsive desire for her would ever fade. He doubted it.

Taking his cell phone out of his pocket, he decided to make some reservations for tonight. She promised to be off work no later than seven and he was aware of an urge to wine and dine her. Perhaps, he'd take her to one of his favorite seafood restaurants. He was interested to find out if oysters were an aphrodisiac for Angels also.

"I see you and Sabryna are seeing each other again," Barclay remarked when Marcus snapped the phone shut.

Marcus shot him a sharp glance. Was that disgust he heard in his voice?

"I heard you mention her name." Barclay pointed to his cell phone.

"I don't see how it's any business of yours." Marcus slid the phone back into his pocket.

"She's my friend," Barclay responded.

"So I've been informed."

When Marcus said nothing more Barclay added, "We've been friends

147

for a long time."

Marcus shrugged. "I guess some accidents are unavoidable."

"Don't be an ass," Barclay sneered. "I don't know what your intentions are, but Sabryna doesn't deserve your particular brand of...caring."

The look Marcus shot him could've turned stone to ice. "What Sabryna deserves isn't your concern."

"She's my..."

"Spare me the 'she's my friend and I don't want to see her hurt' lecture. As far as I or Sabryna is concerned, you have no vote," Marcus replied in acid-laced tones.

Barclay stared at him for a long moment. "If you don't leave her alone she'll--"

Marcus stood up. "Excuse me, I see someone I would much rather be talking to." He left before Barclay could utter another word.

Lying in Sabryna's bed that night, his Angel sleeping curled up in the crook of his arm, Marcus marveled at the peace that held him. Outside, heavy rain hit the pavement and windows. Inside, a quiet peace settled about them, weighing down his limbs and freeing his mind. Freeing his mind to dwell on the magic that was Sabryna.

He was absolutely enchanted by her. The way she laughed. The way she smelled. The way she moaned his name when they were making love. Never in his life had he met someone like her. Many women had come and gone, but none ever inspired him the way she did. None of them made him feel he could conquer the world.

With mild amusement, he thought back to a careless comment that he once made to his brother. Had he really thought that all women were the same, one as good as another, and none worth being distracted by? Well, he believed it at the time. Most of the women who'd paraded through his life, had only one thought on their collective minds, how quickly they could get in his bed and in his wallet. After a few moments of joint sexual pleasure, his interest in them faded quickly, and he moved on. The past taught him well. The selfish, calculating creatures that inhabited his world were motivated by status, lust and greed, always on the look out for the next best thing. Incapable of caring about others, they focused on what others could do for them.

It still blew his mind that someone like Sabryna existed.

Someone who put the needs of others before her own. Someone genuine, good, and kind. Someone whose laugh was real, not fabricated. Someone who respected herself as well as others. Someone who took an interest in who he was as a person not what he could do for them.

To find that in a woman who was smart, funny, and beautiful was like finding buried treasure in quick sand. He wanted to make her his in a way that was irrevocable. He wanted to spend the rest of his life making her as happy and as content as she made him. Every gift of love she gave him he wanted to give it back tenfold. To be the man she saw when she looked at him. He wasn't sure he could, but he was willing to spend every day for the rest of his life attempting it.

With a smile for the darkness, and too happy to sleep, he let his decision sink into his mind, and waited for his Angel to wake up.

He was still smiling when she did. The morning sun peeked through the rain clouds, emanating a soft glow into the room. She stretched, her curvaceous frame moving seductively beneath the sheets. He wondered if she knew how innately alluring she was.

Finishing her stretch she glanced up and grinned into his eyes. "When did you wake up?"

"I never went to sleep."

Her brows furrowed. "Why?"

"I've been waiting for you to wake up so that I could ask you a question."

She pulled the sheet up to her neck and snuggled closer to him. "If the question is, will you cook breakfast, the answer is no."

He laughed as he flipped her onto her back, rising up over her. "It's not pancakes I'm after. It's you."

She flashed him a wicked smile and moved her body suggestively underneath him. "I believe you have me."

"Almost."

"You have my heart. You have my body. What more do you need?" She motioned the best she could to their current position.

He stared into her sparkling brown eyes. "I need your hand in marriage."

CHAPTER TWENTY-ONE

Pushing up on her elbows, Sabryna stared. "A-are you s-s-sure you don't want pancakes?"

"I'm very sure about what I want."

Sabryna's mind reeled. Happiness collided with disbelief. He couldn't be serious. Sitting up she pulled the sheet protectively against her and tried to make sense out of what he just said.

"You know you're the first woman I've ever asked to marry me and somehow I thought it was going to go a little different." His head rested on his elbow.

She still wasn't sure she heard correct. "You want to marry me?"

"Is there another seductive Angel lying in this bed with me?"

Seductive Angel? How did this man turn her mind so easily to mush? She didn't know what thought had gotten into his head, but he looked set to sweep her away on the tide. Marriage? What was he thinking? He was Marcus Cortland, multi-millionaire, use to all the luxuries of life. She thought it a luxury to have enough time for a relaxing bath. They weren't just from different worlds, they were from different universes. "We can't get married."

She didn't realize she voiced the thought out loud until he replied, "Of course we can."

"No we can't." She jumped off the bed and paced about the room, the sheet shielding her nakedness.

He sat up. "Why can't we?"

"Because you're you...and I'm...me." She sounded lame.

His laughed. "I believe that's the point."

She continued pacing back and forth. Thoughts raced and collided in her mind. Could she say yes?

"Sabryna, I love you."

Her pacing came to a dead stop, and she turned to look at him. "I know that."

Marcus scooted to the edge of the bed. "Do you? Do you really believe that?"

She searched his eyes. Saw the truth of his love vibrating in the brown depths. "Of course I do."

"And do you love me?"

"You know I do."

"Then marry me."

Crossing the room, she stopped in front of him. "Marcus, what we have is so great. I love being with you. But, do you think that marriage is the right next step."

"Where did you think this was going?"

He had her there. The truth was she hadn't allowed herself to think past the present. That was the mistake she made last time with him. Ever since they got back together she had been in living for the moment mode. "Marcus, are you sure that I'm the woman you want?"

Smiling, he held up his hands. "I've never wanted any woman the way that I want you."

She couldn't help but smile over that, and still..."Yes, but are you sure that I am the kind of woman you want to spend the rest of your life with?"

Frowning, he grabbed her hands and pulled her down to sit next to him. "Why don't you tell me what's going on in that gorgeous head of yours?"

Not quite wanting to meet his eyes she concentrated on where there hands were linked. Hesitating, she searched for the right words. "I'm not the type of woman that most people would expect you to be with."

"What type of women do...people expect me to be with?"

"You know someone who is...exciting. I'm not rich or extremely beautiful and fashionable. I'm not sophisticated. You're part of a world that I can't even begin to compete in."

His sigh ruffled through her hair. "Sabryna, look at me."

She glanced up and his eyes captured hers.

"I want you to listen to me, okay."

She nodded.

"I don't give a damn who other people think I should be with. The only woman I want, will ever want, is you. And more important, I don't ever want to hear you speak like that about yourself again."

"But Marcus..."

"You're the most fascinating woman I've ever had the privilege to lay eyes on. Ever since I first heard that laughter of yours I've been hooked. You claim you're not exciting, and yet I can think of nothing more enjoyable that simply being where you are. Who cares if you're rich? I have more than enough money for the both of us. Besides, you've no idea how worthy I feel knowing you love me for who I am and not how much money I have. As for you being beautiful and fashionable, it's apparent when you look in the mirror you don't see what I see. You're not just intelligent, funny, extremely opinionated and outspoken, but extraordinarily beautiful, and all I can think of is how and when I can make love to you again.

"As for sophistication, sweetheart, I have come across plenty of woman who are 'sophisticated', and I haven't found one who carries herself with the same self-respect that she gives others. You have a quiet dignity about you that makes people take notice, and a compassion that keeps them noticing. That's what I feel true sophistication is. I know what world you think I live in, but the only world I want to ever be in is one that includes you. You are my world. Am I sure I want to marry you? Angel, my one regret is that we aren't married already."

Tears were streaming down her face. "You have this unique ability to make me cry."

Marcus kissed away a teardrop from her right eye. "As long as they're tears of happiness I'm okay with that."

"I don't think I've ever known true happiness until you," she confessed.

"Does that mean you'll marry me?"

"Yes." She said, and he snatched her into his arms with a shout of happiness. His lips settled on hers and he kissed her long and deeply.

"I swear you'll never regret it," he vowed when he lifted his head.

Her sole response was to raise her lips to his again, and allow him to erase all her worries, fears, and doubts. At least, for now.

The next Saturday, Sabryna stood alone at the window in Marcus's bedroom. Marcus had left about an hour ago to run some errands and she decided to hang out at his penthouse till he came back. If anything, the views would keep her distracted. However it wasn't the city that held her attention that afternoon as she stared down from the 27th floor. The previous Sunday, they'd told Marcus's family their news and she participated in her first family picture taking session. Since then she couldn't help but think of her own family. Or lack thereof. She told Lena and Grant about the engagement and both had been happy for her. Grant was, as usual, reserved in his happiness, but his doubts about Marcus had faded over the last few weeks. Lena of course, had been exuberant, rushing to the store to buy every bridal magazine she could find. Sabryna wasn't quite ready to announce it to the kids, but she was pleased at the support her friends showed her.

However, nothing could top the support of family. Even distant family.

Raising the cordless phone she been gripping in her hand for over twenty minutes, Sabryna dialed a number she knew by heart, despite not having used it in a long time.

The phone rang four times before an achingly familiar voice answered, "Hello."

"Hi, Daddy." Sabryna forced cheer in her voice to over ride the nerves.

"Hello, Sabryna." His voice was monotone, unfeeling.

"How are you? How are things going?" She hated how weird she sounded.

"Everything's okay." Silence ensued.

"Well, I'm good also." Her hand tightened on the phone. "I've been…"

"Sabryna, is there something you needed?" he cut her off abruptly. "I was on my way out."

She took a calming a breath, convinced herself to forge ahead. "Well, I was calling to tell you that I'm getting married."

Silence and then, "Congratulations."

She waited for him to say more. When he didn't, she continued. "He's a wonderful guy. His name is Marcus Cortland. He was raised in Richmont and owns and IT firm."

Her father made no comment.

"We've only been engaged a few days," she ended, unsure of what to say next.

"When is the wedding?" His voice lacked interest but his question held promise.

"We haven't set a date, but we're thinking in a few months." She took a deeper breath than the first. "I was…hoping…wondering, if you would come to give me away."

The silence on the other end stretched so long Sabryna had to ask, "Dad?"

There was a strange clearing of the throat. "I'll see," he told her and then qualified. "But I doubt it. I've been a little under the weather and not much in the mood for travel."

A knife in her heart couldn't have hurt more. "It's my wedding, Dad."

"I said, I'll see. I can't make promises. Look I got to go. I told you I was on my way out."

Dejected, she replied, "I'm sorry for holding you up."

"That's fine. Goodbye." He didn't wait for her response before hanging up.

Sabryna listened to the dial tone for long seconds as though it could explain things to her she didn't comprehend. But nothing could explain why her father refused to love her. Why he pushed her out of his life without a second's hesitation. Pushing the button to end the call, Sabryna sank onto the window seat as tears, once held in control, rolled unchecked down her cheek.

CHAPTER TWENTY-TWO

Marcus walked through the door of his penthouse. When he noticed Sabryna sitting in the window seat, tears cascading down her cheek, he lost all ability to smile. "Sabryna?"

Sabryna glanced up as if she had just noticed his presence, and he was willing to bet she'd been oblivious to everything except what was causing her pain. She didn't move, not even to wipe away her tears. She turned back to the window. "I didn't hear you come in."

He approached her, thankful the seat was large enough to fit both of them, he settled beside her. "What's wrong?"

"Nothing." Her voice was weak.

Reaching up he brushed a tear off her cheek with his thumb. "In our time together you've accused me of many things. Blind was never one of them."

Her smile didn't reach her eyes.

He took one of her hands giving it a gentle squeeze. "What is it, Angel?"

Her eyes never left the window, as she sighed. "I called my father."

"To tell him about me?" Marcus guessed.

Sabryna nodded.

Marcus had an inkling of where this was going. She hadn't mentioned her father since the night she told him about her childhood. As far as he could tell the two of them rarely, if ever, spoke. "What did he say?"

For a moment she was silent. Then she told him what appeared to be a word for word recap of the conversation. By the time she finished her tears flowed anew. Marcus was sure he could commit murder against her unfeeling father. "Baby, I'm so sorry."

She held up her hand. "Don't apologize. It's not your fault that my father doesn't love me."

Marcus bit back a curse. "It's not your fault, either."

Sabryna shrugged. "I thought I didn't care anymore."

Marcus didn't know what words she needed right then. He only knew he wanted to supply them. Releasing her hand, he began to rub her arms and shoulders in a manner meant to soothe. He wanted to pull her close and absorb her pain but he wasn't sure she'd appreciate that gesture. She seemed almost lost inside of herself. "I should be alone."

She started to stand. His hand restrained her. "Why?"

"I'm not very good company right now."

Gripping her hand again, he pulled her back down on the seat. "Don't go."

"Marcus…"

"Stay." His firm interruption halted her. "You don't have to be good company. You don't have to be anything at all. I don't like seeing you like this."

"If I leave…"

"I'll follow you home," he told her. "You wouldn't allow me to turn away from you if I was upset and I'm not going to allow you to do it. Listen, I can't change things between you and your father, but maybe I can take the pain away."

She turned watery brown eyes to him. "How?" Was that hope he saw in the depths?

He pulled her close, she didn't resist. Allowed him to lock her in his arms. His head bent he spoke in a low reassuring rumble. "I can hold you while you cry."

Curling up next to him, she rested her head against his chest. When she relaxed against him, he shifted his position to find his own comfort. He would hold her the rest of the day if that was what she needed.

Sabryna didn't know she'd fallen asleep until she woke up. Curled up on Marcus's lap, his arms tight around her. Stretching, the top of her head bumped his chin.

"I see you're awake," he remarked.

"Mmm hmm." She felt renewed. In no rush to leave her position, she snuggled further into his arms. She hadn't thought it possible, but being able to share her pain and sadness with him had somehow lessened it. It was still there, hovering in the background, but it seemed less prominent, less threatening. Having someone care about the intimate details of her life was a novel experience. One she could fast come to appreciate.

Deciding to give his lap a break, she moved off him.

He stretched. "I don't believe I've ever spent that much time – anytime– in this seat."

She laughed. "Next time I have a minor crisis I'll remember to have it in a more comfortable chair."

"I appreciate that," he quipped. "If I'm going to continue to play the role of knight in shining armor I'm going to have to make a few demands."

Sabryna's eyes wandered over his wrinkled clothes. "Thank you, for being there for me."

"No need to thank me. It's part of the package," he told her.

"I'm sorry I tried to push you away. I'm used to dealing with my problems on my own."

"Sounds like you and I have more in common than we realized."

A slow smile stretched across her face. "You teach me, I'll teach you."

"That sounds fair," he teased. "In fact, I have your first lesson. Consider it a study aid."

Reaching into his pocket, he pulled out a small black box. "Think of it as a visual reminder that you're not alone anymore." He popped open the top to reveal an elegant gold band with a large glittering diamond atop it. There were smaller diamonds inlaid in the gold band.

Her hands flew to her mouth. Her eyes didn't believe what she was seeing.

"I know I'm a little late. But I wanted it to be perfect." He shot her a crooked smile. "Despite what you may think, I've never picked out jewelry for a woman before. It's not as easy as one would imagine."

Sabryna's eyes misted over. She was surprised any tears were left. "It's beautiful."

Taking it from the box, he slid it on her ring finger. "Now, it's beautiful."

Sabryna examined the ring. She'd never been so mesmerized by a piece of jewelry. She now knew why they referred to some diamonds as rocks.

"Do you like it?"

"Like it!" She kissed him, kept on kissing him. "I love it and I love you. I can't wait till I become your wife."

"That-" he inserted in between kisses. "makes two of us."

"Congratulations!" A chorus of cheers rang out as Sabryna reentered the center that Wednesday after completing an errand for Grant. Startled, she stopped in her tracks.

The main room was decorated in a rainbow of mismatched colors. Half-filled colorful balloons floated around. Streamers that read "Happy

Birthday" hung from the ceilings. A beat-up donkey piñata teetered at the end of a string. A large group of kids and teens stood in the midst of it all, holding a large cake, and grinning from ear to ear. The cake read "congratulations on your engagement."

The proverbial cat was out of the bag.

Breaking away from the crowd, Lena came toward her. "The kids insisted on throwing you a surprise…er, wedding shower," she confided in a voice only Sabryna could hear.

Sabryna plastered a huge smile on her face. "I can't believe you all did this."

The kids were pleased at her happiness. "We can't believe you gettin' married," shouted Carlos and everyone laughed.

"Are you still going to work here?" Gabe Lucas asked, a note of concern in voice.

"Of course she is," Latisha slid up to Sabryna. "Do we get to go to the wedding?"

Sabryna laughed at the hopeful expression on Latisha's face. It was impossible to deny her. "You're all invited."

A chorus of cheers went up at her words. The cake was lowered onto a table and a couple of the older kids went to work slicing it and distributing it. The excitement was contagious and Sabryna found herself caught up in the moment as she answered the million and one questions they seemed to have. It never occurred to some of them that she would get married.

She did break away for a moment, long enough to discreetly ask Lena how the kids knew. She didn't wear her ring to work to keep the news from them.

"Next time you want to keep a secret I suggest you not tell it to the papers," Lena teased. "One of the girls noticed and within minutes everyone knew. They started planning this. I was surprised Grant was able to get a cake so fast and the decorations, well it's obvious those are…"

Feeling as though she had missed some vital piece of information, Sabryna interrupted, "Wait…what was that you said about the paper?"

"I was talking about your announcement in the Richmont Gazette," Lena explained. "Everyone saw it."

"What announcement?"

Lena stared. Then she glanced around as if looking for something. Spotting a paper she walked over, grabbed it, and brought it back to Sabryna. Flipping open to the center, she pointed at a picture. "This announcement."

Sabryna stared in utter disbelief at the picture. It was of her and Marcus. The announcement underneath was about their engagement. Sabryna snatched up the paper. "I can't believe it. When…How?" Her eyes narrowed on the photograph. "We took this picture at his mother's house just last weekend when we told his family. How could she have gotten it to the paper so fast?"

Lena shook her head. "I don't know, but it's a good picture."

They were interrupted by the ringing of her cell phone. Reaching into her purse she grabbed it and answered.

Marcus's familiar voice sounded on the other end. "There's something you should know."

"Let me guess. Your mother placed an announcement in the paper."

There was a pause on the other end. "Are you psychic?"

"No I'm surrounded by perhaps the only group of kids who read a newspaper," she teased. "I'm also standing in the middle of my surprise wedding shower."

"And I wasn't invited. I'm hurt," he joked. His voice grew serious. "So, you're not angry?"

She sighed. "No. It's not like it was a secret. I take it she didn't tell you she was doing it."

"No, I would've warned you. Or stopped her."

"That's what I figured." She glanced around at the kids eating cake. "Well, because of her actions I'm having a very nice party. Why don't you come and join us."

"I'm tempted, but I'm going to have to pass," he told her. "I was calling to tell you that I need to leave town. I'll be back late tonight, so I'll see you tomorrow."

Missing him already, she asked, "Where are you going?"

"I have to take care of some business down south. But don't worry I'll be back before you have time to miss me."

To late for that. Not wanting to appear clingy, she kept the thought to herself. Besides, best she get used to his traveling. It was part of his business. He'd be back tomorrow. She could survive one night.

It was 2 a.m. when Marcus stepped off his private jet back in Richmont. His first thoughts were of Sabryna. He been away a few short hours and he missed her more than he thought possible. Checking his watch he decided it was too late to go over to her place.

He imagined her curled up in bed. Long lashes resting on her soft cheeks. Her curvaceous frame wrapped in blankets. A smile flirting about her lips as she dreamed. Hopefully, about him.

She was unaware of the real mission behind his trip, and he hoped she never found out. He didn't know how she would react if she knew he'd gone to see her father.

Her father was a supreme jerk.

How a man, blessed with such an Angel for a daughter, wouldn't want to have a relationship with her he couldn't understand. He hoped to get to the bottom of what was going on with her father. Her pain the other day had disturbed him on some primitive level. Sabryna was going to be his wife. It was his responsibility to take care of her, make her happy. He wouldn't let anything prevent that. Unfortunately, her father didn't care a lick about his daughter or her happiness.

Reaching his car, he slid into the driver seat. He started the engine and popped in an Anthony Hamilton C.D.

Only then did he notice the white card lying on the passenger seat.

Rolling his eyes, he picked it up. He considered tossing it out the window. He wasn't in the mood for more vague threats from his would-be-stalker. A strange feeling of dread settled over him. Surprised at the feeling, he opened the card and read the words:

She's so beautiful.

She loves you so much.

But your love kills.

She'll die tonight.

Sabryna! His heart hammered in his chest. Fear and rage gripped him. His feet flew to the pedal and as he sped through the streets he tried to call her. He got the busy signal. He couldn't think of a single soul she'd be calling at this time of morning. Hanging up he made another phone call.

And prayed to God that is wasn't too late.

CHAPTER TWENTY-THREE

Marcus's tires squealed as it ripped around a corner less than a block from Sabryna's neighborhood. In the rearview he could see flashing red and blue lights on an unmarked police car following close behind him. Thank God his brother had been on duty! The sound of the siren drowned out by the thudding in his heart. Not once did he consider slowing down to pull over. The rational part of his mind told him the cops could get there faster, but the other part of his mind, the one that had a direct connection to his soul, focused on one thing. Get to Sabryna before it was too late.

He parked his car in front of her apartment. Leaving it running, he jumped out and raced up the hill. His brother and another detective, at his heels.

Running up to the door, Marcus prepared to knock it down. Rough hands grabbed him by the shoulders, pulling him back.

"Let us handle this," David commanded and motioned to his partner.

"Let me go. I have to get in there." Marcus bucked against his brothers restraining arm.

David's partner, gun drawn, was already stepping past them. He tried the door knob and it swung open.

That was all the confirmation Marcus needed that something was wrong. Breaking David's hold, he raced ahead of them into the dark apartment, screamed Sabryna's name. His brother cursed and followed.

Marcus headed straight for the bedroom and burst through the door. "Sabryna?" A frantic Sabryna lay on her bed, struggling against a pillow and blanket wrapped around her head.

"Marcus?" Her voice was weak and terrified at the same time.

Rushing to the bed he made short work of the bed spread around her head. The pillow fell off revealing her crazed brown eyes wide with shock and fear. Snatching her into his arms, he buried his face in her curls. "Oh, God. Are you okay?"

Shaking and sobbing, Sabryna clutched at him as if her life depended on it. And in those few seconds he was sure that his did.

"I-I c-couldn't breathe," she sobbed. "I couldn't breathe."

Hearing the note of hysteria in her voice, he pulled her onto his lap, stroking her back. "You're safe."

Tucking her head underneath his chin, she continued to cry as Marcus murmured gentle words to let her know she was okay. Soon her sobs died down to a hiccup and she relaxed in his arms.

"Whoever it was must've heard us and gone out the window," David stated. Glancing up at his brother, Marcus frowned. He'd forgotten anyone else was there. In his arms, Sabryna stiffened. Raising her head she looked at David and then back at the window. It stood open. She shuttered. Marcus instinctively tightened his hold.

"Are you okay?" David squatted down in front of her. She nodded. "Can you tell us what happened?"

Marcus watched her visible fight to regain composure. David's partner and two additional cops entered the room.

Marcus pulled her closer. "Let's go into the living room. She can tell you everything there."

Sabryna told them all she could remember. But first, she was checked out by the medics while David and Jeff took a look around. They declared that she was okay, but suggested she go to the hospital just to be sure. When she declined, Marcus set his jaw, ready to argue with her. She diverted him by asking him to stay with her as she was questioned by David. In the face of her need, he relented.

Sitting on the couch, Marcus's arm draped protectively around her shoulders, she recounted what she knew. David sat perched on the coffee table in front of her, jotting down notes in a tiny notebook. His partner, whose name she learned was Jeff Kinsey, sat on the loveseat, listening to the short story. Around them activity ensued. Several more officers had arrived on the scene, and now were engaged in a meticulous search of her apartment. As she observed the scene she felt as if she wasn't in her own body, but suspended above the action, watching as her place was treated as a crime scene. The truth hit her hard. Someone had tried to kill her.

Coldness spread throughout her, threatened to engulf her. Her body registered Marcus's warm solid weight anchored by her side. Her respiration returned to normal.

"You said your door wasn't unlocked when you went to bed, so chances are he picked the lock," David said, bringing her attention back to them. "You go to bed shortly after twelve, he picks the locks, and shuts the door behind him, so as not to alert any neighbors that might pass by. Then he enters your bedroom and attempts to smother you. But he hears the sirens, and not wanting to risk that we might be coming here, he flees out the window."

"They found signs that the lock was picked and footprints in the ground out back leading away from your window. I assume you don't often leave out your window?" Jeff asked. Turning her attention back to Jeff, she took in his large frame, brown locks, and piercing blue eyes.

Sabryna shook her head. "Do you think it was a robbery gone wrong?"

David and Jeff exchanged a glance. David looked back at her. "I don't think so."

"So he came in here just to kill me." Sabryna heard the horror in her own voice.

"Are you sure it's a man?" Marcus asked.

David nodded. "The size of the footprint suggests that her attacker was wearing a man's shoe." He gestured toward the cops moving about her apartment. "They're looking for any prints that might have been left behind and anything else that might give us an idea as to who this perp is."

"Did you hear anything at all before the incident?" Jeff asked.

"No. I was asleep one minute and the next I was being strangled."

"Smothered," Jeff corrected. Then explained, "If you'd been strangled you might have gotten a glimpse of your attacker. The fact that he chose to cover up your face tells us that he didn't want you to see his."

Sabryna thought and didn't like what she came up with. "He didn't want me to recognize him."

David shook his head. "He wasn't worried about you recognizing him. Dead women can't talk. My guess is he didn't want you to know who was attacking you."

"Are you saying that it was deliberate? That someone came in here with the intention to hurt me?" She read the truth in his eyes. "Why? Why would someone do that?"

"Do you have any enemies? Is there anyone you can think of that might want to hurt you?" Jeff asked.

Sabryna thought then shook her head. "I can't think of anyone...I... wait. There are gangs in this area. I've even run a few off from the center. Maybe it was one of them, seeking revenge or maybe it was a...

an initiation"

David glanced at Marcus. "That is something we could look into." He didn't sound convinced.

"It has to be that. Nothing else makes sense," she asserted.

"When was the last time you had a run in with any of these gang members?" The question came from Jeff.

Searching her memory, she replied, "About six maybe seven months ago."

Jeff frowned. "They usually wouldn't wait this long for revenge. We can check it out, but I doubt that's it."

"I can't think of anything else I've done that would cause someone to hate me so much that they'd try to kill me." Once again Marcus and David exchanged a look. There was something about it that registered with Sabryna as odd. She studied Marcus. His face was unreadable. "What are you thinking?" she asked.

Marcus stared into her upturned face. It was then that she saw the expression in his eyes before his face cleared. It was the same look he'd worn when talking about how responsible he felt for his father's death. Guilt and shame. She looked at David, he sent a pointed glance to Marcus. "You two both know something," she accused. "What is it?"

Marcus took a deep breath. "It wasn't anything that you did." He relaxed his left fist to reveal a crumbled white card. His eyes came back to meet hers. "It's my fault. I'm the reason you almost died tonight."

"You've been getting these for the past seven years?" Sabryna's dismay was obvious. She lifted the card and read the words again.

"Yes. But none that have ever alluded to anyone but me." Marcus shifted, uncomfortable. They were still seated on her couch. "This was the first time a threat was made against someone else."

"Why did you keep this from me?" Sabryna's hurt showed in her eyes and tore at his heart.

"It wasn't a conscious decision," he told her. "I've been getting these things for so long that I don't even think about them until one pops up."

"How do you put death threats out of your mind?"

"None of them have threatened death," David interrupted.

"Until now," Marcus pointed out, his tone grim. "I want to know who this bastard is." He wanted to rip him to shreds.

"We'll find him," Jeff responded.

"How?" Sabryna looked at all of them. "You said yourself that

David's been investigating this for years and hasn't found anything. You've no idea who he could be."

David placed a calming hand on her knee. "We know something we didn't know before. We now know he's a man."

"And when the test come back from the lab we might know more," Jeff offered.

"Do you think he's going to try to come after me again?" She trembled.

Marcus pulled her closer into his side. "He's not going to get anywhere near you."

"Why don't you get some sleep," David suggested. "We can talk more about this tomorrow...well, later today."

Sabryna looked around her apartment as if she didn't recognize it. David broke the silence. "It's best if you don't stay alone. Not until this is resolved."

"You'll stay with me," Marcus decided.

"The security is tight at your building, but I'll put a car out front." David stood up.

Sabryna came to her feet. "I'm going to go pack a bag."

Both brothers watched as she disappeared into the room on feet that were still a little unsteady.

"If I hadn't gotten home when I did..." Marcus started

"Don't think about it. You did and that's what counts," David interrupted.

Marcus looked his brother in the eye. "I can't allow anything to happen to her."

David placed a comforting hand on his brother's shoulders. "She's family. We'll do whatever needs to be done to keep her safe."

Marcus jaw set with grim resolution. "That's exactly what I plan to do."

Sabryna stood at the window of Marcus's penthouse and gazed out at the early morning sky streaked with purple and pink rivers. Far below her, the city was waking up to a calming morning peace. Inside, Sabryna experienced the quiet in a different way. After the initial shock had worn off a decided numbness had settled over her as she realized all that she had almost been robbed of. Her life – which now had so much more meaning to it. Now that she stood on the threshold of being happy for the first time.

Marcus and Sabryna arrived back at his place two hours ago. Neither said much in the car, each lost in their own thoughts. Despite his silence, Marcus wasn't inclined to let her out of his sight. He whisked her upstairs and insisted she drink a shot of brandy. "It will help," was all the explanation he offered. She realized that he thought she was in shock. She decided to humor him, until she noticed the hand that reached for the glass trembled. Then she swallowed the brandy for herself.

Next, they called Grant. There was no way she was ready to go to work. Grant's alarm had been real. He had wanted to rush over. She assured him she was okay, that she was safe. Sabryna's assurance must not have been enough, because Grant asked to speak to Marcus. She listened to Marcus' side of the conversation as he confirmed all of her information and then reassured Grant that the police were on top of it, and that he was taking care of Sabryna. Sabryna appreciated his concern too much to grumble, but she was starting to feel like a child.

Telling Marcus she was going to take a shower, she almost stumbled over him when he followed her. Explaining she needed a moment alone, he conceded. She had a deep suspicion that he sat in the bedroom staring at the closed bathroom door.

The truth after spending so long alone, it had become a comfortable habit to process her feelings in isolation. With Marcus's hovering, she couldn't think. The only way to reduce her shock was to analyze the situation until it made sense to her. Marcus had a stalker. His stalker had attempted to kill her. Marcus rescued her...in the nick of time. After an hour in the shower, the thing she kept coming back to was how much she'd almost missed out on loving and being loved by Marcus.

She promised herself in that moment she wouldn't waste another second of her life on fear. She would live and love every minute as though the next wasn't promised. As she had learned tonight, it wasn't.

After she'd come out of the bathroom, and indeed found him sitting on the bed staring at the door, he decided to take a quick shower. Slipping on a black tank and pair of shorts, she wandered into the living room. Thoughts of a not so innocent nature floated through her mind. She needed a confirmation of life and love that could surpass all others.

Mere inches from her, Marcus stepped up behind her. Catching sight of his reflection in the glass, she smiled. Fresh from the shower, he smelled of soap and his own distinct masculine scent. His broad bare chest radiated heat, licking at her back and igniting an answering fire in her. Lifting her head, she met his smoldering eyes in the window.

His lips relaxed into a smile. The first one tonight. And, even better, it was a wicked one. "Enjoying the view?" he teased, his voice husky.

Her eyes never left his. "Mmm-hmm."

With his right hand, he caressed her bare arm. His left hand lifted the knot of curls at her neck and he set his lips to tease the soft skin underneath.

She moaned her pleasure.

His other hand locked around her waist and pulled her back against him. His need pulsated against her lower back. Her own grin turned wicked. Feeling more wild and reckless than ever, she turned in his embrace and set her own hands to exploring his chest, let her fingers roam over the expanse of muscle. He was rock hard beneath her fingertips. Everywhere she touched, his muscles jumped and flexed in reaction. His hands still loose around her waist, but other than that he allowed her to play.

Allowed her to explore her territory.

When her lips connected with his nipple, Marcus groaned. She tasted him, mimicking the way he tortured her, caressing first with her hands, smoothing the way for her lips.

"I can't stop thinking about how close I came to missing out on this." She raised eyes ablaze with desire to meet his. "To missing out on you."

"Don't think about it." His voice was rough with emotion and something else she couldn't put a name to. "You're safe now."

Marcus's head was swimming in a storm of need and arousal. His blood heated at her soft touches. Her lips settled on to his. A kiss that was filled with such longing, it triggered his instinctive response as he locked his arms about her.

"Do you know what I thought about in those seconds when I thought I was going to die?" she asked, when she raised her head. At the moment he was beyond words.

"All I thought about was you. About how much I didn't want to leave you." Her fingers stroked the hard edges of his face. "My mind was consumed with thoughts of you. Then you were there. It was as though you'd come because you knew I needed you."

"I'll always be there when you need me."

Her smile was all woman. "Good." She placed butterfly kisses along his chest. "Because I need you now."

She pushed against him, wanting to be released. Reluctantly, he let her go. But she didn't go far. Stepping back, she pulled at the string holding up his cotton pajama pants. Her nimble fingers sneaked inside of them and before he could blink she had his erection in her hand, caressing him with sweet possession.

His groan was torn from his soul.

All of a sudden, she released him, pushed him toward the couch. Feeling he would give her the stars if she asked, he complied. When his legs hit the back of the couch, he followed her gentle guidance and sat. Relaxing back into the leather, he pulled off his pants and boxers and waited to see the next act in her play.

He didn't have long to wait. She stepped back and with the grace of a Russian ballerina pulled her tank over her head, baring her beautiful breasts. Her eyes never leaving him, she lowered her shorts over her hips and let them drop on the floor. Stepping away from them she stood proudly in front of him in nothing but a pair of red bikini panties. Allowing him to look his fill, her eyes conveyed what didn't make it to her mouth, "This is all for you."

He heard the words as clear as if she had spoken them out loud. Desire pumped through his blood. Still locked in his gaze she skimmed her hand over her smooth, flat stomach.

He had to remind himself to breathe.

With deliberate slowness, she walked toward him, lowering herself to her knees between his legs. Stretching up they enjoyed a kiss aflame with their joint desire. She broke the kiss first, and began to trail light kisses down his neck, chest, and waist. When her lips kissed the inside of his thigh, he groaned. When she took him into her mouth he almost convulsed with desire. His head lolled back on the couch. The sensation of him inside of her warm, sweet mouth was almost more than he could handle. It took every ounce of control he possessed not to release himself into her mouth. His last thought, before thinking became impossible, was that his Angel was sensual innocence personified.

When he could take no more, he grabbed her by the shoulders and lifting her up, roughly placed her on the couch. Every demon he owned was begging him to take her right there. To bury him self inside of her till he was so deep there was no separation between their souls. But first he wanted to pleasure her. She almost lost her life tonight because of him. He was determined to replace every ounce of pain she experienced with a pound of pleasure.

He turned to her, she rested against the arm of the couch facing his profile. Reaching out he took her panties and slid them down her legs, revealing her treasures. Turning so he was facing her, he spread her legs wide and placed kisses on the inside of her thigh just as she had done his.

She laughed low in her throat as she realized he was following her lead…and what the outcome would be. Laughter soon turned to moans of pure delight as his lips kissed the very core of her. He licked and laved, exploring every part of her until she held no more secrets. Only then did he allow his tongue to enter her, tasting the sweetness of her core. He probed her until she was sobbing and begging for more.

"Marcus." She demanded.

He cupped her breast. Giving each one a tender squeeze as he pressed deeper into her. She screamed his name and shattered around him. He continued licking as her climax raced over her. When he sensed she was coming back to earth, he found her sensitive nub and began to suckle, gentle at first and then with greater demand. Once again her climax came upon her, nails dug into his shoulders, bracing herself through the storm.

This time as her climax receded, he lifted up and worshipped her breast. Circled each nipple with his tongue until she was again writhing beneath him. He was already between her legs, shifting, he slid in, filled her to completeness. She took him in as though she were welcoming him home. A soft satisfied sigh escaped. He drank it off her lips.

Sabryna's pleasure knew no limits. His thrust, deep and sure, filled her. Their bodies moved to a rhythm as though they were two similar notes in the same song. He covered every inch of her skin with his own and Sabryna thought there was nothing that could compare with being this close to him. When her orgasm came, even stronger than the first two, she was aware that he was soaring over the edge with her. Their hearts connected, their souls entwined, their spirits forever bonded.

CHAPTER
TWENTY-FOUR

Rolling over in Marcus's large bed, Sabryna wasn't surprised to find herself alone. Turning her head, she glanced at the alarm clock perched on the night stand. It was mid-afternoon. Sitting up in bed, she looked around the room and allowed the previous nights activities to drift through her memory. Pushing the covers back, she got out of bed with new determination. It was time to locate a stalker turned attempted murderer, make sure he ended up behind bars, marry the man she loves, and enjoy the happiness that had long eluded her.

After taking a quick shower and throwing on a pair of jeans and a t-shirt, she found Marcus in the kitchen. He was sitting at the counter, his back to her, talking in hushed tones to David and Jeff.

"Is this a private conference?"

Three pairs of eyes stared back at her, and she was sure there lowered voices hadn't just been to keep from waking her up. She looked at her fiancé but his dark eyes were unreadable and gave nothing away.

David was the first to break the spell. "Good Morning. We were wondering if you were going to sleep the day away."

Walking up to stand next to Marcus, she kept her eyes locked on his. There was something in his expression that didn't sit right with her. She looked to Jeff. "Any news?"

Jeff shifted. "Well…"

"Do you want some coffee or something to eat?" Marcus interrupted.

Sabryna glanced at him before replying, "I'll take some coffee." When he got up to get it she took over his seat and met David square in the eyes. "Did you all find the guy?"

David shook his head. "We haven't yet. But don't worry we will."

"I know you will. What can I do to help?"

David looked at Marcus. Marcus handed a cup of coffee to Sabryna. "David and Jeff are on it." Marcus's tone held a dismissive note.

Now she was getting annoyed. "As the person who almost got killed last night I'd like to know what's going on."

Jeff cleared his throat. "We weren't able to find any prints at your place, but we did find some hair. Right now it's at the lab being tested. We'll compare it with samples from both of you and if it's not a match we'll run it through our database."

"That's great." Sabryna breathed a sigh of relief. "Then you'll know who this guy is."

David shook his head, "Not necessarily. We can't rule out that the hair might be from someone else who might have been in your room with an invitation. Also, we only have matches in our system for people who have priors."

The air went out of her balloon. "So in other words, it wouldn't matter even if we had a whole tube of his blood."

"It will help us with a conviction once we catch him."

"Okay, so we need to catch him," Sabryna insisted.

"And we will," David told her.

"And I'm going to help you." Sabryna leapt off the stool and retrieved a pen. She came back and settled on her stool. "I have a pen, do you have a notebook?" Since she was looking at Jeff he slowly took out the small notebook he carried with him. Grabbing it out of his hand, she flipped it open to a blank page. "Okay, the first thing we need to do is make a list."

"A list?" David asked.

"Yes, a list," she confirmed. "A list of all the people who would want revenge on Marcus. That'll help us narrow down the field of suspects. Then we can divide up the list and start questioning people."

"I don't think that's a good idea." David's eyes darted between her and Marcus.

"Of course it is. It's the next logical step." Sabryna looked from one to the other. Why weren't they jumping on this? They were detectives, she'd seen enough cop shows to know that this was a standard question. Realization was slow to come, but when it did it brought her temper with it. "Of course it's the next logical step. But you know that, because ya'll have already discussed it. You've also discussed how to best leave me out of it." Her accusation rang out in angry tones. When no one was quick to tell her she was wrong, she exploded. "I can't believe you."

"Sabryna, we can talk about this when they leave," Marcus told her.

He reached out to her but she backed away. "No. I'll not be treated like a child. I'm a grown woman. I don't need or want to be shielded."

"Sabryna…"

"In case ya'll forgot, it was me who almost died last night and I have every right to help track down the bastard who did it."

"Sabryna, it's not that we don't want your help, we need your help in order to catch him," David replied.

"But?" Sabryna asked hearing the hesitation in his voice.

"But, as you pointed out you were the one he tried to kill. So that means you are the one he will come after again."

"We don't know that," she asserted.

"Yes, we do." Marcus slid a white card on the counter. For a second, Sabryna just stared at it. "I found it taped over the peephole when I woke up."

Sabryna picked it up. Silently, she read the card.

Consider last night a blessing -

I can't allow you even the mercy of watching her die.

You don't deserve her love. You never did.

I'm not her killer - you are.

The card fell from her hand. She couldn't stop the sound of distress that escaped her throat. Marcus folded her in his arms. "It's okay. You're safe."

"I know." She clutched at him anyway. Maybe a few days ago a note like that wouldn't have the same affect on her. But for all her bravado about finding this jerk, she couldn't forget how close he'd come to reaching his goal. She couldn't let him. Not just for herself, but for her future, the future she was determined to spend with Marcus.

David and Jeff stood up. "We have to go."

Marcus nodded, turning toward them with one protective arm still locked around Sabryna. "I'll call you."

Jeff looked at Sabryna. "There will be an officer outside your door 24 hours. If you should decide to…stay somewhere else, let him know, he'll go too."

Sabryna smiled. "Thank you."

Sabryna waited until Jeff and David left before turning to Marcus. "Why did Jeff say 'if I should decide to stay somewhere else'?"

Releasing her, Marcus took a deep breath. "Because he knows you won't be staying here."

"And why wouldn't I?" Sabryna asked, puzzled.

Marcus briefly looked away as if steeling himself for some tough event. When he turned back to look at her, his eyes were dark with intent. "You won't be staying here, because I'm ending this. You and I are over."

A punch to the gut would've been less painful and definitely more expected. For a moment, Sabryna just looked at Marcus as if he had grown a third head. "We're over," she repeated as if she hadn't heard the words correctly.

She half expected him to tell her not to be foolish, that she misheard, misunderstood, anything. Instead he turned his back on her and walked around the counter. Her heart sunk even lower. After a moments hesitation, Marcus turned back around to face her, grim resolve etched in every line of his face. "Yes, we're over."

"We can't be over," she reminded him. "We're getting married."

Folding his arms across his chest, Marcus stated in even tones, "No we're not."

"What do you mean – no we're not?"

"The wedding is off. We are off."

"Just like that?"

"Yes."

Sabryna searched his face. But it remained blank of all emotion. Walking over to him, she put her hands on his arms, implored him, "Tell me what is going on."

He moved away from her. "Just accept that we're over."

When he turned away from her, she almost cried out. He never rejected her touch before. All the hurt from weeks past began to resurface. So this was how it was going to be. One minute he loved her and the next he wanted her out of his life. No, she wouldn't allow it. "I will not accept it unless you tell me why you're so ready to turn your back on us."

When he didn't answer her, she asked in a soft voice, "Have you stopped loving me?" Her question was met with silence. "Have you?" She demanded with more force.

"No, damn it." Agitation rang in his swift reply. Finally, he turned to her and she could see the anguish he was hiding in his eyes. "Sabryna, someone tried to kill you."

"I know. I was there."

"You don't understand. Someone tried to kill you because of me." His voice was softer, filled with guilt. "Someone wants you dead because of your connection to me. I can't allow that."

It seemed he made his own promise. "Neither can I. That's why we have to find this guy."

Marcus shook his head. "It's not that simple."

"We find him, put him behind bars and live the rest of our lives in peace."

"We haven't found him yet. We haven't even come close."

"It's been one day."

"This jerk didn't appear overnight. He's been in my life for seven years. And after all this time the only thing I know about him is that he's able to get around me, into my personal life and space, without anyone noticing him. He's smart and dangerous."

Frustrated, he began to pace. "He's been in my car, in my office, and even in my home. Hell, the security in this building is tight and there was even a police car stationed out front. But that didn't stop him. He's been waiting for the last seven years to make a move and now he has... against you. Somehow, he figured out the best way to hurt me is to hurt you. So now you're his target. I can think of one way to take you out of his sight."

"By breaking my heart?"

"By protecting you. If I, we, end things, he'll lose his motivation for coming after you. You weren't in danger before we got together."

"We've been together for weeks and nothing has happened." Sabryna was tempted to pace her own line of frustration across the tile.

"Yes, but now our picture is in the paper announcing our engagement. Boasting to all the world how happy and in love we are."

Sabryna's mind began to put the pieces of the puzzle together. "So, the stalker sees the picture and decides to get revenge on you by killing me."

"Exactly."

"And your best solution is to break things off so that he won't come after me." She didn't sound impressed.

Marcus gave a stiff nod.

"How can you be so sure that would work?"

"If he thinks you are no longer important to me he'll leave you alone," Marcus explained.

"So what do we do, announce our disengagement in the paper?" she asked with clear sarcasm. "Maybe we can throw in a tag line – 'Attention killer we are no longer in love. Your attempted murder has helped us to see that maybe we aren't right for each other."

"This isn't a joke, Sabryna."

"Trust me, I know," she shot back. "I realized the seriousness of the situation last night when I was struggling to breathe."

"Sabryna," Marcus infused patience into his tone. "I'm doing this to protect you. It's temporary. When we catch him then we can pick back up where we left off."

"And what if you never catch him?" Sabryna crossed her arms. "You said yourself it has been seven years and you haven't had a single clue. What if instead of working he just waits another seven years for something else to use against you. Then what?"

His silence was her answer.

"Then it's not so temporary, is it?" She didn't need verbal confirmation to know he already thought through that conclusion. He was prepared to sacrifice everything in the face of this stalker's threat. Even if it meant spending the rest of his life figuratively, if not literally, running from this psycho. "It won't work. It won't stop him. He has to be forced out. And the way to do that is to set a trap."

"With you as bait?" Marcus spit out the words as if they were foul.

"David said that last night was the first time they had any kind of lead on this guy. That was because now he feels he has a purpose. He can't hide and act at the same time. If he has a reason to come after me he will, and then we'll get him."

"I won't risk your life."

"It's not your choice."

"The hell it is," he growled. "It's my right to take care of you."

"Not if we're not together," she pointed out.

"Sabryna, please understand," Marcus pleaded. "I couldn't stand it if anything happened to you. I can't lose another person that I love."

The pain in his voice stabbed at her heart. "So that's what this is really all about."

"Of course, I'm trying to protect you," he agreed.

"No, you're trying to protect yourself," she contradicted.

"What the hell does that mean?"

"You're so afraid to be hurt that you don't want to take a chance that it might happen again. Better that you push me away before I can be taken from you." She wasn't just angry now. She felt almost…betrayed. "That is just what my father did to me. As soon as he got hurt and afraid, he pushed me away."

Marcus looked as if he'd just been slapped. "Don't ever compare me to your father."

"Why shouldn't I? Aren't you doing to me now what he did when my mother died? You're faced with a challenge you don't feel you can handle so the first thing you try to do is let me go and get rid of the potential for any future pain."

"I have my reasons," Marcus defended.

"He had his reasons to." It was Sabryna's turn to raise her voice.

"That's not fair. My intention is to protect you. His intentions were, still are to pretend you don't even exist."

"Were? Still are? What is it you're not telling me?" She demanded to know.

He hesitated and then, "I went to see your father."

Shocked, she sputtered. "What? When?" Then she realized. "When you were supposedly out of town on business." She gripped the counter for support.

"Yes," he confirmed. Marcus stopped pacing and looked her square in the eye. "You were so upset after that conversation. I thought if I talked to your father maybe I would understand why he is the way he is. Then I could help you make peace with it. Maybe I could even find some common ground between the two of you."

The sentiment was nice but, "Why didn't you tell me?"

"I didn't think you needed to know."

The words were enough to make her explode. "You didn't think I needed to know! He's my father. I have a right to know. You should've told me."

"Well I got a little distracted when somebody tried to murder you," he shot back.

The fight flowed out of her and she took a seat at the counter. Resting her head in her hands, she massaged her temples. After a moment she looked up at him. "Well, now you've seen for yourself just what my father thinks of me. And maybe you can understand just a little why I'm not jumping at the chance to be pushed away, even if it is for my own safety. When I was younger, I had no control over my life, no defense against a father who resented my very presence. He went from loving me to hating me and things have never been the same since." She locked her eyes with him. "I can't stop you from doing the same if that is what you're determined to do. But, I won't stick around this time waiting for my love to be returned."

"What are you saying?" Marcus asked.

"Either we face this challenge together or we end things...forever. Nothing in between and no going back."

CHAPTER TWENTY-FIVE

Sabryna's words crashed into Marcus. Did she have any idea what she was asking? What she was asking him to risk? Her life meant more to him than his own. He couldn't allow her to be in jeopardy and do nothing about it. But to save her he would have to risk losing her forever.

The vise locked around his chest clinched tighter.

He couldn't handle it that she was in danger. Especially since that danger was because of him. He hadn't slept. Preferred instead to hold her in his arms and watch over her. In his mind he hadn't been able to block out the images of her struggle to stay alive. If she had died, he would've gone insane. He hadn't realized what loving someone meant. Even now the emotions rocking him were more than he could handle. He would be a liar to claim that he wasn't terrified, for her as well as for himself.

He stood in the middle of his kitchen and looked at the first woman he'd ever loved wait for him to tell her he was willing to risk her life. If he did he could lose her. If he didn't he would lose her. "You don't know what you're asking."

Sabryna didn't say a word, just watched him.

"My father died...because of me. Kari died...because of me."

Standing up, she walked over to him. "I won't argue the past with you, Marcus. What's done is done." She took his hand and put it over her heart. The warmth of her skin permeated through the shirt. "This is the present. And I'm here now, fighting for our future." She raised luminous brown eyes to meet his. "I can't do it alone."

Pulling her into his embrace, he rested his chin on the top of her head. Breathed in her sweet fragrance. "God help me." There was nothing more he could say in that moment and she seemed content to rest in his arms.

There was no telling how long they stood there, locked in each other's embrace. For just a moment he allowed himself to pretend there wasn't a killer out there trying to take her from him. He wished he could freeze time and keep her safe in his arms forever. He doubted she would agree to stay locked in his penthouse until this creep was caught.

But he couldn't deny the pound of truth in her words. There was no guarantee this psycho would leave her alone if they ended things. He might see right through the ploy and still come after her. His plan might just make her an easier target. There was another option.

"Have you ever been to Europe?" he asked, his mind churning with ideas.

"No." Confusion rang in her tone.

"Would you like to go?"

"Sure, someday."

"How about tomorrow?"

"Tomorrow?"

"Yes," he replied. "My mother loves any excuse to go to Europe, I'm sure she'd be willing to go with you. You could shop for the wedding."

"And are you coming with us?" Sabryna asked through gritted teeth.

"No, I have too much work to do here."

"And a killer to catch," she added, pulling out of his embrace. "It won't work. He'll just wait till I get back." She searched, suspicion etched her face. "Or were you thinking I would go away until he was caught?"

He stayed silent, sensed that was the safest bet.

She stood there staring at him for a few seconds and then turned on her heel and walked out of the room.

"Where are you going?" he called after her.

"I'm leaving."

"What the hell do you mean you're leaving?" he demanded to know following her into the bedroom where she was throwing clothes back into her overnight bag. "What happened to us doing this together?"

"Is this your idea of together?" she snapped at him. "I go to a foreign country for God knows how long while you search for a stalker."

"We'd still be together."

Sabryna looked at him, an incredulous expression graced her face. "How can we be together a million miles apart?"

"It's more like twenty-five hundred miles."

She glared at him. "Don't be smart about it."

"Damn it, Sabryna," he shouted. "I'm handling this the only way I know how. I love you. You know how much I love you. And yet you treat me like a jerk for wanting to protect you."

Sabryna dropped the jeans she was holding into her bag and sat down on the bed. He was right. She was being unreasonable. "I'm sorry. I know this isn't easy for you."

Marcus walked over and sat next to her. "So, you'll go to Europe."

"No." Sabryna felt him tense up beside her. "I have a job. I can't just leave the center for an indefinite amount of time."

"I think Grant would understand."

"Grant might help me pack," she agreed. "But, it doesn't change the fact that I'm not allowing some psycho to chase me away from my life. The kids depend on me to be there. Can you understand how important that is to me?"

Reaching over, he enclosed her hand with his own. "Do you understand how important you are to me?"

She kissed his cheek. "I do."

Roughly, he pulled her onto his lap. Hard brown eyes stared into hers. "If anything happens to you…"

"It won't." She cut him off with her words and a kiss, one that went from tender to passionate. She pulled back until there was the barest amount of space between their lips. "You won't let it. Between you, David, and the police, I'll be safe enough."

The arm around her waist tightened to an almost painful degree. "I'm willing to play the game your way, but don't doubt that I'll do whatever I have to do to protect you."

"I know you will," she assured him and continued kissing him. His hands roamed over body possessive, aggressive. Everywhere he touched a fire lit to life inside of her. She spread her kisses to his neck, nipped.

In an instant, he shifted and threw her back on the bed. He made quick work of his clothes, and sensing his urgency she did the same with hers. She had the last item off in the same second he covered her naked skin with his. Kissing her, touching her, freeing her soul and claiming her body all at the same time. He was not the tender companion who awakened her passions slowly. He was her rough, seductive lover, who demanded and gave with equal strength, who branded her body, heart, and soul. The man who loved her with a tender aggressiveness that caused her toes to curl.

She had once called him Sin.

That word seemed too tame when he entered her so deep she felt he pierced her heart. Too simple, when every thrust threatened to erupt in her a tide of pleasure. She couldn't get enough of him, get close enough to him. She wrapped her legs around his waist and arched her pelvis up wanting to take more of him inside of her and he responded with a deep surge into her body. They were both mindless in their need to please the other. For the first time, his climax came before hers, and she knew he'd lost all control. He continued to rock in her, wanting to spill every ounce of seed into her body, and she gripped her thighs closed holding him there, allowing her own climax to send her soaring over the edge.

"First thing we need to do is make a list of anyone who might want to hurt you." Sabryna looked at Marcus from her position on the floor, a notebook in one hand and a pen in the other.

Sitting not to far away on the sofa, Marcus eyed the notebook. "Do you think you're going to need that much paper?"

She shrugged with mock innocence. "Do you think I need more?"

He tossed a pillow at her head. Laughing, she ducked it. "This is serious."

He leaned back on the couch and stared up at the ceiling. "This isn't how I want to spend my evening."

"And how do you want to spend your evening?"

"Take off your clothes and I'll tell you."

It was her turn to toss the pillow at him. He caught it but didn't lose his devilish smile. They already spent most of the afternoon making love and sleeping. They were both still tired from the night before. They roused about an hour ago and ordered Chinese food. Eating in the living room, in front of the big bay window, watching as the rain started to pour down outside, creating a feeling of safety and seclusion from the outside world. In unspoken agreement they both decided not to discuss her would be killer while they ate, but as soon as they finished Sabryna jumped up to retrieve her notebook. It was time to take action.

"You think of names and I'll write them down." She stared at him.

He noted her focused expression, and let out a resigned sigh. "That is the very same question David always has. The truth is I can't think of anyone." When she raised a challenging eyebrow he continued, "I'm not claiming to have been an angel all my life. I'm sure I've pissed off tons of people. But, I can't think of anything that would cause someone to seek revenge."

"Well, there must have been something," she responded. "Maybe something that doesn't seem like a big deal to you but to someone else was a matter of life and death, literally."

"So I have to think of every petty event that ever happened in my life?" The task seemed insurmountable.

"No, just the ones that you feel might've been more than petty to someone else."

He groaned. "There's got to be an easier way."

Sabryna folded her legs under her. "Well, let's look at what we already know. We know that the event happened prior to seven years ago, before the first card. We know that whoever it is has a serious grudge against you they want to take out on someone close to you."

He shook his head. "They want to hurt someone I love."

She thought then shook her head. "No, it's not as simple as that. Most people who know you know you come from a close family. If they wanted to hurt someone you love they could've done it way before now."

He followed her train of thought. "Instead they waited until I was in love with someone." He looked at her. "Which didn't happen until now."

She smiled at that. "So I become the target. And the killer knows where I live. Which means in all likelihood he's someone close to you."

"Or someone whose been watching me. Watching us."

Sabryna shivered. "I wish we had those cards then I could look through them and see if anything pops out."

"David said he'll bring them by in the morning," he reminded her. "But, don't expect too much. They aren't very revealing."

She stood up and stretched. Marcus's arousal stirred to life as he admired the sensual shape of her body. "And that's why we have to read in between the lines." She walked over and sat cross-legged on the couch near him. "I have a thought."

He looked at her and waited.

She hesitated, biting her lip. "You said before that when you were in college you…used a lot of women. That you told them things that you didn't feel but knew they wanted to hear. Well…"

"Hell hath no fury like a woman scorned," he quoted.

"Exactly."

For a second he delved into his memory. Then he shook his head. "Doesn't fit. We know it's a man."

She looked disappointed. "I had a feeling that was too easy." Her expression perked up. "Maybe she hired someone."

"Let's not make this more complicated than it already is." Last thing he wanted to do was recite a list of his former lovers for her. "Besides, I don't think they'd wait seven years for revenge only to hire someone else to do it."

"Maybe, it's the boyfriend or husband of someone you used," she suggested.

He laughed. "I'm not sure I like your opinion of me. But I've never been interested in other men's women. If she belonged to someone else, and I knew it, I left her alone."

"Okay, then we're back to people, men, who have a reason not to like you."

He flashed a crooked smile. "I can think of one. Steven Barclay."

Sabryna's pen froze mid air. "Steven!"

The look he shot her was all innocence. "Well, he doesn't like me."

"Yeah, but that's no secret. You don't like him and he doesn't like you. That doesn't make him a killer. Besides, he's my friend. He wouldn't try to kill me."

"It's my list of enemies not yours."

"You're just being childish."

"Maybe." He snatched the pen and paper from her and jotting down his name. "But we need to consider all potential suspects. Besides, he does have an unstable personality."

Sabryna burst out laughing. "He does not."

"And he's not very nice."

A sly grin wreathed her face. "He is to me."

Marcus wasn't happy to hear that. "Now he definitely stays on the list."

She giggled. "Could it be anyone out to get you for breaking down your father's company?"

He gave that serious thought. "I thought about that, but I don't think so. His associates were upset, but they knew I could do far more damage if I chose to go public." He shifted so he faced her. "Keep in mind that it's been so long I'm sure they're all rich old farts by now. Even if they had a motive I doubt they would have the energy."

Sabryna didn't look convinced. "I wouldn't be so quick to discredit people with a motive that they feel is powerful enough."

"True. But, this person is targeting me. My father's associates wouldn't know that no one else in my family is involved."

"I wouldn't count on that," she replied. "I knew your family for a short time and got the impression that they didn't know. It would be a simple thing to deduce."

He was quiet, staring pensive out of the window. "I prefer not to have to expose that unless I must."

She reached for his hand, gave it a gentle squeeze. "I understand."

Marcus looked down at their hands and then raised his eyes to meet hers. "I want you to know the secret about my father isn't more important to me than your safety. Nothing is. If I have to expose it to protect you, then I will."

Shaking her head, she replied, "I don't want you to worry about that. I'm going to be your wife, which means this isn't your secret alone anymore. It's for both of us to protect our family."

Smiling he pulled her closer to him and placed a kiss on her lips. "For someone who claims to have never been part of a family before you sure have this down."

She lifted her shoulders in a light shrug. "I've been learning from a natural."

He kissed her deeply and they both knew there would be no more talk of secrets, revenge, and killers that night.

CHAPTER
TWENTY-SIX

"I didn't know she was coming she just showed up," Sabryna explained into the phone as she watched Madelyn in the center.

"What the hell is she doing there?" Marcus's grumbled on the other line.

Sabryna looked out the window of her office at her future sister-in-law who was talking to a few of the younger girls. "Remember she asked if she could volunteer here? She wants to beef up her resume for her college applications. I told her anytime, but I didn't realize she would just pop up."

"Well, tell her now is not a good time. Hell, I don't even want you there today."

Sabryna was glad Marcus couldn't see her rolling her eyes. That morning she woke up and announced she was going to work. Marcus reacted as if she suggested she was going mountain climbing without a rope. He pointed out she was the target of a killer and she pointed out that she had a job and people depending on her.

"Marcus, it's Monday," she had attempted to reason. "I have tons of work piled up and for that matter I'm going a little stir crazy." They hadn't left his penthouse for days. She hadn't been back to her own place since the night of her attack. She and Marcus had a brief talk about going back there this weekend to pick up some more of her clothes. They both agreed she should stay with Marcus until the stalker was caught. Besides, the security was better at his penthouse.

"Grant will understand."

"It's not Grant I'm concerned about. Besides, I'm sure you need to get some work done also." It was a low blow, playing on his responsibility to his company, but it worked. He gave his grudging agreement to let her go as long as she promised to go straight there and back. The center was safe, there was always someone around her.

So, she returned to work that morning, feeling as though she was reclaiming yet another piece of her life. After an interrogation from Grant, an hour spent reassuring Lena, and few moments attempting to evade Damon's questions about where she'd been, things were starting to seem normal again. An uneventful day was what she needed.

And then Madelyn walked in, a bright smile on her face.

She'd spoken to Sabryna before about assisting at the center, perhaps helping out with homework. Sabryna, happy for any help, agreed.

When Madelyn sailed in she had been pleased to see her. Madelyn was fast becoming one of her favorite people. Then reality hit. There was psycho stalker out there waiting for his perfect opportunity to strike. It was one thing for her to take a risk, she was involved. But, Madelyn was young, she needed to be protected. However, Madelyn's enthusiastic personality had bubbled over in excitement at being there and Sabryna found herself being swept away on the tide. Besides, she reasoned that Madelyn was as safe as she with being there.

"Marcus, I'm not going to kick your sister out," she returned into the phone. "There's nothing wrong with her being here and we could use the help. You should've seen how excited she was and the younger girls are fascinated by her."

Marcus's resigned sigh came clear through the other end. "How did she get there?"

"She said that your mother's driver dropped her off."

"How long is she planning to stay?"

"I'm not sure. But she's surrounded by people, as am I. What could happen?" Sabryna questioned.

"You say that now. But wherever my sister goes drama tends to follow," Marcus grumbled. "Please keep an eye on her."

"She's sixteen, not seven." Sabryna looked out her office window again and noted Madelyn still standing there talking to some of the girls. Madelyn glanced up and waved at her. Sabryna waved back. "Don't worry, I'm counting on an uneventful afternoon."

"Who's that girl?"

Sabryna looked up at Damon standing in the doorway of the room she was setting up for group. His voice sounded...hostile. She took in his posture, stiff. His expression was stormy as he stood there, arms crossed, and waited for her to answer.

She shot him a look of innocent confusion. "Which girl?"

"That girl. Upstairs in the red. The one helping Latisha and Shondra with their homework." He didn't bother to hide his impatience.

Sabryna turned away so that Damon wouldn't see her smile. "Oh, that's Madelyn."

"Madelyn?"

"Yes, she's my future sister-in-law."

"She is?" Damon sounded like he was choking on the words.

Sabryna turned back around to face him. "Yes, she is. Why, is there a problem?"

"No." Damon said a little too quick. He continued in a more casual manner, "Is she gonna be here long?"

"From time to time. She's a new volunteer." Sabryna turned away to greet the kids who were starting to come in for their anger management group. "Are you going to sit in?"

Damon straightened away from the doorway. "Uh, no. I think I better help out in the homework room upstairs. Just in case there's too many kids."

Sabryna fought to contain her smile. "If you think that's best."

Damon's nod was curt, then he left.

As Sabryna rode home that night, she allowed her mind to roam. It had been an exhausting day, but after Sabryna's unscheduled time off it felt good to be exhausted. She got off work later than expected and discovered Madelyn needed a ride home. Marcus had already called a dozen times. She was sure he would have shown up at the center if he hadn't been working late also. His work had gotten backed up. He wasn't thrilled to hear she was driving Madelyn home, but after all her help that day, Sabryna didn't have the heart to tell her no.

When they arrived at Madelyn's, Marcus's mom had wanted to talk about details for the wedding. She was a little upset they hadn't already set a date. She couldn't tell her they were occupied with trying to keep her alive, so she promised that she would get right on it. As she drove down an all but empty highway she daydreamed about being a June bride. She was so locked in these pleasant thoughts that she didn't notice that another car was driving along beside her on the right.

Until the car swerved to the left, swiped her side, and sent her almost flying off the road.

Panic raced through Sabryna with an alarming jolt that brought her crashing back to the present. She gripped the wheel with both hands and turned to straighten herself back out. Managing to stay on the road, she adjusted her speed to a slower pace to let the car that hit her drive past. They had to be drunk, she thought, or not paying attention.

She glanced over at the other car. It was black with tinted windows. She couldn't see inside, but she could tell that the car was also slowing down to match her speed.

For a moment confusion reined. She sped up and the car sped up also. She was about to reach for her cell phone, when the other car once again slammed into her side.

She just managed not to scream, concentrating on staying on the road. Her cell phone went sliding off the seat and landed on the floor. Reality sank in. The person in the car wasn't drunk. They were determined to run her off the road.

The stalker was attempting to kill her. Again.

Both cars slowed as they rounded a curve. Sabryna's mind raced with possible solutions. She knew she wouldn't be able to reach her cell phone and keep control of her car. She considered braking, but that would just make her a sitting target. Better she remained on the road until they drove into more populated areas. Then she could pull over and get help.

Her car was rammed again. She screamed and went spinning out. Her head rocked from side to side and she slammed on the brakes, attempting to stop the vehicle. However, it was no longer in her control. The car went sailing into a ditch off the side of the road.

CHAPTER TWENTY-SEVEN

Sabryna didn't lose consciousness, but for a few moments she was dazed. She was still strapped in the seat belt. She looked to her left and realized her car had lodged itself against a tree. A few of the branches were sticking through her broken passenger side window. Her right side seemed clear, even the window was intact. She needed to get out of the car, but for a moment, she just listened. When she didn't hear any sounds she assumed that her killer had driven off. Probably assuming he'd accomplished his goal. But, she couldn't be too sure. She would need to get out as quick as possible and find her cell phone so she could call the police.

Bracing one hand on the ceiling, to protect her head, she undid her seatbelt with the other. She fumbled around as much as she could reach searching for her cell phone, but to no avail. Deciding it might be easier to look for from outside the car, she reached for the door.

And saw the smoke rising up from her engine, filling the inside of her car. Any second now her car was going to go up in flames.

Coughing, she popped the lock and attempted to open the door. It didn't budge. She smacked at it, frantic. The air in the car thickened with smoke. In wild urgency, she pushed against the door with both hands, putting all her energy into it. That failed.

Please God, she prayed, don't let me die trapped in this car. Fear and terror engulfed her. As the smoke inside the car became thicker, tears smarted her eyes and her vision started to blur.

She reached down and beat on the glass attempting to break it. She was more than willing to cut up her hand if it meant saving her life.

"Move away from the glass."

Shocked to hear a voice, Sabryna looked out and saw a pair of black men's leather shoes. Her panic reached new heights. So, the killer hadn't driven off after all. Instead, he returned to make sure he finished her off.

"Move away from the window," the voice yelled again. It was a strong male voice.

"No!" she yelled back. She wasn't going to make this easy.

The killer dropped peered through the window. She had a clear picture of him, a black male, with a bald head and large forehead. Her heart almost stopped when she saw the cold look in his eyes.

"I'm trying to help you," he said to her.

"Like hell you are," she retorted. Anxious, she looked around for anything she could use as a weapon.

"Marcus sent me," the stranger called out.

"Sent?" Confusion mixed with mistrust.

"I'll explain later. Right now you need to trust me. This car is going to explode. Now move away from the door so I can get you out."

If he was lying, he'd kill her when he got her out. But if she stayed in the car, she would die. She had a better chance of surviving if she let him help her and then ran like hell.

"Okay," she called out. Backing up, she covered her head. A few seconds later the glass shattered and rough hands reached in and yanked her out of the car.

When the chimes on the clock signaled ten, Marcus picked up his phone and once again dialed Sabryna's cell. He slammed the phone down when it went straight to voice mail. No sense leaving a tenth message. Where the hell was she and why was her phone off? Alone in his kitchen, Marcus told himself that everything was okay. However, his shoulders were tense and there was a mild sinking feeling in the pit of his gut. Something wasn't right.

He looked up when he heard his front door slam. Please God let it be Sabryna, he thought.

"Have you heard from her yet?" David asked as he rounded the corner into the kitchen.

Marcus shook his head. "I was hoping you were her." He'd already made some calls to get answers. David had been one of those.

David's cell phone rang. He flipped it open. "Cortland."

Marcus studied his brother's expression waiting for any sign that something was wrong.

David glanced up at his brother, then spoke into the phone. "Where?"

Marcus's heart constricted. He stopped breathing.

"Call me as soon as you know more," David instructed into the phone. He flipped it closed and looked back at Marcus. His face was blank. "Jeff got a report of an accident on 95. A car was on fire. He went to investigate."

"Is it Sabryna's?"

David opened his mouth to speak when the sound of the door slamming shut caught their attention. They both froze and looked up.

"Marcus, where are you?" she demanded in clipped tones. There was no mistaking the sound. Both brothers breathed a sigh of relief.

Sabryna came striding into the kitchen, hair disarrayed, khaki's stained, shirt torn and a fire burning in her eyes. She stopped as soon as she saw them. "I'm going to kill you."

Marcus reached her in a second and pulled her into his arms. Squeezed her so tight she coughed. "Thank God, you're okay."

Sabryna maneuvered her hands between them and pushed against his chest. "Let me go. I haven't decided yet if I want to scream, kiss you, or kill you."

"I thought you voted on killing him," David offered, a teasing light in his eyes.

Marcus ignored her pushing. "What the hell happened?"

"I'll tell you what the hell happened," Sabryna yelled. "You're once again making decisions and trying to run my life without me." She used all the extra strength she had to push against his chest. He released her.

"Was that your car they found?" Marcus moved to pull her back into his arms.

Sabryna walked further into the kitchen, tossing her purse on the counter. She turned back around to look at Marcus, found he was just two inches behind her, and bumped into him. "First you have some explaining to do." She poked him in the chest.

"Me?" Marcus's shock was evident.

"Yes, you. You're the one who keeps trying to run the show. You're the one who keeps forgetting I'm your partner, not your employee." No matter how happy she was to be alive he was not going to get away with this one. She looked toward the door and sighted the source of her frustrations.

"Sabryna, what the hell are you talking about?" Marcus demanded.

"I'm talking about him." She pointed at the large silent man leaning against the door frame. He was shorter but stockier than both brothers. His muscular chest attested to many days at the gym. He was dressed in all black, and with the scowl that seemed a permanent fixture on his face, he looked more like Satan's bodyguard. "My watchdog."

"The bodyguard you hired." David's voice rang with recognition. He went over to greet Cole.

"You told your brother but you didn't tell me." Outraged, Sabryna didn't wait for an answer. She turned on her heel and left the room. She had no clear destination in mind. Her sole goal was to get away from the infuriating man that thought nothing of making decisions without her. Finding herself in the master bathroom, she slammed the door, locked it, and fell back against it. She took a deep breath and then let the terror of the night wash over her. Shivers raced down her spine.

"Sabryna open the door," Marcus ordered from the other side.

"No."

"Sabryna…"

"Who's Cole?" she interrupted.

"Didn't he tell you?"

Sabryna attempted to keep her temper in check. She gritted her teeth. "I want to hear it from you. As I should've before."

There was a moment of silence and then, "He's an old friend. I called him a couple of days ago and he agreed to help."

"You mean he agreed to watch me." Sabryna turned her head toward the door so he could hear the anger in her tone. "And were you going to tell me?" When silence met her questions she added, "Now is the time to speak up."

She heard him take a deep breath. "I was hoping you wouldn't find out."

"Like when you visited my father," Sabryna accused. Was this foreshadowing for their future? Every time there was a problem, would Marcus solve it how he saw fit without consulting her? Would she be his partner or his dependant? Or, would he be like her father, decide what was best for everyone. She wouldn't live that way. What if one day he decided it wasn't in their best interest for them to be together. Hadn't he already tried something similar?

"This isn't the same situation." His voice cut through her thoughts. "I didn't know how you would feel about someone looking after you. So I called in someone I could trust."

"I don't need a bodyguard."

"You needed one today," Marcus asserted. "David and I talked about it and…"

"It should've been me and you talking about it," Sabryna interrupted.

"Sabryna, please open the door." His tone held a note of pleading.

She didn't care. "Marcus I want to be alone."

"And I want to know what happened tonight," he shot back, in unconcealed anger.

Enough was enough. Sabryna stood up and flung open the door. She and Marcus stood almost toe to toe. "I'll tell you what happened," she snapped. "The psycho that you failed to tell me about attempted to run my car off the road. I spun out and got caught inside. Luckily, the watchdog, that you failed to tell me about, was working hard. He rescued me. Well, actually, he rescued me and then I tried to run away from him, so he had to tackle me. Then I scratched him a few times, which didn't seem to bother him at all. But he did have to use more than two words to explain himself, which did bother him. I don't think he enjoys talking. But anyway, it took him forever to convince me he wasn't there to kill me. I was positive that the man I trusted wouldn't go behind my back after he had promised that we would fight this as a team." She pushed past him and stomped into the bedroom. "Yet, every time I turn around you're either trying to push me away, lock me away, or send me away. And now I find out this guy has been hired to dog my every step. A fact that might not bother me so much, considering someone is trying to kill me, if I'd known about it." By the time she finished her rambling tirade she was shouting at the top of her lungs.

Marcus folded his arms across his chest. "I'm sorry."

"I'm sorry. That's all you have to say?"

"Sabryna, what more do you want from me?" It was his turn to let his frustration vent. "There is someone trying to kill you. Because of me. Doesn't it make sense that I would want to protect you?"

She sat on the edge of the bed. "Protect me, yes. Treat me like a child, no. I'm a grown woman. Why can't you understand that?"

He stopped his pacing and looked over at her. "I love you. More than I've ever loved anything or anyone in my life. Nothing means more to me than your happiness and safety. And here you are in danger and everything that I do to try to keep you safe you read it as me pushing you out of my life. The thought of anything happening to you causes something ugly to churn in my gut. I have to do everything I can to protect you. Why can't you understand that?"

All of a sudden, she felt like a spoiled child. What was wrong with her? He wasn't trying to alienate her like her father had done. He was trying to protect her so that they could enjoy a life together. Maybe, if she was more understanding he wouldn't feel the need to go behind her back and act. She walked over to him and took hold of his hand. "I do understand."

Marcus looked down at their joint hands then back at her. He reached up and brushed back her hair. "I should've told you about Cole."

"Yes, you should've," Sabryna agreed. "I know I haven't made it easy for you."

That earned her smile. "You're right about that."

"But, if I'm going to be your wife, I need you to treat me as your partner." Sabryna's eyes locked on his. "You don't get to decide what is best for us both. We do that together."

Reluctantly, he nodded.

"Promise me," she prodded.

He leaned down and placed a soft kiss on her lips. "I've spent most of my adult life making all the decisions. It won't be easy. But, I promise to try."

She hugged him tight. "Don't worry, when you overstep I'll let you know."

He laughed. "I don't doubt it." He pulled back from her so that he could see her face. "Are you sure you're okay."

She nodded. "I am now."

"Where are we going?" Sitting in the passenger seat of her car, Sabryna peered out at the passing buildings. "We missed the turn to Marcus's."

"I know." Cole continued driving and said nothing more.

"Are you going to tell me where we're going," she prompted. It was dark outside but the illuminations of the street lights were casting a bright glow over the city streets. It had been a long day of work and she was tired and anxious to get home.

Cole took the car around another turn and said nothing. Realizing he wasn't going to answer, Sabryna wondered if she should start to worry. She knew Marcus trusted Cole but she had only known him for a short time. She decided to ask. "Are you taking me somewhere to kill me?"

"No."

"Good," She remarked stifling a yawn. "Because I'm too tired to fight you."

For a moment, the corner of his lips appeared to be lifting upward, but when Sabryna blinked they were in their usual straight line. Great, she thought, now I'm so tired I'm hallucinating. Her bodyguard was an interesting person. He never smiled, or initiated a conversation. When she did attempt to speak to him he was short and abrupt with his answers. At times she teased him just to see if she could get a response, but it never worked. Other times she forgot he was there. Until he stepped out to block an action he didn't approve of as safe. But despite his lack of a social IQ, she felt safe. He was super vigilant when it came to his job and for that she was appreciative.

The car pulled up in front of the Grand Regency Hotel. A valet hurried to open the door for her. Cole was already out of the car and around to her side before she took a single step. He tossed the keys to the valet.

Sabryna stared up at the large hotel. Then she turned back to Cole. "If I ask you why we're here do I have any chance of getting an answer?"

"Let's go." He gestured for her to proceed him.

"I guess not," Sabryna mumbled. Cole ushered her through the elegant lobby to the elevators. He punched in a button and they went up to the top floor. When the doors opened he led her down a short hallway. There were two doors on this floor. Both on either side of the elevator. He led her to the one on the right. Reaching around her he opened the door and with a tiny push to her back, sent her in. She turned back around to protest his behavior, but found him shutting the door in her face. She couldn't believe her bodyguard had just left her alone in a strange room. Maybe she did have reason to be concerned. Not sure what she was going to find she turned back around.

CHAPTER
TWENTY-EIGHT

Sabryna eyes scanned the large suite. To her right, a beautiful dining table with seating for twelve rested under a glittering chandelier. She spotted a kitchen area just beyond. Spread before her, a spacious living room area, appointed with comfortable looking couches and chairs in a soft sky blue color. Beyond the living room, a door to a bedroom stood open. At every end of the room were large windows boasting breathtaking views. The only illumination came from the soft glow of candles upon every surface.

Sabryna stepped into the room, a smile of wonder beginning to inch its way across her face. The soft sounds of jazz music pumped onto the scene. Startled, she froze in her tracks, searching for the source.

"Looking for me?" A low voice asked.

Sabryna's head twisted toward the bedroom door. Marcus leaned against the frame, looking handsome, dressed in a dark blue suit which fitted his muscular frame to perfection. His tie hung loose around his neck, a bottle of wine dangled in one hand and two glasses in the other.

"You planned this," she accused, but pleasure rang in her tone.

He raised an eyebrow. "What was your first clue?"

Sabryna shook her head. "I can't believe you did all this."

"I thought you could use a little change of scenery." Marcus's eyes continued to watch her. "Do you like it?"

When he stood there staring at her like he wanted to lick the skin off her body she liked everything. "My regret is that you didn't tell me. I feel somewhat under-dressed for the occasion." She motioned down at her jeans and green V-neck cotton shirt.

Marcus pushed away from the door and came toward her. Circling her until he stood behind her. His chest hard against her back. She leaned into the feel of his solid body surrounding her. He lowered his lips to her ear and she shivered with delight as his breath fanned her neck.

"For this occasion you're extremely overdressed." He extended his arms past her and poured wine into both glasses.

"I'm impressed," Sabryna quipped, eyeing his maneuver. She accepted one of the glasses and then turned to face him.

He took a sip from his glass. "Baby, you ain't seen nothin' yet."

Her laugher rang out in the room.

Marcus couldn't help but smile when she laughed. He remembered how it had first caught his attention. How the sound of her joy made his heart thump with wild abandon. In the past few days, he hadn't heard it enough. They'd been so caught up in tracking down psychos and dodging murder attempts. No time to appreciate what her presence in his life meant. Or to show her that having her by his side had made his world right, whole.

For tonight, that was his sole purpose.

Sitting the bottle of wine down on the nearest table, he took her hand. Without any words, led her into the bedroom. This room was also illuminated by a multitude of candles. He'd lit each one himself, wanting to create a scene worthy of an Angel. Worthy of his Angel. With each candle he lit, he contemplated how gorgeous her naked skin would look in its soft glow.

Sabryna's breath caught in her throat when she caught sight of the large sleigh bed in the center of the room. The white coverlet generously sprinkled with pink rose petals.

Sabryna felt as though she were the main character in a fairytale. She noted the plate of chocolate covered strawberries lying on the night stand. The scent of rose petals hung heavy in the air but nothing blocked out the smell of the man standing beside her. His sandalwood cologne aroused her senses. She met his deep brown eyes. "Thank you."

Marcus turned and pulled her toward him at the same time. He didn't put his arms around her but she felt his presence wrapping around her like a sensual cloak. He bent his head and touched his lips to hers. "Thank you," he whispered.

Her lips curved upward. "I didn't do anything."

Marcus's bent low and scooped her up in his arms. He took a couple of steps and then laid her on the bed. He followed until he was leaning over her on his elbows. He looked down on her with an intense expression on his face. Then he dropped his head and placed a kiss on each eye. She closed them with a sigh. Marcus let one finger trace her lips. "Yes, you did," he said in the same whispered tone. "Yes, you did."

Sabryna locked the front door after she ushered the last child out of the center. She caught sight of the clock on the wall, 8:00 p.m. She promised herself tomorrow she would leave by 6:00. She had earned it. It had been a long day, but after Marcus's surprise last night she was still feeling satisfied in every pore of her body.

She looked over to where Cole sat on one of the couches in the common area. "I've some things to finish in my office but it should only take a half an hour. I think Damon might be upstairs, if he hasn't left. I'll call Marcus and let him know I'm going to be late."

Cole nodded.

Sabryna hadn't expected anything more. Not containing her smile at his predictable behavior, she went to her office and called Marcus. She didn't expect too much of a fuss because he'd told her earlier that he had some late meetings. She got his voice mail and left a quick message, then took a seat at her desk and got to work.

A loud thump emanated from upstairs.

Engrossed in her work, she wondered for a moment what Damon was doing upstairs. She should tell him to finish whatever it was tomorrow and go home.

Another thump filled the air. This one louder than the first. This time she glanced at her window expecting to see Cole move past to investigate. When no large image appeared she shrugged and turned her attention to the paperwork. If Cole didn't think it merited a check then neither would she. She just hoped Damon wasn't hurting himself. That thought gave her pause. What if he'd dropped something heavy and injured himself? What if he needed help but couldn't call out. She stood up from her desk. She wouldn't be able to concentrate until she knew he was okay. She almost reached her door when she heard a whiz, a pop and then the center was cast into blackness.

Startled, Sabryna froze, her hand on the knob. "Don't be stupid," she whispered to herself. "It's just a blackout. The backup generator should kick on any minute." She waited. Nothing happened. When she realized the generator wasn't going to come on, panic started to crawl up her spine. With slow precision, she cracked open her door. "Cole!" she called out in a loud whisper.

No answer.

"Cole!" This time her voice was louder. Still no answer. Alarmed, she shut the door and locked it. She moved as quick as she could in the dark over to her desk and picked up the phone to call for help. She wasn't sure yet if she needed it, but she wasn't going to wait around to find out. She lifted the headset and pushed the first button. Nothing.

She pushed the receiver button. Still nothing. There was no dial tone. She checked all the lines and got nothing on them either. The chance that the phone, electricity, and back up generators had gone out at the same time was slim to none.

And, it seemed so were her chances for surviving the night.

"Don't panic," she told herself even as her heartbeat sped up to an unnatural rhythm. I have a cell phone, she thought with relief. It didn't pick up reception in her office, but if she could get by a window she knew she would get a signal. She felt her way to the file cabinet. It was pitch black but her eyes were starting to adjust. Her hands gripped the handle of her top file drawer and she yanked it open, found her purse and fumbled inside for the cell phone. Then realization hit.

Her cell phone had gone up in flames inside her car. She hadn't replaced it. Her knees went weak and she sank to the floor. She was frozen with fear. But she knew now was not the time to let that emotion take over. She could do that much later from the safety of Marcus's arms.

God willing!

She needed a weapon. Something heavy or sharp. Reaching up, she opened her drawer and searched until she touched her letter opener. It wouldn't do much damage, but if used correctly it would serve its purpose. Summoning every vestige of strength and courage she possessed she rose to her feet, the letter opener gripped like a life line in her right hand.

On quiet feet, Sabryna walked to the door. Took a deep breath, unlocked it, and opened it a crack. She listened.

Quiet greeted her. Opening the door further she peered out. The room was draped in dark shadows, but it appeared empty. The moon provided a small amount of light. Sabryna stepped out, holding the letter opener out in front of her in defense. She waited. When nothing happened she felt her way over to the common area.

She found Cole lying facing down on the ground in front of the couch.

With a silent cry she dropped down beside him. Concern for him shot through her body. "Cole?" Putting her hands under his shoulders, she attempted to turn him over, but he was too heavy. She set her face next to his and tried to hear if he was breathing. She prayed to God that he still was. When she couldn't tell, she felt for a pulse, and found it beating strong and steady.

Thank you God, thank you God, thank you God. Now she just had to get them out of this alive. Reasoning that Cole would have a cell phone clipped to his belt, she attempted to reach under him and was grabbed from behind by a pair of rough hands that lifted her up and away from the body.

One arm held her tight around the waist, the other hand reached out and wrestled the letter opener from her grasp. Sabryna snapped. She knew from the way she was being handled, it wasn't a friend. She began kicking, and screaming like a wild woman, hitting any and every surface on her attacker's body she could locate.

"Aagh!" emanated from her attacker as her elbow connected with his jaw. She was released and didn't waste any time. She went running for the back of the center. There was a way out from there. The door stayed locked to entry from the outside but it wouldn't be chained until the night custodians came in at 10:00p.m.

Hearing heavy footsteps behind her, she increased her pace. She knew the layout of the center better than her attacker did, but she didn't want to trip over anything and slow down her progress. The door was a few feet in front of her. Reaching it, she pushed it open and ran into the night. Her eyes needed another moment to adjust to the change of darkness, but hearing the door open behind her, she knew she had to move with all speed. She went right, rounding the building. There was a fence around the yard area and the only way out was through the side gate on the right.

Sabryna pushed the gate open and broke into a full sprint. She rounded the last corner, her intention to run straight for the apartments across the street and bang on the first door.

Instead she ran straight into a hard male body. She screamed. Arms locked around her. "Sabyrna! It's me." The voice penetrated her terror and in overwhelming relief, she collapsed into Marcus's embrace.

His hold tightened. "What were you running from?" He pushed her back toward the safety of the front wall all the while scanning the shadows behind her.

She pushed out of his hold. "We have to get help, the killer is here. Cole…Damon…they're still inside. Cole's hurt. Damon….Oh my God, I don't even know." She looked behind her, scared her attacker would emerge from the shadows and kill them both.

Marcus pulled her close. Searched for any danger. The sounds of police sirens reached Sabryna's ears. She looked to the street and saw two patrol cars and one unmarked car pull up. Seeing them the cops come over, David and Jeff at the lead.

"Are you both okay?" David looked from one to the other.

"He was here. He might still be. Sabryna said Cole and a kid named

Damon are both inside. Cole is hurt," Marcus told them. His soothing hand massaged her back. She was still locked against his frame and it was then that she realized she was clinging to him like a child. She felt the tears stinging her cheeks.

"You two go stand by the patrol cars with Officer Murphy." David gestured toward one of the cops. "We need to secure the building."

Marcus nodded and led her away. An ambulance arrived a few minutes later and David and Jeff came out to report that Cole, although embarrassed about being knocked unconscious, was okay. There was no sign of Damon or the attacker. Sabryna called Damon's house on Marcus's cell phone and found that he was at home and had left work before the blackout.

"It seems he cut all the power and phone lines to the building," Jeff announced. "This bastard is crafty."

Sabryna shuddered. More police cars were now parked out front. She needed to call Grant, but she wasn't up for it at the moment. It wouldn't be long before a crowd gathered.

As if reading her mind Marcus said, "I'll have David call Grant. Let me get you home before the crowd gets here."

She didn't have the words or the heart to protest. They left.

There was blood everywhere. It was a familiar scene to Marcus. He stepped into the room, eyes trained on the body face down on the carpet. A red river of blood flowed from her head. The gun limp in her fingers. Her eyes were glazed over in eternal slumber. Terror and the helplessness gripped him, he cried out as he dropped to his knees beside her body. In slow motion, he reached and stroked her beautiful brown curls. When he pulled his hand back, it was covered in blood.

"Why?" he screamed.

"I think you know why," a light feminine voice sounded beside him.

Startled, Marcus looked up into Kari's bright green eyes. How was it that she stood next to him, looking ethereal and beautiful when he had seen her.

He looked back at the body slumped beside him and saw that it was Sabryna. "NO!" he screamed, gathering her up in his arms. "No, not her. Please, God, no."

Kari squatted down beside him and placed a hand on his shoulder. "Tsk. Tsk. You shouldn't act so surprised," she chastened him as if he was an errant child. "She loves you. Of course she had to die."

"No, I won't let her."

Kari laughed. "Oh, Marcus, it's too late. You can't stop it. You couldn't save me and you won't save her. Do you understand? She'll die because of you."

Marcus shot up in bed, his heart pounding. With trepidation, he looked to his left. Sabryna slept, peaceful, curled up beside him. His heart calmed just a little. It was a dream. No, it was a nightmare. One that he hadn't had since he and Sabryna had gotten back together.

On silent feet, Marcus left the bed and went to the bathroom to splash water on his face. He guessed it was a couple of hours until morning. For a moment, he stared at his reflection in the bathroom mirror. How was it that his life had gone from paradise to hell in such a short time?

And how was he going to bring himself to do what he knew must be done?

He pushed away from the sink and walked back into the dark room. He sat down on the edge of the bed and looked at his Angel. She rested on her right side, facing him. One hand lay under her head and another on the sheet where his body had been, as if she was seeking his warmth. He brushed a strand of hair out of her face. She looked so innocent and peaceful that for a moment he couldn't believe anyone would want to harm her. But the truth had been thrown in their faces three times now. It was time to take serious action.

Earlier when they returned to his place, Sabryna had been exhausted. And more shaken by this latest attempt on her life than he knew she was willing to admit. When David and Jeff got there, she could barely keep her eyes open. However, she kept it together long enough to give them the details of what had occurred. It had been enough to make Marcus want to scream out in rage. He had to protect her. No matter the cost.

Sabryna murmured something in her sleep. The lines between her brows furrowed and then once again relaxed into slumber.

Thank goodness there had been one question she hadn't thought to ask. He knew she might later think of it, but he hoped by then it wouldn't be necessary. She hadn't asked how he had ended up at the center at that time.

Marcus's fist clenched in the bedcovers just thinking of it.

It happened not long before he'd found her at the center. He was at his office finishing up his last meeting. He was anxious to get home to Sabryna, he didn't know she wasn't there yet. Most of his workers had already left for the night. Marcus's plan had been to check his email and then follow suit.

The box was waiting for him in his office chair.

He almost sat on it. It was a small plain white box. Thinking it was something Marie had left for him, he picked it up and began to open it as he logged into his email. Once his email started up, he reached into the box to retrieve its content.

And pulled out a handful of pink rose petals.

For a moment he just stared in confusion as the petals flitted from his fingers and fell to the floor. He stared at them and then at the box. Tipping the box over, the rest of the contents fell out. More pink rose petals and a small white card. Everything in him went cold. The rose petals sent more of a message than whatever could be in the card. They could have been the same petals that he'd lovingly sprinkled over their hotel bed the night before. It told him the psycho was close, he knew their every move, that Sabryna was never safe, not even with him. The card was the exclamation point on the statement:

As long as you love her; she'll never be safe.

I will take her from you.

Poetic justice has never been so sweet

He hadn't wasted time. While racing to the center, he called David and Jeff to meet him there. Once again, Sabryna's life was in danger. Once again, because of him. What he'd encountered at the center hadn't reassured him. No sooner had he stepped out of his car than Sabryna came tearing around the corner in blind terror.

The situation was getting out of control. So far the stalker had gotten past all of their defenses, proving locks, walls, guards, and even Marcus's presence was not going to stop him from getting to Sabryna.

Marcus had one choice. He couldn't allow her to be hurt. Not because of him. Not if there was still one thing he could do to stop it. She was his life. And he had to save hers.

Even if it meant sacrificing his own.

CHAPTER
TWENTY-NINE

Sabryna was just walking into the kitchen when Marcus placed the phone back on the receiver. She went straight to the coffee maker and poured herself a cup. Sabryna turned back around and leaned against the counter. "Was that David?"

Marcus's back was to her as he shoved files in his briefcase. "No."

Sabryna took a sip of her coffee. "Who was it?"

Cole came into the kitchen before Marcus could answer. He looked at Sabryna dressed in a pair of light gray crop pants and a pink sleeveless sweater. "Work?"

"Yep," Sabryna answered.

Cole looked at Marcus's back. "That's okay?"

Sabryna rolled her eyes. Marcus hadn't said anything to her this morning about not going to work, but then she hadn't bothered to discuss it with him. He'd already left the bed by the time she woke up.

Marcus turned to Cole. "You heard the lady."

Sabryna blinked in surprise. Marcus walked to the fridge and poured a cup of orange juice. She studied his face. Sensed a change in him. A difference that she couldn't quite put her finger on. He seemed stiff. Almost like he was just keeping himself from exploding. Sabryna decided to leave it alone. He had a right to feel wound tight after the events of last night. If he wasn't going to argue with her about leaving the penthouse then she wasn't going to make a fuss about his strange mood.

Cole grunted something that sounded like he would wait by the door and left the room. Sabryna walked over to Marcus and embraced him from behind. His muscles were rigid under his hands. She squeezed tighter and he relaxed.

"Last night was not your fault," Sabryna told him.

He sighed and turned, wrapped his arms around her. "It should've never happened."

"No, it shouldn't have," she agreed. "But it did and now it's over."

He bent and rested his chin on her head. "How can you be so

203

sanguine about this?"

Sabryna laughed. "I'm not. But I refuse to let this jerk take our lives from us."

Marcus set her away from him. His eyes bored into hers. "I won't let him get to you."

Sabryna searched his eyes. What was he trying to tell her? "I know that. I trust you."

Marcus pulled her tight up against him and seized her mouth in a soul devouring kiss. His tongue sank inside her mouth, not to play with hers, but to mark her, possess her. She kissed him back, with all the love and desire swirling in her soul, leaving her own mark. When he pulled away, their breaths were ragged.

"I better get to work." Sabryna stepped back. "I'll see you this afternoon. I'm going to leave at about six today."

Marcus followed as she headed for the door. "Sabryna," he called before she disappeared.

Sabryna looked her question.

"Why don't you meet me at the office? We'll have dinner at The Cascades."

Sabryna smiled, blew him a kiss. "I can't wait."

Marcus leaned back in his office chair and watched as dusk spread over the city. The sun created an orange glow that lingered on the rooftops and obscured the people on the street. Everything was the same color. For just a moment everything seemed so simple.

He turned back in his chair and the numbness settled back over him. Better that he couldn't feel for the ordeal ahead. When he found this psycho he was going to rip him limb from limb.

Marcus looked at his desk. He had accomplished nothing. His thoughts had been too bleak to concentrate on work. What he needed was a distraction.

As if on cue the intercom on his desk beeped. Marcus reached over and pushed the button. "Yes, Marie."

"Mr. Cortland, Miss Adrina Howell is here to see you." Marie didn't sound pleased.

"Send her in."

Marcus heard the hesitation. For a moment he thought Marie was going to drop her professional shield and ask, "Are you sure?" But then she stated, "Yes, sir."

It took five seconds for Adrina to walk through his door. From his seat, he eyed her. She was dressed to kill in a tight red mini skirt and matching jacket. Every alluring curve of her body was displayed to advantage. Her hair was pulled up in a stylish twist that accented her high cheek bones. He didn't have to look down to guess she was wearing a pair of heartbreaking red stilettos. The long lines of her legs said it all.

Marcus found his first smile. "Adrina, you always live up to expectations."

Adrina's answering smile was all cat that found the cream. And was planning to enjoy every delicious lick. Her slender fingers begin to unbutton her jacket revealing a lacy black brassier underneath. "I'm glad you noticed, and…" She walked to his desk, dropping her jacket on the floor. Adrina leaned over his desk on her elbows, revealing her deep cleavage. "I'm glad you called."

Sabryna watched as the numbers on the elevator panel flashed with each floor they passed on the way up to Marcus's office. Cole stood beside her, quiet as usual. There had been a brief moment of awkwardness when he apologized earlier. She knew he was horrified that he had been caught unaware and left her unprotected. Sabryna tried her best to reassure him. As a result, Cole had been super vigilant all day and even less inclined to talk. If that was even possible, Sabryna thought with a smile.

They reached their floor and stepped off the elevator. It was late, the floor was quiet and most of the lights were turned off. Marcus's office suite was still well lit and Sabryna headed in that direction.

Cole placed a restraining hand on her shoulder. Sabryna looked up at him. "Once you get in the office, I'm going down the hall to get a soda. Will you be okay?"

Sabryna placed her hand over her heart as if dying of shock. "Do you realize you just used a complete sentence?" she teased. "Are you okay?"

A scowl was her only response. Sabryna laughed and turned to head into the office. "I'll be fine." The understood rule was that whenever Sabryna was with Marcus, Cole could relax his guard. Sabryna waltzed through the double glass doors, noting Marie had already left. She headed toward Marcus's office. The door was ajar and she could see his light was on. More than likely he was bent over his desk absorbed in his work. Her lips rose upwards as she imagined getting him absorbed in her.

Sabryna pushed open the door and was halfway across the room before she realized Marcus wasn't alone.

He was already absorbed in someone else.

Sabryna froze. A sound of shock and distress emanated from her soul and alerted the other occupants of the room they had company.

Marcus looked up. He'd been bent over his desk. But he wasn't pouring over a report or tapping away at his computer. Instead, he was absorbed in the half naked woman lying on her back on his desk. Marcus's face buried in the crook of her neck.

Marcus stepped away from his desk. His expression was one of cautious resignation. "Sabryna, let me explain."

Sabryna barely heard the words through the buzzing in her brain. Her heart dropped to the ground, hitting every organ along the way. Nausea welled in her stomach. Her feet wouldn't move from the spot on the carpet. She waited for her eyes to adjust, to show her it was an illusion, to blink away this nightmare.

The half-naked woman sat up, unhurried as she re-hooked her bra. Sabryna recognized her as Adrina Howell. "I thought she was at work," Adrina spoke to Marcus. Her dismissive tone suggested she was irritated at the interruption, not ashamed. Other than fixing her bra, she didn't move from Marcus's desk.

The words Sabryna thought she would choke on came with vehemence. "What in the hell is going on?"

Marcus stepped around the desk and headed toward her. "Sabryna, I know what you're thinking."

"So you're also wondering how fast can I purchase a gun?" Sabryna shot at him.

"Sabryna, don't get dramatic," Marcus chastised.

"Dramatic!" Sabryna jabbed her finger at him. "I just walked in to find you sexing that slut on your desk and I'm not supposed to get dramatic. You must be crazy."

"There's no need for the insults," Adrina called out sarcastically.

Sabryna decided she would shoot her first. She turned on the witch, thinking she would claw her eyes out just to get warmed up. Then she checked herself. It was Marcus she needed to be angry with.

Marcus stepped closer to her. "Sabryna, calm down."

Sabryna held up a warning hand. "I swear to God if you tell me to calm down or not get dramatic one more time…"

"All right, All right," Marcus interrupted. "Let me explain."

"How can you explain that?" Sabryna pointed at the naked floozy on her fiancé's desk. "I trusted you. I believed in you. I loved you.

How could you do this to me?" She hated that her voice broke on the last question.

"Sabryna, this has nothing to do with us," Marcus explained in that firm voice that Sabryna was starting to hate. "It doesn't make me love you any less. I still want to marry you. But you have to understand, affairs are very common in our world. They don't mean anything, it's just helps add variety. When you understand that, you'll feel better about them."

Had Marcus morphed into a dinosaur, Sabryna could not have been more shocked. Was he telling her that he loved her, but that he would still engage in affairs? Did he expect her to play the perfect society wife and just roll over and accept it? She would sooner jump off the nearest building.

Sabryna shook her head, feeling the first rivulets of tears roll down her cheeks. Angry, she swiped them away. "After everything we've been through over the past few weeks, I can't believe you would jump into bed with the first slut ready to take off her clothes."

"Again with the insults," Adrina called out from the desk.

Marcus walked over and held her by the shoulders. "It's because of everything that's happened," Marcus told her. "I was feeling stressed out and I needed a distraction."

"Why didn't you call me?" Sabryna demanded, furious, beating on his chest as tears poured from her eyes. "I'm your fiancée. If you needed someone you should've called me."

Marcus looked into her eyes and said as if she were a slow-witted child, "Like I told you…variety."

Sabryna pushed away from him. Slid her ring off her finger and threw it at him. "Well you can take me off the menu." She turned, and ran from the room.

The tears were coming so fast she couldn't see where she was going. Somehow she made it to the elevator. She had no idea where she would go, but she had to get out of there. She stepped onto the elevator and punched the lobby button. As the doors slammed shut, she heard Cole calling out to her. Sabryna didn't care. She wanted to be far away from anything dealing with Marcus Cortland. Unbidden, the memory of the last time she'd fled his office after finding him in the office with a woman came to mind. That woman had been Adrina. Why hadn't she learned her lesson then? Why hadn't she seen that bastard for who he was? She was sure she would feel stupid when the overwhelming pain of watching her dreams crush wore off.

She stepped off the elevator and dashed across the lobby. She did think Marcus was following her this time, but she didn't want to take any chances. It wasn't until she got outside that she realized Cole had her car keys. *I'm not going back up there, I'll call a taxi.* She swung around to head back into the building and ran into a large male body.

She stifled her scream.

"Sabryna, it's me." Two large hands shot out to grip her by the shoulders, giving her a little shake.

Sabryna looked up into a familiar face. "Steven!" she exclaimed in relief. Steven was her friend, he would help her. "I'm so glad you're here."

"Sabryna, what's going on? Did something happen?" Steven stared at her.

Sabryna shook her head. It was too many questions and her head was spinning so fast. Any minute now Cole would come downstairs. "I need your help," Sabryna told him. "I need a ride to…." She had no idea where to go.

The grip on her shoulders increased until it was almost painful. "First, tell me. Did that bastard do something to hurt you?"

He ripped my heart out and squashed it like a bug. "Please, just get me out of here."

Steven looked at her for a second as if he could see it all in her eyes and then gave a decisive nod. "Come on, my car's right here."

He led her to the Jaguar sitting by the curb, ushered her in, then rounded the car and slid into the driver's seat. The engine revved up and Sabryna turned her head to glance back at the building. She noticed Cole tearing out of the building just as Steven pulled away.

"Where do you want me to take you?" Steven maneuvered the car into the traffic.

Sabryna stared unseeing out the window, her purse clutched like a life-line in her lap. At Steven's words, she turned to look at him. She hadn't been back to her place since the attack and she wasn't ready to spend the night there alone. She knew she could go to Lena's or Grant's but they would want to know what happened and she wasn't ready to deal with that just yet either. She turned back to look out the window. "I don't know."

Steven let out a deep sigh. "Okay." A long moment of silence passed in the car. "Why don't I just drive for a little while until we figure ~~out?"~~

~~yna~~ nodded. She looked down at her hands clutching her purse.

"Thank you."

Steven reached out and patted her knee. "That's what friends are for." The car revved forward as he took the exit for I-95.

With each mile that distanced her from Marcus, Sabryna felt the hole in her heart expand a little wider. Had the last few weeks of her life been one big lie? Did he love her? Had he ever loved her? Had she risked her heart and her life to be with a man who thought cheating was just another way to add variety to a relationship? She looked out into the night, hoping to find the answers in the shadows. Wondered why happiness always seemed just beyond her reach.

Sabryna glanced over at Steven. Quiet as he drove, not pressuring her to speak. She was lucky to have a friend like him. And lucky that he'd been where she needed him tonight. Her brows furrowed together in confusion. That had been a strange coincidence. "Steven, what were you doing outside of the Cortland building tonight?"

"Looking for damsels in distress to rescue, obviously."

Sabryna gave a self-deprecating laugh as she wiped the rest of the tears from her face with the back of her hand.

"Ah, a smile. That's much better," Steven murmured.

Sabryna opened up her purse to look for a tissue for her face. She wondered what he must think of her now. "Steven, I'm sorry to drag you into my mess."

"It's all right. I'm your friend." Steven glanced over at her. "At the risk of bringing you more pain, can I ask what happened tonight?"

Sabryna took a deep breath and then recounted what occurred when she walked into Marcus's office. The retelling of the story caused a fresh wave of tears to flow from her eyes and she once again dug through her purse to locate a tissue. "I feel like such an idiot."

Steven remained quiet through the retelling. His eyes still locked on the road. Both hands gripped the steering wheel. "I tried to warn you."

"I know. I wish I'd listened," Sabryna responded. "It's just that…I loved him…I still do. And I thought that he loved me. But how can he if he can be with another woman?"

Steven seemed to consider her words. His tone hesitant when he spoke. "Sabryna, I know it sounds strange, but chances are he does love you."

"Don't defend him," Sabryna warned.

"I'm not," Steven said with vehemence. "But he is right. Affairs are very normal in our world. Most people turn a blind eye to it."

Sabryna shot him a look of outrage. "Do you expect me to turn a blind eye to being played for a fool?"

"No, of course not. You're different." Steven smile was grim. "It's unfortunate Marcus couldn't appreciate how special you are and just leave you alone. I'm guessing he's back in his office trying to figure out how to get you back."

A tiny spark of hope ignited in Sabryna's heart. She gave herself a mental kick. She didn't want him back. "It would be a waste of time." She kept her face turned to the glass not wanting Steven to see the indecision in her eyes.

"I wish I could believe that." There was a strange note in Steven's voice that made her turn back to look him. She searched his face but it was expressionless.

"I told you what happened," she reminded him.

Steven nodded. "Yes, and you also told me before that nothing was going on between you and Marcus." Steven moved the car into an exit lane. "You lied."

Sabryna was surprised at his words. Why did he care what occurred between her and Marcus? He was taking the protective friend role a little too far. It was at that time that she noticed the car was in an exit lane. "Steven, where are we going?"

When he didn't answer, apprehension niggled down her spine.

"It doesn't matter what happened tonight." Steven ignored her question. This time the strange note in his voice was unmistakable. It sounded like resignation mixed with steel. "He loves you. To my knowledge you're the first woman he's ever loved. Everything in his behavior to you proves that. He treats you so different than all the others."

Sabryna wondered at Steven's words. She remembered he never explained how he came to be outside the Cortland building. Then she remembered what anger and distress caused her to forget. Someone was trying to kill her. But not Steven, she chastised herself, he's my friend. She looked out the window and noticed they were getting off on the exit for the Marina. "Steven, I want to go home." Sabryna struggled to keep her concern out of her voice. "I'm feeling better now."

Steven didn't look at her. "I can't take you home. Marcus might find you there."

"I…I'm okay with that. I…ca--can deal with him," she stuttered. That niggling of apprehension was now full blown suspicion.

Steven shook his head. "I can't allow that to happen. He can't have you. He loves you too much." Steven turned the car. "I have to take you from him."

Sabryna slipped her hands into her purse. "Steven, I don't know what's going on, but I would like for you to take me home." Inside her purse, Sabryna felt her cell phone clutched in her fingers. Thanked her stars that Cole had given her a replacement phone that morning. None of her numbers were programmed in it yet, but Cole's was. She knew all she had to do was hit send, and then send again, and it would go to him. She didn't dare risk taking it out of her purse, so she pushed the buttons to connect the call, praying it went through. She waited a few seconds, and then as loud as she could without causing suspicion, said, "Why are we going to the Marina?"

Steven looked over at her with hard, haunted eyes. It took Sabryna's breath away, fear lodged in her heart. "She loved the water. She would've wanted this."

Sabryna raised the phone closer to the top of her purse without removing it. "Who is she and what would she have wanted?" she asked. But God help her, she already knew.

Steven's lifted his lips upward. "Kari."

"Oh, God," Sabryna breathed. "It was you, wasn't it? All this time it was you."

Steven shrugged. "Guilty."

"Why would you try to kill me?" Sabryna asked. "We're friends?"

"Oh, Sabryna," Steven replied and in his voice Sabryna swore she heard regret. "This isn't about you. It was never about you. That's why I tried to stop you from getting involved. But you wouldn't listen and I've waited too long too allow anything to stop me. I like you Sabryna, I always have. But I loved her. And that bastard took her from me." He looked over at Sabryna, his eyes like shards of ice. "He took the woman I loved from me. And now I'm taking his. Which means, my dear, you have to die."

"Well, that was easy." Adrina hopped off Marcus's desk and slipped back into her brassiere. "Now that we've gotten ridden of the baggage, lets get dinner. I'm thinking Chinese."

Marcus stood rooted to the spot. The same spot from where he watched Sabryna, heartbroken and destroyed run out the door. He couldn't move. Couldn't think. Couldn't feel. "What have I done?"

"The right thing," Adrina answered. "You said so yourself. If she's as smart as you claim, she'll understand. Besides..."

Her words drifted past Marcus. Ice formed in every corner of his body. He clutched Sabryna's engagement ring in his hand. In his mind, he could see the look of shock, disgust, and anger that had washed over her features when she walked into his office. He could still picture the tears dropping from her eyes and breaking his heart. He hadn't hurt her, he'd devastated her. She would never forgive him.

But, at least she would be alive to hate him.

Adrina walked over and slid her hands up his chest interrupting his thoughts. "Well, now that that business is taken care of, why don't we…"

Her voice broke off as Marcus grasped her wrist in a gentle hold and pushed her away from him. "You knew what this is all about."

Adrina sighed. "You can't blame a girl for trying."

"No, I can't." Marcus turned his back on her and walked over to his desk. "Thank you, Adrina. The bra was a bit much, but thanks for coming through."

Adrina retrieved her jacket from the floor. "You said you wanted it to be believable." She shrugged into her jacket and looked back up at Marcus. "I'm glad you asked for my help. Surprised, but glad. Just remember, if ever you're interested in more than a fake make out session I'm…"

"-Adrina," Marcus's tone issued a warning.

Adrina laughed and headed for the door. "Marcus, I'm sorry about this stalker business. I hope you catch this guy before he can do any real damage."

Marcus had no words. Nothing was more real to him than this.

Adrina opened the door just as Cole burst through. "What the hell is going on?" He glared at Marcus, and then Adrina. "Why did Sabryna just run out of here?"

"What do you mean? Why aren't you with her?" Marcus demanded to know rushing over to Cole. "You're supposed to be with her."

"She jumped in someone's car before I could catch up with her." Cole looked his accusation at Adrina. "She was upset."

"Whose car did she get in? Where did she go?" Marcus asked.

"Do you think if I knew that I'd be standing here?" Cole ground out. "All I know is she wasn't going against her will. I don't know what the hell is going on, but I hope it's not what I think. That woman is dodging bullets for you and this better not be how you repay her."

Marcus walked to the center of the carpet and began pacing. "It's not what you think." Marcus explained how he decided the best course of action was for Sabryna to break things off with him so that the psycho would leave her alone. Since Sabryna was unwilling to do that, he staged a scene with the help of Adrina that would ensure that she did.

"You should've told me," Cole said when Marcus was finished. "I need to be prepared for anything."

Marcus dropped his head. How had he screwed things up so badly? "I'm sorry. I just thought of this last night. But it was what I had to do."

"Well, I hope you know what you're doing because now she's out there alone and unprotected," Cole informed him.

Marcus froze in his pacing. "Describe the person that she left with."

Cole gave a quick description of the car and the driver.

"Steven Barclay," Adrina shouted. Marcus forgot she was there. He and Cole stared at her with blank expressions. She flung her hands in exasperation. "He fits the description, and never misses a chance to show off his Jag."

Marcus sighed with relief. "It's okay. She's safe. He's her friend. But I want you to stick with her until we're sure this plan works."

"Do you think he'll take her home? If so --" Cole stopped talking when his phone rang. "It's her." He flipped it open. "Hello? Sabryna? Sabryna?"

Marcus stepped closer. Anxiety crept over him. He needed to know she was safe and the strange feeling inside of him wouldn't rest until he did. Cole had gone quiet and still. His eyes darted to Marcus. "What's going on? Is she okay?" Marcus demanded but Cole held up a finger for him to be quiet. Holding on to his patience was getting more difficult by the second. For long minutes, Cole listened without speaking. Marcus couldn't ignore the fear that was slithering up his body. Something wasn't right.

Cole moved the phone from his ear and looked at it. "Damn, it hung up." He called back and got no answer. He looked up at Marcus. "You're sure Barclay is her friend?"

"What's going on?"

"Well, if I heard correct, her friend is taking her to the Marina right now," Cole informed him. "To kill her."

CHAPTER THIRTY

Steven didn't bring out the gun until the car came to a stop at the Marina. "I never did show you my boat. I'm just sorry you have to see it in these circumstances." He pointed the gun in her face. "Make a sound and I kill you now instead of later."

Sabryna tried to keep her purse with her. She didn't know if her phone call was successful. However, as Steven pulled her from the car, her phone rang. Snatching the purse out of her hand, he flung it back inside the car. Slamming the door, he pushed her toward the dock. It was quiet, but for the gentle lapping of the waves. The smell of salt water assaulted her nostrils. He ushered her along the dock until he came to a medium size yacht. She didn't get a good look at it before he pulled her on board and down into a posh stateroom. "Have a seat," he instructed, gesturing toward a chair on the far side of the room.

Sabryna did as she was told, her mind swam with possibilities. The chances were small that anyone was coming to her rescue. She'd have to get herself out of this one. Steven was busy searching through a desk by the stairs. The room, decorated in hues of blue and gold, didn't appear to have any ready weapons. Everything was either too small or nailed down. She looked over to the small kitchen. It seemed sparse. She looked back at her captor. Perhaps she could talk her way out of this one. "What are you planning to do with me?"

Steven paused in his search and looked at her. His eyes were clouded, lost in mania. "I thought I explained. I'm going to take you from him."

"The way he took Kari from you?" Sabryna infused understanding into her voice.

"Exactly." Steven resumed his search.

"I thought Kari committed suicide."

Steven's head popped up, and he approached her with lighting speed. She cried out as he stuck the gun against her head. "No!" he screamed. "Don't ever say that. She didn't kill herself. She never would. She loved me too much to leave me. It was Marcus. He killed her. He convinced her she couldn't live without him."

"I'm sorry," Sabryna sobbed, desperate to get him back to the other side of the room and calm once again. "I didn't know. I didn't understand." It was clear Steven was insane.

Her words appeared to mollify him and he stepped back. "It's okay. All you know are the lies that he told you. You don't know how his love kills. But you soon will." Steven walked back over to the desk.

"Te—te--tell me about Kari." Instinct told her to keep him talking.

He paused at her words. A wistful smile spread across his face and he leaned back against the wall. For a moment he looked like Steven, her caring friend. "Kari. Kari was beautiful and perfect. I loved her from the moment I laid eyes on her. We were just eight, you know."

"How did you know each other?"

"Her family lived in Virginia Beach. My family had a beach house on the same street and we would spend time there in the summer." Steven laughed as though they were sharing stories over a beer. "Everywhere Kari went I went with her. My parents used to joke that I wanted to be her shadow."

Sabryna spied a knife holder and wondered if she could get closer to it. "How did Kari feel about it?"

Steven shrugged. "Kari always played hard to get. It made her more interesting. I loved her anyway. She was my first, you know. I swore I would love her forever."

"What happened?"

Steven straightened from the wall. Anger dropped like a veil over his features. "What do you think happened? She went to college and met that bastard Cortland. He tricked her into falling in love with him and he used her. Took advantage of my sweet, innocent Kari. And then he killed her." Steven walked toward Sabryna. He stopped in front of her and caressed her hair. "He took her. And now I am going to take his. I've waited seven long years for this moment. Seven years for my revenge."

"Steven, you don't want to hurt me," Sabryna pleaded. "We're friends. Why don't we go somewhere and get a cup of coffee. We can talk about what to do?"

"Don't try to change my mind," Steven yelled. "I hate that it has to be you, but I warned you. You should've listened. Now I can't help you. I owe this to Kari. I should've saved her from that bastard before things went too far, but I didn't and now I have to avenge her death."

Steven resumed his search in the desk, and locating what he needed, looked up. "I've got it." He held up a pen and notepad. He walked over and dropped them both into Sabryna lap.

She stared at him. "What am I supposed to do with these?"

"I assume you'll want to say goodbye," he informed her. "Kari left a note. She dropped it in the mail to me. Told me all about how she'd fallen in love with Cortland and how he kicked her aside."

Sabryna looked at him in horror. "You want me to write a suicide note."

The look Steven shot her was patronizing. "Well, of course. After all, I'm not going to prison for your death."

"And how are you going to explain my dying on your boat?"

Steven walked over to the kitchen island and leaned against it, his gun still pointed at her. "Well, it's simple. I took you here after you caught Marcus with another woman. I offered to let you stay the night and at some point during that time you shot yourself out of grief. I, of course, will find your body in the morning and call the police."

"Steven, the police aren't stupid. They know someone has been after me. They'll suspect that something fishy happened if I turn up dead." Sabryna infused steel into her words. "You'll never get away with this."

"You let me worry about that." Steven cocked the barrel. "Now write."

Sabryna realized there was nothing left of her friend inside of Steven's warped, vengeful mind. She picked up the pen and pad, wondering what her next move should be. There was no way in hell she was writing a suicide note to help cover up her own murder.

Out of the corner of her eye, she saw a movement on the stairs. Praying it wasn't wishful thinking, she glanced at Steven. He was pouring himself a glass of brandy, not watching her. She looked back to the stairs. This time she was sure of what she saw. Someone was on the stairs. There was no telling who it was, Cole, David, or even Marcus. However, one thing was for sure, with Steven waving his gun around, there was no way anyone was going to get down those stairs without getting shot. Sabryna knew she'd have to get Steven to lower his guard, turn his back, and then she could make a mad dash for the stairs and safety. Sabryna looked toward the kitchen area where her captor stood, brandy in one hand, gun in the other. "Steven, could I please have a glass of brandy?"

He cocked an eyebrow. "I've never known you to drink."

"I think we both agree this is an extenuating circumstance," Sabryna responded.

Steven chuckled. "That's the Sabryna I know, always rising to the challenge." He turned away to retrieve a glass. "I'm very sorry that things have to end like this. I've always liked you…"

Sabryna ignored his words, keeping her eyes trained on him. He still held the gun, but he seemed to have relaxed his guard some. Slowly she stood to her feet. When he poured the drink without turning around, she took a cautious step forward.

Then bolted for the stairs.

"Sabryna, get back here!" Steven's yell blended with the sound of glass crashing on the floor. She charged up the stairs screaming, and ran straight into a hard male body.

"Marcus!" she exclaimed, breathless. Marcus clutched her, looked over her head, and then flung them both toward the deck, twisting so that his body would take the impact. A shot rang out.

Hitting the ground, he rolled until they bumped into the side of the boat.

"Stay down," Jeff ordered. He and David crouched by the doorway, guns drawn. Sabryna clung to Marcus. He shifted, covering her as much as possible.

Out of the corner of her vision, she saw Jeff and David slip down the stairs. Seconds later, they heard David yell, "This is the police, place your hands where I can see them." There was silence and then David yelled again. "Drop the gun and put your hands where I can see them. Do it now."

The sound of a gunshot shattered the air.

"Oh, God," Sabryna sobbed, clinging tighter to Marcus.

"David?" Marcus yelled at the same time.

There was an ominous silence. The sound of footsteps climbing the stairs reached their ears. Sabryna felt Marcus tense. "It's all right," David said. "He's dead."

Marcus rose, helping Sabryna to her feet. For a moment they stood there and stared at each other. David turned away and went back down the stairs.

"Are you okay? Did he hurt you?" Marcus asked.

Sabryna shook her head. "No. You all got here in time." Sirens sounded in the distance coming closer and closer.

"Everyone okay?" Cole asked from the dock, his brows furrowed in concern.

Sabryna turned to him, a shaky smile on her face. "I guess you got my call."

Cole's features relaxed. He nodded. "The police are coming. I'll make sure they find the right boat." He turned to walk away and looked back over his shoulder. "The trick with the cell phone was clever." She started to thank him for the compliment, but then he finished, "But running off like that was stupid."

Sabryna remembered what had led her to being on a boat with a former friend turned psycho aiming to kill her. She looked back at Marcus.

She opened her mouth to speak when Marcus grabbed his shoulder and collapsed at her feet.

"Marcus?" Sabryna cried out, dropping to her feet beside him. He'd fallen on his side and when she moved his hand away from his shoulder she saw that it was covered in blood.

David and Jeff came running at her screams. "I don't know what's wrong with him." They both dropped down beside her to examine Marcus.

Jeff pulled out his cell phone and started dialing. David turned his eyes to Sabryna, fear and anxiety burning in the depths. "He's been shot."

After taking the bullet meant for Sabryna, Marcus needed emergency surgery. Sabryna paced in the waiting room, blazing a trail in the carpet. She ignored suggestions to eat, to sit, to go home, or to stop worrying. She didn't want to hear that Marcus was tough and would pull through it. She didn't want to hear that the bullet hadn't pierced any major organs so the surgery should be simple. She wanted to hear his confident steps as he walked down the hall, ordering the hospital staff to do what he wanted.

Cole leaned against the far wall and David sat in a chair, both watching her as she paced. She knew David concealed his fear and worry behind a wall of confidence. It was what his brother would do, Sabryna thought. David decided not to call his mother. He didn't want her to worry. His plan was to call her after Marcus got out of surgery. Sabryna didn't think Elaine would be pleased with her son's decision, and she prayed that Marcus recovered, so that David's news would be positive.

Jeff had stayed behind at the crime scene. David explained to her that Steven had taken his own life. Sabryna didn't want to hear all the details. It pained her to think of what had become of Steven. That someone she trusted for so many years would try to kill her. At least now, maybe Steven had found some peace.

David stood up, interrupting Sabryna's thoughts. "I think I should call my mother," he told her. This must mean David had lost his confidence, Sabryna thought and she almost doubled over in pain at what that meant when Dr. Simmons walked into the room.

"He's fine," Dr. Simmons said as an anxious David and Sabryna approached him. "I won't lie to you. He's in ICU and he hasn't woken up yet, but we got the bullet out and stopped the bleeding."

Relief flooded through Sabryna's body. "Can I see him?"

Dr. Simmons nodded. "Of course, you both can. But please keep in mind. We aren't out of the critical stage until he wakes up."

They were directed to his room in the ICU. "Go ahead in," David told her. "I'm going to call my mother and check in with Jeff. I'll be right back."

Sabryna nodded and pushed open the wooden door. She paused as her eyes went straight to the bed. Marcus lay there, unmoving, attached to all types of medical equipment. She stepped further into the room never taking her eyes from the bed. Any second she expected him to open his eyes and smile at her. When he didn't, tears slipped down Sabryna's cheek. Determined, she walked over to the bed, pulled a chair over and sat down. Her hand searched for and found his hand. His skin was cold, lacking its usual heat. She squeezed his fingers and tears dropped on her face. At the moment she didn't care what he'd done or how he hurt her. He was the man that introduced her to love, taught her how to love, and saved her life in more ways than one. Even if they were never together, she wanted him to live.

"Marcus Alan Cortland, I want you to know something." Raising their joined hands, she kissed his. Tears fell from her cheek onto their hands. "I want you to know tha-that I've decided not to cry over you anymore. I've cried more tears for you than most people produce and I don't believe it's fair for you to make me do it again. Do you hear me?" She raised her voice with the last question, infusing it with love, anger, and determination. "I'm done crying over you. So, I need you to wake up so I can tell you that."

Sabryna searched his closed lids. "Wake up, please," she begged. He remained still. Holding on to his hand, she rested her head on his chest. Listened for his heartbeat and found it weak but steady. Her tears flowed like rivers.

"He did it on purpose, you know?"

Her head popped up at David's voice and she glanced toward the doorway where he stood. She looked back at Marcus. She didn't know what David was talking about and she didn't care. She only cared that Marcus opened his eyes. She wouldn't leave until he did. Then she would thank him for saving her life and find a way to rebuild her own, without him.

David walked to the other side of the bed and looked down at his brother. After a moment, he stirred and pulled up a chair for himself. "He needs his rest All that plotting and planning can get pretty darn exhausting."

"What are you talking about?" Sabryna's tone was laced with confusion.

David leaned back in his chair and regarded Sabryna. "The scene between him and Adrina. He did it on purpose."

"I don't care about that," Sabryna dismissed.

"Don't you?" David eyed her with skepticism. "Isn't it why you gave him back this?" He held up her engagement ring.

Sabryna looked at it in surprise.

He extended it to her. "The nurse gave it to me. She said it was in his pocket."

Sabryna turned away without taking it. "It doesn't belong to me."

"To my knowledge there's only one woman my brother wants to marry," David told her. "Only one that he loves."

Sabryna kept her eyes on Marcus. "Your brother has some interesting views on marriage and love," she said with derision. "Let's just say that we don't see eye to eye. But that doesn't matter anymore, does it? All that matters right now is that he'll be okay."

"And do you think he'll be okay without you?"

"He'll have to be."

David sighed. "Sabryna, what you saw with Adrina was intentional. Marcus staged it to make you break up with him. He called Adrina and asked for her help. He knew it was the one thing that would make you leave him."

No, he wouldn't, would he? They had talked about him not pushing her away. He'd promised he wouldn't. She shook her head in disbelief. "David, don't cover for him."

"I'm not," David assured her. "Marcus would never be unfaithful to you. Especially with Adrina Howell, he wouldn't touch her with a ten foot pole."

"That was the shortest ten foot pole I've ever seen."

"Marcus told me what he planned before he did it. He wanted to make sure that everything was in place and that we kept a watch on you for a while after, to make sure it worked Think about it. Do you think he would get it on with some other woman when he knew he'd told you to come to his office? My brother's not stupid."

The puzzle pieces started to fit together and Sabryna couldn't deny the truth. David's story made perfect sense. Except..."Why then? What made him do it then?"

"The night before he received another note from Barclay. This time it was accompanied with a box full of pink rose petals." David searched her face. "I can tell from your expression you know the reference. Marcus didn't feel you would be safe if you stayed with him."

Sabryna's relief that he hadn't cheated on her, never intended to do so, was eclipsed by another feeling. A deadening sensation that settled into her bones. Marcus had done what she expected all along. He pushed her away. The risk had gotten to be too much and his first step was to cut her off. Just like her father. Her hand slipped from his on the bed.

"Sabryna, don't be angry."

She heard David's voice as if from a distance. Hadn't she expected this all along? All her fears over getting close to someone came down to this moment. If she let someone in, if she trusted someone with her heart and soul, how long would it be before something happened and they decided is wasn't worth the effort? How long before they decided that walking away was easier than staying? Her father had set the precedent. When he'd lost her mother, he felt it would be easier to distance himself from Sabryna. God forbid that something happened and he had to experience that grief twice. Then there was Marcus. He promised to love her forever, to be her partner. But when the situation got out of control, he took the safest way out. After all, loving someone came with pain, and who wanted to be exposed to that.

"My brother loves you. He loves you so much he was willing to sacrifice his happiness for your life." David's words penetrated Sabryna mind.

Sabryna thought on the words. Thought on what they meant. And knew without a doubt what she had to do.

Marcus felt as though a huge weight was sitting on his eyelids. He attempted to open them but the effort was exhausting. His head was fuzzy and his thoughts jumbled together. He wanted to stretch but his brain refused to communicate the message to his body. What was he forgetting? He struggled to recall it and when he did it hit him like a ton of bricks.

Barclay was trying to kill Sabryna.

He lurched up. Gentle hands pushed on his shoulder. Heard the sweet voice of an Angel telling him to take it easy and lay back down.

Marcus's eyes snapped open at the same time he registered a burning in his chest. Sabryna was there, her liquid brown eyes staring into his. It was her gentle hands on his shoulders, anchoring him to the world. He looked her over. She'd been crying, but she didn't look hurt.

Marcus lay back down. Fatigue washed over him. He remembered getting shot and reasoned he was in the hospital. Nurses rushed in the room, checking his monitors, checking him, but his eyes remained locked on Sabryna. She stepped back out of the nurse's way and he wanted to call to her. He needed to feel her touch. But she was so far away and he was so tired.

His eyes drifted shut.

The next time he awakened his mother was there. She sat stiff by his bed, gripping his hand. He raised his eyes and smiled at her. "Hello, Mother."

She didn't smile back. "Hello, Son."

Marcus studied her face. "Why are you frowning? I survived."

"Yes, you did." His mother sigh was resigned. "And that's why it's unfortunate that I have to kill you."

Marcus chuckled. "I guess David filled you in."

"This is not funny," Elaine snapped. "I can't believe there was someone trying to kill you and Sabryna and you failed to inform me. Really, Marcus, this keeping things to yourself is getting out of hand. I could've helped."

"Well, if we'd known who it was I would've asked you to send a cake to the Barclay residence. That would've solved our problems."

"I'm ignoring that young man." Elaine relaxed back in her chair. "I can't believe it was Steven Barclay. His parents are such nice people. I can't imagine what they must be going through. David said Steven was out of his mind."

Marcus thought about it, but he couldn't bring himself to care. Steven had come to close to reaching his goal.

Elaine leaned over and kissed Marcus on the cheek. "I count my blessings that you're okay."

"Do you have any spare blessings for me?" David quipped from the doorway.

Elaine glanced at her middle son and hmmphed. "I might have some on back order."

"Uh, oh…how did you get in the dog house?" Marcus asked his brother as he looked to see if Sabryna was with him.

David shrugged. "Apparently, I encouraged you to keep secrets from mom."

"And you didn't call me until he was out of surgery," Elaine added. "Your brother Alex would never have done that." Elaine stood up. "Speaking of him, I need to call and let him know everything's okay. Madelyn was upset I didn't bring her with me, but I wanted to make sure all was well first."

Elaine sailed out of the room as David took a seat next to his brother. "Feeling better? You should, you've been asleep for hours."

"Where's Sabryna?" Marcus asked as soon as they were alone.

David looked down. "She's gone."

Pain gripped Marcus, he rose up.

"She left as soon as you woke up," David explained.

She was okay. Marcus relaxed. "Where did she go?"

"I don't know. She didn't say." David pressed a small object into Marcus's hand. "But she left you this."

Marcus opened up his palm to reveal her engagement ring. His eyes shot to David.

David just shook his head. "I explained everything to her. Told her it was all a setup, but I think it just made her angrier. I'm sorry."

Marcus stared at the ring. "It's all right. It's not your fault it's mine. I did the one thing she asked me not to do. I pushed her away." And now I've lost her forever.

CHAPTER THIRTY-ONE

Sabryna stood on the sidewalk and stared at the small brick house in front of her. The house sat on a quiet street, surrounded by an overgrown yard. There was a black SUV in the driveway, and she hoped that meant her father was home. The Georgia heat was at its hottest, and she felt beads of sweat pop out on her forehead. Or was that from anxiety?

Summoning her courage and tucking it away in her determination, she walked the few feet to the door. When she reached out to push the doorbell, she realized her hand was shaking. But she pushed it anyway and felt the gong echo in her soul.

After a few agonizing moments, the door swung open to a familiar face. "Sabryna? What are you doing here?"

"Hello, Dad." She stepped past him and into his house. John closed the door and turned to look at her. She twirled around, viewing the room. She was standing in a sparsely decorated living room. A couch, an easy chair, and a big screen television seemed to be the main items. There were no pictures or small touches to make it feel homey. Sabryna turned back to her dad.

"Are you going to tell me why you're here?" He hadn't moved from his spot by the door.

She studied him. Every angle of his face seemed so achingly familiar and yet so new to her. She noted the marks of age on his caramel colored skin. His frame was still slim, but now carried a slight stoop. She couldn't remember the last time she'd seen him. "I came to see you."

He shuffled past her and settled in the easy chair. "Do you want to sit?" He motioned toward the couch.

She walked to the couch and sat down. Looked for the words she needed to say.

Her father's patience ran out. "Well, you wanted to say something."

"I…I…uh," Sabryna started, hating that she was stuttering over her words, but as she looked into her father's hardened face, devoid of any emotion the questions she wanted to ask wouldn't come. She wanted to ask him why he didn't love her. To find out what made it so simple for him to turn his back on her. Before she moved on with her future, she needed to understand her past. As she stared into her father's face, watched as he attempted not to meet her eyes, the questions didn't seem so important. She looked around the empty room. At once, she understood her father better than she ever thought she could. It wasn't that she was unlovable. There wasn't something about her that made it easy for people to walk away from her.

The problem was her father's.

He lived in a bubble of fear. He hadn't come to Georgia to avoid her. Not even to rebuild his life. He might have gotten sober, but he still wasn't living. He'd run away from her, from the world, because he was too scared to get stung by fate again. Now he lived isolated, in a web built on weakness.

She'd done the same thing, albeit differently. She'd avoided getting too close to anyone. She'd drowned herself in her work, because it was something concrete. Something she understood and a job couldn't hurt her. She could focus on the pain of others and never have to face her own. She was living in her own protective bubble, afraid that someone would pop it and all the hurt would tumble in. Like him, she isolated herself. Until one kiss from Marcus Cortland changed that. Changed her forever.

Straightening, she looked her father square in the eye. "I came to ask for your forgiveness."

"For...for what?"

Her lips lifted in a sad smile. "For being so distant. For not calling you more. For not coming to see you more."

Her father shifted in his seat. "You want my forgiveness for not calling?"

She nodded. "Yes, I do."

He cleared his throat. "Well, I guess I could've called more also."

Sabryna shrugged. "Yes, that's true. But it still doesn't excuse my behavior. You're my father and I should've called and visited."

Her father looked down at the floor. "No one would blame you for not doing it."

Sabryna stood up and walked over to him. She squatted in front of him and waited until he met her eyes. "I blame me. No matter what has happened, we're family and nothing can change that. Being family means you get unconditional love and acceptance no matter what you've done. We should support each other and be able to depend on each other. And I want you to know that you can always count on me. No matter how far away I am. If you need me, I'll be there." Sabryna rose and walked back to the couch.

Her father stood from his easy chair. "I...uh...I don't know what to say."

She smiled. "You don't have to say anything. Just don't forget what I said."

He scratched the back of his head. "Maybe, uh...we could...forgive each other."

Sabryna nodded. "I'd like that." For a moment father and daughter just looked at each other as a silent understanding passed between them. Sabryna was the first to stir. "I have to go. I have a plane to catch."

She grabbed her purse and headed for the door.

"Sabryna," Her father called and she turned around. "I'm glad you came."

"Maybe, you'll come visit me. We can spend some time getting to know each other."

Her father nodded. "I'd like that."

Unable to resist, Sabryna walked over and embraced him. For a moment, he was stiff in her arms and then squeezed her back. It was the first time she'd embraced her father in over fifteen years. With an awkward pat on her back, he wished her a safe trip back home.

She wished she could see the rain clouds clearing from her spirit. With light steps, she left the house and headed for her rental car. It was time to start living.

"Welcome home, big brother," Madelyn exclaimed, her arms outspread. She stepped back as Marcus and their mother came through the door. Two days had passed since the shooting and he had insisted on coming home. He still felt a little unsteady on his feet, but he was much improved. He looked around at what he could see of his condo. He pictured a Sabryna coming around the corner, arms wide open.

He blinked and the image was gone. Sabryna was gone.

"Do you want something to eat? I made some chicken soup." Elaine hovered around him like a mother hen. Although he loved her for it, he needed some time alone. Some time to come to grips with the choices he had made and their consequences.

"No, I'm good," he assured her.

"Yeah, Mom he just left the hospital, the goal is to keep him out of it," Madelyn teased.

"My soup was delicious." Elaine helped Marcus to a couch in his living room. "Besides, you all should enjoy these home cooked meals while you can. I've decided to give up cooking."

"What are you going to do now?" Madelyn perched on the arm of the couch.

Elaine shrugged. "I haven't decided. Although I'm toying with the idea of pottery. I better call Alex and let him know you made it home okay."

Madelyn watched her mom leave the room and then turned back to Marcus. "Can you picture all the misshapen figurines in our future?" Marcus chuckled. A cloud of sadness dropped over his sister's delicate features. "I'm sorry about you and Sabryna."

Marcus turned to stare out the window. News sure did travel fast in his family. "I am too."

"Do you think she'll come back? Maybe you should call her. I'm sure if you apologize she'll forgive you."

"It's a little more complicated than that," Marcus told her.

Madelyn hummmphed. "Love is too confusing. Remind me never to fall in love."

Marcus's lips twitched. "Believe me; I'd be quite happy to do that. At least until you're thirty."

After his family left, Marcus grew restless. It was late, but he didn't want to sleep. Couldn't bring himself to lay in the bed he had shared with her. He wandered around his penthouse, wishing for a drink. Anything to numb the pain. Deciding he needed to clear his head, Marcus wandered up to the roof. He stood there for over an hour feeling the slight summer breeze on his skin, watching the world pass by under him, staring into stars that appeared close enough to touch. Yet, still he felt no peace.

"I thought I might find you up here."

At the sound of Sabryna's voice, Marcus spun around. Almost as if in a dream she stood before him wearing a white flowing summer dress. Her curls draped over her shoulders, her beautiful eyes shining like rich amber.

He started to move toward her and then stopped himself. He didn't know why she was here. It might simply be to collect her clothes.

Slowly, she walked toward him but stopped when they were about ten feet apart. "Hi," was all she said.

"Hi." He jammed his hands in his pockets to keep from reaching out for her.

"How are you feeling?" He couldn't tell anything from her tone.

"Much better. It's going to take more than a bullet in the shoulder to stop me." He touched his arm. "Thanks for staying with me when I… when I got out of surgery."

She nodded, walked over to the edge. For a moment, she peered out into the darkness.

Aching to hold her, he stared at her. "Sabryna, you were gone when I woke up, but I wanted to say…"

"I went to see my father." She faced him.

That surprised him. "How did that go?"

She leaned back and let her lips curve upward. "Let's just say we reached a very satisfying understanding."

"You seem happy about that. I'm glad for you."

She pushed away from the wall and stepped closer to him. "It's not my relationship with my father that I feel so happy about. It's something else that I realized."

"What is it?" He asked, although he wasn't sure he was prepared for the response.

Once again she stepped past and walked a little to his right. He turned following her progression. "You know, when I found you with Adrina, I could've ripped her eyes out. And when David told me it was all a set up, I could've ripped your eyes out. But then I realized, it wasn't anger that I felt, it was relief. All along I expected you to push me away. And so when you did, I was relieved because then I didn't have to be afraid anymore. I was afraid to be happy.

"My father taught me a long time ago the dangers of getting close to anyone. So I never did. I thought that staying away from them saved me from any potential hurt. Sure I wanted to be loved, but I didn't want to take the risk of what could happen. So I built walls around myself that kept everyone out. Even you didn't stand a chance, because eventually I would've found a reason to keep you out." Sabryna raised her luminous eyes to meet his. "I don't want to be alone anymore. I don't want to be afraid anymore."

She took another step closer to him. Her eyes caressed his face. "I love you and no matter how many walls I throw up in front of you, I'll always love you. And I hope…" Her voice broke on a sob as tears started pouring from her eyes. "I hope that you never get tired of busting through my walls."

"Sabryna." Joy exploded in Marcus's chest. Tears smarted in his eyes.

Sabryna didn't appear to hear him as she swiped at the wetness off her face with the back of her hand. "I know I'm not making any sense… and I'm probably babbling…and I never babble…"

"Sabryna." His voice was loud and firm, she stopped talking. He looked at the space separating them. "If you take about three more steps in this direction I can wrap you in my arms and tell you I don't care how much sense you make as long as you promise to love me forever."

She was in his arms before he finished speaking. Clinging to him, she drenched his shirt with her tears. He did as he promised, and wrapped her tight in his embrace, pulling her as close as possible, telling her how much he loved her, and begging for her forgiveness.

After a moment, her tears stopped. She leaned back and looked at him. "If you ever think of touching another woman again, I'll cut off your hands."

"My hands are holding the only woman they need." He leaned down and kissed her with all the love and passion clamoring in his heart and sensed her answering response. Their kiss left them both gasping for more, but they stood on the rooftop, locked in each other's embrace, holding on to the moment. There would be time later to hash out the details and talk about all that had occurred, but for now it was enough for them to be together.

Marcus was the first to stir. He took her ring out of his pocket, reached for her hand and slid it back on her finger. She gave him a wobbly smile. "My ring."

He squeezed her hand. "Don't forget that again."

She kissed him. "I won't."

He sighed and rested his cheek on her hair. "My mother is going to be thrilled."

Sabryna laughed. "She'd be more thrilled if we set a date."

Marcus thought. "Why don't you let me take care of that? I have the perfect date in mind."

"When?" Sabryna pulled back and peered at him in clear skepticism.

"Will you just trust me?"

Sabryna rested her head back on his shoulder. "I do."

Marcus smiled and stared up into the heavens. Silently, he thanked God above for sending him an Angel. He didn't know what he'd done to deserve her, but he promised he would spend his entire life making her happy.

EPILOGUE

The next evening Marcus stood next to his mother, sister and brother on the rooftop.

"I raised such an impatient son," Elaine Cortland adjusted her pale green Donna Karen dress. "I think you should know I'm not happy with this at all."

"Is that why you're crying?" Marcus handed his mother a tissue.

"I'm crying because this is the sweetest, most impulsive thing I've ever seen," she told him sharply. "Who knew I raised such a romantic son."

Madelyn rolled her eyes and looked at Marcus. "She makes you dizzy, doesn't she?"

Marcus laughed and hugged his mother. "Yes, but its part of her charm."

"Well, I hope you find this charming. When you come back from your honeymoon I'm throwing you a huge party to celebrate," His mother informed him.

"I'll even pay for it," Marcus offered.

"Well of course you will," Elaine told him before moving away to talk to the minister who was standing with Grant Morganfield and his wife Grace. Marcus looked around and noted Lena Martinez, her husband George, and Damon. All had come at a moment's notice to be a witness at his and Sabryna's wedding. There hadn't been time to get his brother Alex there. However, her father was in attendance and he walked her down the aisle. A surprise Marcus arranged that had greatly pleased Sabryna.

The minister drew them all together to begin the ceremony. When Sabryna stepped out onto the roof, Marcus's eyes, heart, and soul were riveted on her. She looked like a vision ripped from the pages of his deepest fantasy, dressed in an elegant white gown that hugged every curve. Her curls were pinned to the top of her head, and her love shone in her eyes.

Sabryna didn't see anyone but Marcus, standing in front of her in an elegant black tuxedo. His large frame, the only home she would ever need. He was her friend, her lover, her soul mate. She had finally found the place where she belonged.

When she stepped up to him, he took her hand and slid it onto his arm. Bending down, he whispered in her ear, "You take my breath away."

She scanned him from head to toe. "You're not so shabby yourself."

He laughed and the ceremony proceeded. When it was time to exchange vows, she said hers first. They were the standard vows as they didn't have time write any. She wondered if she would spend the rest of her life getting caught up in Marcus's whirlwinds. And then decided she didn't care, as long as he rode the waves beside her.

When it was Marcus's turn to say his vows, he repeated them in a confident voice. Sabryna listened, mesmerized by his tone. She heard him promise to love and honor her, through sickness and through health, until death did them part. Yet, Marcus didn't stop there. He continued without the minister, "And I promise to treat her always as my partner."

Startled, Sabryna eyes flew to his.

Marcus looked back, his gaze unwavering. "To treat you as my equal in all things, to never turn away or forsake you, no matter the circumstance. To be your family, helpmate, and friend until death do we part."

Sabryna burst into tears and threw her arms around Marcus and kissed him with everything she possessed. Later she would tell him how much she loved him. How he had changed her life and taught her what it meant to love and be loved in return. Later she would thank him for giving her a family. But for now, she simply kissed her husband, her way of thanking him for giving her forever.

ABOUT THE AUTHOR

Jasmine Alexander developed a passion for writing when she was in elementary school. She loved creating a world of characters with fascinating lives and complex relationships. She was born in Madrid, Spain but raised in Virginia where she currently resides. Her dream of writing became a reality when she joined the Chesapeake Romance Writers. She works as a school counselor, a job which she loves because she never has the same day twice. She received her B.S. and M.S.Ed from Old Dominion University and is currently pursing a PhD in Counselor Education. Her ultimate goal is to spend her days training school counselors and writing passionate love stories. When she has free time, she loves to read, write, travel, and shop!

Jasmine loves to hear from readers. She can be reached at jasminealexanderwrites@yahoo.com